The Winds of Heaven

JUDITH CLARKE

The Winds of Heaven

HENRY HOLT AND COMPANY

NEW YORK

Henry Holt and Company, LLC
Publishers since 1866
175 Fifth Avenue
New York, New York 10010
www.HenryHoltKids.com

Henry Holt® is a registered trademark of Henry Holt and Company, LLC.
Text copyright © 2009 by Allen & Unwin
First published in the United States in 2010 by Henry Holt and Company, LLC
Distributed in Canada by H. B. Fenn and Company Ltd.
Originally published in Australia in 2010 by Allen & Unwin.

Library of Congress Cataloging-in-Publication Data
Clarke, Judith.
The winds of heaven / Judith Clarke.—1st American ed.
p.   cm.
Summary: Clementine and her cousin Fan both grow up in 1950s Australia but
have very different lives, Clementine coming from a stable, city family and Fan
from a broken, country home, and their destinies are also strikingly divergent.
ISBN 978-0-8050-9164-9
[1. Cousins—Fiction.   2. Single-parent families—Fiction.
3. Family life—Australia—Fiction.   4. Australia—History—
20th century—Fiction.]   I. Title.
PZ7.C55365Wi 2010   [Fic]—dc22   2009051780

First American Edition—2010
Designed by April Ward
Printed in the United States of America

1   3   5   7   9   10   8   6   4   2

To the Wiradjuri Country

Contents

2009

These days Clementine has visions. There's nothing exotic or heavenly about them: they're made of the most simple stuff. A ragged chorus of "Happy Birthday" is enough to bring back her mum's young face, bright with love above a pink-iced cake she's spent all day making. "Happy Birthday Clementine" is spelled out in tiny sugar flowers.

A skein of crimson embroidery silk in a craft shop window can make Clementine stop short with a little gasp: she'll see the bright cross-stitched border of her mother's favorite linen tablecloth, feel the coolness of its cloth beneath her smoothing hand, hear the sweet sound of her dad's homecoming bike purring up the side path as her nine-year-old self sets the table for their tea.

A hot summer day with a certain harsh light in it, dust in the air, an old song of Johnny Cash's on the radio—any of these will bring back her cousin Fan.

And however disparate, there's one quality all Clementine's visions have in common: the people and places in them are lost and gone forever.

Most times these visions come when Clementine is alone, but today she's with her friend Sarah, walking around the lake in Flinders Park as they do each Thursday morning—two old ladies taking their exercise: three times around, with a rest on the green wooden bench after the second lap.

It's late January, the very height of summer.

"Hot!" puffs Sarah. "Lord, it's hot today!"

They've been around only once but already she's heading for the bench and the shade of the rustling she-oak trees. "Early break!" She grins at Clementine. "Can't take the heat anymore; I'm not as young as I used to be. Sixty-seven next birthday!" Sarah punches a fist in the air and flops down on the hard wooden bench, flicking a hand at the small black flies that hover around their faces and settle on the shoulders of their T-shirts like an embroidery of shiny black beads.

Clementine sits down beside her friend. Sixty-seven! she marvels.

Sixty-seven is the exact age Fan would have been if she hadn't gone away. And though it's almost fifty years ago, the thought of her cousin's going away fills Clementine's eyes with tears. Throughout her life, even in the happiest times there's always been a sadness at the bottom of her heart, like a small cold pebble lying in whispering reeds.

"Are you okay?" asks Sarah.

"Fine," answers Clementine, and she leans back and gazes up at the hard, pewter-colored sky of January. There are no clouds in it, she notices, none of those clouds in fantastic shapes that she and Fan used to watch from the grassy bank above Lake Conapaira. She can't imagine her cousin being sixty-seven, any more than she and Fan could have imagined such a thing when they were children—in those days even forty was impossibly old to them. It was ancient. Disgusting, even.

Now she hears her cousin's voice, quite clearly. It's hoarse, the voice of a child who's been crying. "She's forty!" Fan is spitting out contemptuously. "She's old!"

A picture comes next, a little vision: Fan is standing in the middle of the small bedroom they shared in the old house in Palm Street; in each hand she holds one of her thick blond plaits, and with a small, quick gesture she lifts them onto the top of her head and twists them into a crown.

"O-old!" Fan's voice is mocking now. "So old!"

It's her mother she's talking about, Clementine's scary aunt Rene.

"She's got wrinkles! Imagine! Imagine having wrinkles!" Fan pulls a wrinkly face and lets the heavy plaits fall; they tumble down over her pointed shoulder blades and settle at her waist. She flings herself onto her bed crosswise, head hanging over the side, plaits sweeping the floor, and walks her small, slender feet up the grubby wall. The tops of them are speckled with the red dust of Lake Conapaira, and her soles are stained with it, crimson as an Indian bride's. "I'm never going to get wrinkles," vows Fan, and then Clementine hears her own nine-year-old self protest, "But everyone gets wrinkles when they get old."

"Not me," says Fan. "Everyone else will, but not me." The utter certainty in that childish voice, remembered half a century later on this hot summer morning in a suburban park, makes Clementine's blood run cold.

A small breeze ripples the sluggish surface of the water; a flock of black cockatoos swoops over the lake toward a bank of trees.

"Bilirr," Clementine hears Fan saying now, and at once that other lake swims into her vision, the real one, Lake Conapaira. It's huge—on hot, hazy days like this one you couldn't see the other side. They're lying in the grass at Fan's hidey watching the clouds race grandly over the sky. Then the cockatoos come shrieking and Fan reaches over and lays one fingertip lightly on her cousin's lips. *"Bilirr,"* she says again, smiling. "Now you say it, Clemmie."

"I can't."

"Yes you can. It's easy. Go on."

"Bilirr," whispers Clementine, and is rewarded by a memory, so exact it's almost painful, of her cousin's laugh, a sound that always made her think of a handful of bright water flung into the air.

On the green bench beside the artificial lake Sarah turns her head. "Belair?" she asks. "Is that what you said? I'm afraid my hearing's not what it used to be."

"Bilirr," replies Clementine. "It's an Aboriginal word for the black cockatoo. Fan taught it to me."

Sarah puts her head on one side. "Fan?"

Way down in Clementine's heart the small cold pebble seems to shift and stir. "Oh, Fan," she says. "Fan was my cousin. My cousin from Lake Conapaira."

PART ONE

1952

CHAPTER

1

"Mum?" whispered Clementine. "Mum, when will we be there?" She was whispering because her mother sat so very still and quiet, her knitting abandoned in her lap, her head resting against the back of the seat, eyes closed. She might even be asleep.

"Mum?" Clementine shifted along the shiny seat until she was right up close, reached out a hand, and lightly brushed her fingers across her mother's soft cheek. "Mum?" she said again, so softly it was hardly more than a breath. Mrs. Southey sighed and moved her head a little but she didn't open her eyes. She was asleep.

Clementine slid back into her own seat. She rested her elbow on the windowsill and stared out at the gray-gold paddocks rushing by—paddocks and paddocks and paddocks and then a single twisty tree, quite gray and leafless, a dry creek bed full of stones, more paddocks, paddocks—"Aa-aah," yawned Clementine, and, stretching her legs out, she began to swing one foot, slowly at first, and then faster and faster until a shoe fell off and plopped onto the floor. "Aa-ah-aaah!" she yawned again.

Oh, it was such a long way to Lake Conapaira! So long it seemed they'd been traveling for whole nights and days, for weeks and months, like the explorers Mrs. Carruthers had told them about in history, who crossed the mountains and the deserts and the whole of Australia, from sea to shining sea.

But Clementine knew it had only been a day. Only a day since Mum had woken her this morning, so early that it had still been dark outside, with the moon down low in the sky, a raggedy old moon that looked as if something wicked had taken a big ugly bite from its side. It was still dark when the taxi came to take them to the station, and the rattling old train that hurried them into the city was well past Auburn before Clementine saw a single lighted window. The window had no curtains, and Clementine could see inside a kitchen where a lady in a green dressing gown, with pink curlers in her hair, was putting a kettle on for tea. By the time they reached Burwood there were lots of lighted windows, and the tiny lamps of shift workers' bicycles coming home along the streets, and at Central a pale light was creeping into the concourse, thin and gray as the gruel fed to orphans in fairy stories.

The pigeons! Clementine had never seen so many, whole flocks of them, strutting and squabbling, rising with a great clattering sound when a long luggage trolley rattled by, and feathers like gray snowflakes drifting down from a sky that was plainly morning. She cupped her hands and a single feather landed gently on one palm; it felt warm and mysterious, soft as thistledown.

"Clementine! Hurry up! What are you doing dawdling about back there?" Mrs. Southey was wearing her hot-and-bothered look, her face flushed, and her second-best hat with the bunch of fat cherries slipped sideways on her curls. She frowned at the feather in Clementine's hand. "Put that down, it's dirty!"

"No it isn't, it's new, it hasn't been anywhere!"

Mrs. Southey snatched the feather and sent it spinning down onto the tracks, where it would get run over by a train. "Your hat's on crooked," said Clementine coldly, but her mother took no notice. She grabbed her daughter's hand and tugged her along the platform where the Riverina Express stood waiting, its huge black engine making short, sharp spurting sounds, as if it were eager to be off. A long string of carriages trailed behind it, skirts of bright red dust beneath their windows.

"Where's Dad?"

"He's in the train. Oh, hurry, Clementine."

In the train. A small butterfly of hope fluttered inside Clementine's chest. "Is he coming, then? Is Dad coming with us?"

"You know he isn't. How many times do I have to tell you?"

"So why is he in the train?"

"He's seeing to the luggage. In you go now!" Mrs. Southey pushed Clementine up three small steps and into a carriage marked Car D. A row of open doors along a narrow passage showed tiny rooms neat as ships' cabins, and Clementine saw her dad in one of them, hoisting their big suitcase up onto the rack.

"Is that our room?"

"Compartment," corrected Mrs. Southey, stepping briskly inside it, taking off her crooked hat, running her fingers through her mussed-up hair. She opened one of the tall cupboards set into the wall and Clementine caught sight of herself in the big mirror on the inside of its door: a skinny little kid in a tartan frock with tartan bows in her hair, standing in the doorway as if she wasn't certain whether to stay out or come in. The little room didn't look big enough to hold three people, though Clementine was so small for her age that people often mistook her for seven, or even six, instead of nine. Her eyes were gray, a dark gray that was almost the color of charcoal, and there was a faint dusting of freckles over her cheeks and the bridge of her nose. Her bobbed hair was the most ordinary sort of brown, so straight and smooth and slippery that the lovely hair ribbons Granny Southey bought for her wouldn't stay on; they slid down and fell into the dirt and lost their bright new shine.

Her father pushed the big suitcase as far back on the rack as it would go. Then he turned around, wiping his hands down the sides of his trousers, and said to her mum, "When you get to Coota, make sure you call the guard to get it down for you. Don't want to start your visit with a strain."

A strain sounded awful to Clementine. "What if the guard doesn't come?" she blurted. What if he didn't come and they couldn't get the suitcase down and Mum got a strain and then they got carried on past Coota to other places where they didn't want to go?

"You're such a little worrier, Clementine," said her mother, but her dad winked and said cheerfully, "Of course he'll come! No doubt about it!"

She took a small step into the compartment. Outside a sharp whistle blew and the pigeons rushed up in a clatter. "Better be off then," said Dad, kissing Mum on the cheek and catching Clementine up in such a fierce hug that she could feel the buttons on his shirt press hard into her skin. Before she'd got her breath back, he was gone. He was outside on the platform smiling in at them, a beautiful smile that had a kind of sadness in it, as if she and Mum were going away forever instead of only for the summer holidays. The train began to move, and his face disappeared from the window like a light that had been turned out. She pressed her nose against the cold glass and saw him standing among the pigeons and the empty luggage trolleys and the little groups of people waving, getting smaller and smaller and farther and farther away, until the platform vanished, and the station itself, and the railway workshops—and they were rushing past the dark little houses of Redfern with their cluttered yards and skinny cats and sooty, sickly trees.

And after Redfern came Macdonaldtown and Newtown and Stanmore, their narrow streets bathed now in soft buttery light, with whole crowds of men on bicycles riding off to work, and a green bus pulling away from the stop outside Ashfield station. Croydon and Burwood, then Strathfield, where their train stopped to take on more passengers—all these were places whose names were familiar to Clementine, stations they always passed when she and Mum came in to do shopping in town. Homebush and Flemington, Lidcombe, Auburn and Clyde. Granville and Merrylands—that was theirs, that was home—and how strange it seemed that the train didn't stop there, but raced on swiftly by as if the place where they lived was nothing special after all.

She could see the Avenue, and the big house on the corner, with its glassed-in veranda, where all day long old Mrs. Cowper sat in the sun and waved to passersby. And there was Carlyle Street, and the Catholic school, and the old wooden house where the Brothers lived, and behind it the tops of the big trees in the park, and across from the park—though you couldn't see it—was Willow Street, where Clementine and her parents lived at number 33. And all of this passed in such a narrow moment there was barely time to clap your hands: you looked, and it was gone. The train rushed on through Guilford and Yennora, places that were still familiar because Yennora was where Granny Southey lived, but then it was stations whose names Clementine didn't know, and orchards and market gardens and thick green bushland that went on and on and on. If the train stopped and they had to get out, how would they ever find their way back home?

"Mum, do you know how to get home from here?"

Her mother glanced carelessly out the window. "I suppose so, at a pinch," she said.

"Will Dad be home?"

"Of course not." She consulted her little watch. "He'll be at work by now."

Work was why Dad couldn't come with them to Lake Conapaira. While they were away at Aunty Rene's, he would go to the factory in the mornings, the same as any day. He would make his own sandwiches in the kitchen like he did when Mum had been sick with flu, cutting the bread too thick and the corned beef raggy, then he would ride off on his bicycle, and in the evening he would come home again. He always came home at the same time, five thirty, and as she set the table for tea, Clementine would listen for the soft *tick-tock* of the chain as he wheeled his bicycle up the path, past the kitchen windows and down toward the shed. He would come home in the same way tonight, only there would be no one to listen for him: the kitchen would be all shadowy when he walked in through the door and the table wouldn't be set, because it was Clementine who always did this, smoothing the creases from the tablecloth with the red cross-stitched border which Mum had made for her glory box when she was a girl, laying out the place mats and the knives and forks and spoons. Tonight the table would be bare and shiny, and there wouldn't be anything for tea.

"Mum?" Clementine grabbed at her mother's arm. "What will Dad have for tea tonight? What will he eat?"

"I don't know, Clementine."

Clementine pulled anxiously at a strand of her slippery hair. She dragged the end of it toward her mouth.

"Don't chew your hair! How many times do I have to tell you?"

"But, Mum, if Dad doesn't have anything to eat, then—"

"Your father will have plenty to eat. He's having tea at Aunty Rita's place while we're away."

"Oh." Clementine sank back into her seat with a small sigh of relief.

Aunty Rita and Uncle Jim were Mum and Dad's best friends; they lived in Randall Street, only one suburb away, in an old house with a big palm tree in the front yard.

"And then will he come back to our house, to sleep?"

"Of course he will."

Their house would be dark by then, dark and empty and sitting silent in the street. But that didn't really matter because Dad wasn't scared of the dark—whenever Clementine woke from a bad dream it was always Dad who came to comfort her and he never bothered to switch on the light. He sat on the edge of her bed and held her hand in the dark and the dark became soft and friendly and he would stay there until Clementine had gone to sleep, even if that took a long, long time.

And now uneasiness took hold of Clementine again, like a small cold wave creeping over sand. "Mum?"

"What?"

"Will he be there when we get back?"

Because they were going away for a long time, a whole four weeks, and what if he forgot about them, and went away? There were girls in her class whose fathers had gone away: they had gone out the door and never come back again. And Lizzie Owens had never even had a father.

"Who?" asked her mother, frowning. "Do you mean your father?"

Clementine nodded.

"Of course he'll be there. Whatever made you think he wouldn't be?"

"Nothing," whispered Clementine.

"You shouldn't worry so much, Clementine."

"But I have to ask things, don't I?" cried Clementine. "I have to know things, so I won't worry."

"Yes, but—" Her mother sighed, leaned closer, and placed a soft little kiss right in the middle of Clementine's forehead, like you might fix a stamp, very neatly and exactly, on a very important letter.

"You're a funny old thing," she said, and then she pushed down the arm of the seat between them, took a big pillow from the narrow cupboard, and made a little bed for Clementine. "Take your shoes off, sweetheart," she said. "Try and have a little sleep."

"But I'm not tired."

"Just try. You don't want to be all sleepy and cranky when we get to Cootamundra, do you? When we change trains?"

"No." Clementine took her shoes off and curled up along

the seat. There was just enough room for her to fit, and the pillow was so big and soft and deep that in no time at all she was fast asleep.

When she woke again, the world outside the window had changed so completely she thought for a moment she was dreaming. The green bushland had gone; in its place were broad paddocks of gray-gold grass and dry, cracked creek beds rolling away to a line of distant rounded hills. There were big stones that looked like sheep, and gray sheep that looked like stones, and dead trees that took on fantastic shapes like clouds sometimes did in the sky: here was a big rooster, over there a kangaroo, and leaning against a crooked fence a twisted thing that could have been a Hobyah with a bag on his shoulder, waiting to catch a little child. The sky was bigger, it was huge, and the way it arched above the paddocks made you see how the world really was round.

Clementine rubbed her eyes. "Where are we?"

Her mother looked up from the gray cable sweater she was knitting for Dad. "Just out from Harden."

A sudden patch of oily green appeared beside the railway line, its tussocky grass all spiky like a crowd of porcupines.

"What's that?"

"A swamp."

"If you walked there would you sink? Over your head?"

"Oh, Clementine!"

"I just wanted to know. Are we nearly there? At Aunty Rene's place?"

"Of course we're not. We're not even at Cootamundra yet. Do you remember your aunty?"

Clementine shook her head. She'd only been four last time they'd visited.

"Your cousin Francesca?"

Francesca. Clementine felt a jolt of sheer astonishment at such a lovely name. It was so beautiful you wouldn't expect an ordinary person to have it. "Francesca," she whispered.

"Yes," said her mother. "Only everyone calls her Fan. Don't you remember her?"

Clementine closed her eyes to concentrate. She concentrated on the single thing she could remember from that long-ago visit: the shady back veranda of her aunty's house, and the screen door that opened onto its smooth wooden boards. She held this picture in her mind, waiting to see if someone would come through the door.

And someone did. "A big girl with black hair?"

"That's Caroline, Fan's big sister. Fan is fair, and she's only a year older than you."

"Fan is fair." As soon as her mother said this, Clementine saw her younger cousin's face exactly: a pale oval where everything—her eyes and nose, her finely arched eyebrows and delicate rounded lips—was quite perfect, like a dish full of precious gifts. She remembered Fan—Francesca—standing in the sunlight and how the silky hairs escaping from her long fair plaits had glittered around her head like golden wire. She was as beautiful as her lovely name.

"Oh!" She'd remembered something else. She heard it: someone calling Fan's name in the kind of scream that meant someone might get hurt, that made you want to run away somewhere safe where the screaming couldn't get inside you, into every little nook and cranny. She put her hands up to her ears.

"What's the matter?" asked her mother.

"I can remember someone screaming."

Strangely, because the memory was so scary, Clementine's mother smiled. "That would be Fan all right; your cousin can be quite a handful when she wants to be."

"It wasn't her. It was someone else." Clementine gazed at her mother with big frightened eyes. "A lady. Someone yelling at Fan." A small, spiky lady, Clementine remembered suddenly: all sharp edges, with a long thin nose and little pointy teeth that might have belonged to a bad child. Small black eyes you felt might burn like coals if they rested too long on your skin. "Aunty Rene," she whispered. "Aunty Rene was screaming at Fan."

Her mother frowned and looked out the window, tapping her nails on the armrest of her seat. "Ah well," she said at last, mysteriously, "your Aunty Rene has had a lot to put up with."

"What? What has she had to put up with?"

"Never you mind." Mrs. Southey's voice was low and serious. "Now listen, Clementine. I want you to be especially good while we're at your aunty's place." She reached out a hand and retied the tartan ribbon that was coming loose, as if a little neatness might actually be the start of good behavior. "And it might be best if you didn't mention your cousin Caroline."

"Why?"

"Well, Caroline left home last year."

"You mean she ran away?"

Although Mrs. Southey didn't know about it, Clementine and her best friend, Allie Lewis, had run away only a few weeks ago. They'd taken Mrs. Lewis's big white china fruit bowl out into the yard to make a swimming pool for their family of tiny pink plastic dolls, and the bowl had slipped from Allie's hands and broken into pieces on the bricks beneath the garden tap. "Oh!" Allie had gasped, and without even thinking of it, they'd simply joined hands and run away, down Walpole Street and Gisbourne Avenue, over the canal to the back of the cement works, where they'd hidden inside a big gray concrete pipe. But when the afternoon began to fade and the pipe got cold and creepy, they'd decided to go home again. No one had even missed them. "Oh, that old thing," Mrs. Lewis had said when they'd told her about the broken bowl. "You're late," was all that Clementine's mum said when she'd walked in through the door. "Hurry up and set the table; your dad will soon be home."

Somehow—perhaps it was something to do with the spiky lady's scream—Clementine knew her cousin's running away would be of a different, more serious kind. She stared out through the window at the empty paddocks racing by. How could you run away up here? You wouldn't know where to go, because everything looked the same.

"Of course she didn't run away," her mother said sharply. "Whatever gave you that idea?"

Clementine looked down at the floor. "I don't know."

"It wasn't like that at all. Caroline's a lot older than Fan, and she left because she found a good job in a bigger town. That's all."

"Oh."

Mrs. Southey pursed her lips and added very quietly, as if she was talking to herself, "But all the same, your Aunty Rene wasn't very pleased."

"Why wasn't she?"

Mrs. Southey shrugged. "Forget I said that—just don't

mention Caroline." She gave a final pat to the shiny tartan ribbon. "There."

Clementine leaned her elbow on the sill and gazed out over the paddocks where Caroline had run away. Because she knew Caroline had done just that, whatever Mum said. Fan's big sister had run away from Aunty Rene and that's why she couldn't be mentioned, because—because if Aunty Rene even heard Caroline's name she'd scream and scream and scream.

The paddocks were perfectly flat and the pale gold color of the grass made you think it would be soft to walk upon, like fur, but Clementine knew it would have been hard and prickly beneath her cousin's feet. Dotted across the paddocks were strange boxy trees with straight trunks and crowns of deep green leaves, like trees in a little kid's drawing. They stood singly or in groups of two or three, like people waiting for someone. Waiting for Caroline, thought Clementine. How creepy it would be alone out there in the paddocks at night, where the trees might come alive and whisper to one another— much more scary than the big hollow pipe at the back of the cement works.

In the middle of the afternoon they reached Cootamundra and changed to the small diesel train that would take them farther west. Once inside it, the day seemed truly endless, the sun bright as ever on the paddocks, the small stations trundling by so slowly: Stockinbingal, Temora, Barmedman. And now her mum had gone to sleep and there was no one to ask how much longer it would be until they reached Lake Conapaira; they had been the only people in the carriage since the big man in the tight blue suit had got out at Stockinbingal.

Bellarwi, Narriah, Rankins Springs—"Rankins Springs," sang Clementine softly, and then, more loudly, "Rankins Spri-i-ings," but still her mother didn't wake. Outside the window the shadows of the boxy trees grew longer, thinner; the grass became a softer gold, the rounded hills in the distance were blue instead of brown.

And then the signs began to appear again, nailed to trees or fences and gates beside the railway line: green signs with big black letters that told you how many miles it was to Griffiths Tea. Clementine had seen them on the other side of Cootamundra. Looking up from her comic, she'd spotted the first one, which had said "65 Miles to Griffiths Tea," and a little while later there was another, "50 Miles to Griffiths Tea," and then it was thirty-five, and twenty; but then, absorbed in the comic, she'd missed it, she must have, for the next sign she saw said "200 Miles to Griffiths Tea."

"What's Griffiths Tea?" she'd asked her mother, but Mum had reached a tricky bit in Dad's cable sweater. "Not now," she'd said, looping wool around her needle. "Not now, Clementine." And then they'd arrived at Cootamundra and Clementine had forgotten about the signs.

Now here they were again: "50 Miles to Griffiths Tea." Fifty miles wasn't far; this time she wouldn't take her eyes from the window—she was determined not to miss Griffiths Tea, because it must be special. Why else would they have all these signs, as if the only point in all those miles and miles the train swallowed up was that they took you closer and closer to Griffiths Tea? It would taste like ambrosia, decided Clementine, ambrosia, which Mrs. Carruthers said was the nectar of the gods. And you would drink ambrosia from thin blue-painted cups, in a special, beautiful place: a jeweled palace, with great halls of silver and gold, with peacocks in the gardens, and a lake with white swans. . . .

"30 Miles to Griffiths Tea." And now the sky was changing, its bright blue grown dimmer, almost pearly gray, and at its edge there were bands of different colors: smoky purple, apricot, and palest apple green, like a layer cake, the rainbow one Mum had made for the Christmas Fete at school.

"5 Miles to Griffiths Tea."

A little farther and the train slowed at a tiny station. Goolgowi, read Clementine, and she watched as a small, white-haired old lady stepped out from farther down the train and was instantly surrounded by a ring of smiling people, men in big-brimmed hats and ladies in print dresses, little kids in pajamas, all ready for bed when they got home. They stepped forward one by one to kiss the old lady, and Clementine thought it looked like they were taking part in a dance.

With a single mournful hoot, the train pulled out from the station. The evening was deepening; the rainbow-cake stripes on the horizon had vanished and in their place was a scattering of big pale stars. But there was still enough light to make out the sign on the fence a little way out from the station, the sign that read quite plainly, "250 Miles to Griffiths Tea."

She'd missed it. She'd missed the jeweled palace where princesses and grand ladies drank ambrosia from cups so fine the light shone through. Griffiths Tea was gone.

Her mother had woken and was sitting up straight, pushing damp curly hair from her eyes. "How much farther is it to Aunty Rene's place?" Clementine demanded in a furious choking voice.

Mrs. Southey yawned. "What was that last station we passed? Did you see?"

"Gool, Gool—"

"Goolgowi." She smiled at Clementine, mistaking the rage and sorrow on her daughter's face for tiredness. "Not much farther now."

Clementine kicked at the seat. "I don't care!" And all at once she was crying—crying and crying like a little kid in Infants instead of a big girl in fourth class—great splashy tears that rolled down her cheeks and fell with a plop onto the front of her tartan frock and the worn shiny fabric of the seat.

"Sweetheart! What's the matter? Are you feeling sick?" Mrs. Southey put her hand on her daughter's damp forehead, and Clementine pushed it away. "No, I'm not sick!"

"Then what is it? Are you tired?"

"No, I'm not tired!"

"Then what?"

"It—it's the Griffiths Tea!" wailed Clementine, flinging herself against her mother's chest.

And it really did seem like that: how it wasn't the long, long way to Lake Conapaira that was making her cry, or the strange dark roaring at the windows and the silent country outside; it wasn't the way her dress felt damp and sticky and her eyes stung and her skin itched with gritty red dust; it wasn't the scary memory of Aunty Rene screaming or Fan's big sister running away across the prickly paddocks—it wasn't even the thought of Dad coming home to the empty house and how he might forget them and go away. No, it really was because she'd missed Griffiths Tea, and the beautiful jeweled palace with its halls of silver and gold, and the peacocks in the gardens and the lake with white swans. It was as if a great wonder, a world more beautiful than you could ever imagine, had been coming closer and closer all the long day, until it

was so very near you could reach out and touch it, and then—
she'd gone and missed it. She'd missed it.

And now she would never see it, and she would never
taste ambrosia, never—"Never ever!" shrieked Clementine.

Her mother held her closer and kissed the top of her slippery hair.

"Oh, Clementine!" She sighed. "What are we going to do
with you?"

CHAPTER

2

They shared Fan's room at the end of the hall, a small room with two beds, a battered wardrobe, and an old chair squashed in beside the chest of drawers. Clementine's bed was beneath the window, Fan's up against the wall, and the space between them was so narrow they could hold hands.

Fan's room. But it had once been Caroline's room too. Clementine hadn't asked Fan about her sister, though she longed to know if Caroline had run away. She hadn't asked because Fan never spoke of Caroline, and this seemed strange to Clementine, who'd always wanted a sister and knew that if she'd had one she'd never stop talking about her, like her friend Allie never stopped talking about her big sister, Meg. Perhaps it was different if you had a sister who'd run away.

Fan told stories. She was in the middle of one now, spinning around in the cramped space in the center of the room while Clementine sat cross-legged on her bed, listening hard, because she'd never heard stories like these.

"And then," Fan cried, flinging her head back so that her two thick plaits bounced and swung against her shoulder blades, waving her arms dramatically, "then, well, the magic kid, he sang the tree—"

"He sang to it?" asked Clementine. "He sang a song to a tree?"

"No, not sang to it. He sang it." Fan stood still for a moment. "That's a kind of magic," she explained. "It's making things. It means he made the tree be there." With small, quick hands she shaped a tree growing, spreading the roots wide and deep, raising the trunk, stretching her arms out to make a thick canopy of leaves and branches, her movements so sure and tender that Clementine wouldn't have been surprised if a real tree had suddenly sprung up through the floor. You could feel a tree.

"So," Fan went on, "so he sang the tree and it flew right up into the sky with all the bad spirits hanging on to it. And when it was high, really high, right up in the clouds"—she stood on her toes and stretched her arms above her head— "then he called the winds of heaven and they made the tree shake like anything, like there was a big storm, a thousand storms, and the wicked spirits all fell down to the ground and changed into great big stones—"

"I've seen those stones!" Clementine burst out. "I saw them when we were coming up in the train! They're gray and they look like sheep sleeping in the grass!"

"And did you see the pebbles? The little white pebbles lying everywhere?"

Clementine shook her head. "The train was going too fast."

"Those pebbles are the bad spirits' teeth. When they fell down, all their teeth got knocked out and turned into little white pebbles and scattered all over the ground!"

"Oh! And then what? What did the magic kid do then?"

"What do you think?" Fan jumped up beside Clementine, and the old wooden bed creaked and groaned beneath them. "Like an old cow having a calf, eh?" giggled Fan. She reached up and yanked the curtains apart and together they peered out into the dark backyard, at the black shapes of Uncle Len's shed and the big gum tree beside it, and beyond the sagging fence the nighttime paddocks stretching on and on, all silvery with the moon. Fan pointed upward to the vast black sky that was filled with stars. They were bigger than the ones Clementine saw in the city; they were as big as the magic dogs' eyes in the story Mrs. Carruthers had read to them on the last afternoon before the holidays; as big as teacups, as big as mill wheels, as big as round towers.

"That magic kid, he climbed up into the sky, of course," said Fan.

A lot of her stories ended in this way, and it was strange how she could make something like climbing into the sky sound natural and easy—as if you could be somewhere quite ordinary, walking around the corner of Main Street into Palm Street, for instance, or standing outside the bank or the post office waiting for Mum and Aunty Rene, and suddenly it would happen: the winds of heaven would blow and the sky would come nearer and there'd be a kind of ladder in it where you could put your foot and climb up and be gone. Just like that. Before anyone else had noticed that something amazing was happening.

"Do you make those stories up?" asked Clementine, because they weren't like the stories she'd read in books or the ones Mrs. Carruthers read to them at school. Fan couldn't have got them from a book anyway, because she hated reading.

She read like a little kid in Infants, or like Lizzie Owens and Christa Jorgensen, big girls who sat in the front row of the class, repeating the year they'd done before.

When Aunty Rene made her read out the shopping list before they went on errands, Fan had to sound out all the bigger words—words like *tomatoes* and *potatoes* and *kerosene*, and when she got them wrong, Aunty Rene would say she was a dummy and make her sound them out again and again until she got them right. Clementine and Mrs. Southey weren't allowed to help; Aunty Rene made Fan do every single word herself, right to the bottom of the list, even though anyone could see how much she hated it. Her face would turn bright red and her eyes would slide in all directions, as if they were trying to run away from the words written out on the list. And whenever Clementine picked up one of the storybooks she'd brought from home, Fan would get this panicky look and she'd grab Clementine's hand and say, "C'mon, let's go outside and play." Even if they'd only just come inside.

She was ten, a whole year older than Clementine, but when school started again in February, Fan would still be in fifth class, the same as Clementine. She'd had to repeat the year, like Lizzie Owens and Christa Jorgensen. "Because I'm a dummy, that's why," she told her cousin.

"No, you're not," Clementine protested.

"Ask anyone!"

It was true that on Clementine's first day at Lake Conapaira, walking down Palm Street with Fan, two girls playing jacks in a dusty front yard had bawled out, "Dummy Fan! Raggedy Fan! Fan's got a face like a frying pan!"

"They're just jealous," Clementine had said indignantly, because Fan's face was as beautiful as ever.

"As if I care!" Fan had retorted, skipping on down the road.

"Do you make those stories up?" Clementine asked again, because Fan wasn't listening, she was still gazing through the window at the star-filled sky where the magic kid had climbed.

"Make them up? Course I don't!" Fan got down from the window and settled herself comfortably against Clementine's pillow, drawing her legs up, resting her chin on her knees. She didn't have pajamas or a real nightdress; instead she wore an old green petticoat that was far too big for her, and which Clementine somehow guessed had also belonged to the vanished Caroline. The lace on the hem was all torn. Raggedy Fan. Her long bare legs were powdered with red dust. She hadn't had a bath tonight; she'd taken off when Clementine's mum had called them—across the yard, through the back gate, down the lane and out of sight. Mum hadn't bothered to send Clementine after her. "Oh, let her go," she'd said wearily. "She'll keep."

"They're true, those stories," Fan said. "They're from the Dreaming."

"The Dreaming?"

"The oldest, oldest time."

"You mean like the Garden of Eden?"

"The Garden of Eden!" said Fan scornfully. "Older than that! They're from when there was nothing"—her two hands shaped a big round zero—"and then the spirit ancestors came out of the ground and they sang up all the world."

"Did you learn that at school?"

"Course I didn't. My friend told me."

There was something so soft and secretive in her voice that Clementine asked, "Is he your boyfriend?"

Fan laughed. She had the most perfect laugh: it seemed to fly upward, like drops of bright water flung into the air.

"Course he isn't. He's old."

"How old?" asked Clementine, because Lizzie Owens had a boyfriend at the Tech who was fourteen.

"Old as them," answered Fan, pointing through the window to where a distant line of rounded hills showed black at the edge of the silvery plains.

They were the same hills Clementine had seen coming up on the train. "The blue hills," Fan said softly, and it was true that in certain lights those gray-brown hills did take on the smoky color of Clementine's mother's best blue dress.

"He's my *miyan*," she whispered.

"What's that?"

"Oh, like—a sort of uncle?" Fan frowned. "No, not an uncle, exactly, more like, like—oh, it's so hard explaining!" She made a small flowing motion with her hands; you could tell that the shape they were making was strong and true and calm.

"Someone who looks after you," said Clementine.

"Sort of." Fan smiled. "Guess what he calls me."

Clementine shook her head.

"Guess!"

"I can't."

"You're right," said Fan unexpectedly. "You'd never get it in a million years. No one would. It's—" A faint flush of color spread across her cheeks. "It's *Yirigaa*," she said. "He calls me *Yirigaa*."

"*Yirigaa?*"

She jumped from the bed and twirled around on the floor. "It means 'morning star.'"

Clementine didn't know what to say. She sat there silently,

sensing that her cousin had some other, richer life, a mysterious life that ordinary people knew nothing about.

"I'll take you to see him one day," Fan promised. "Only don't tell Mum, okay?"

"Course I won't." There was no way Clementine would tell Aunty Rene anything. She was frightened of her aunt's sharp voice and bitter black eyes and the way she made you feel like walking on tiptoe. In the mornings Aunty Rene lay in bed until late, and this, like a kind of queer bad magic, made the whole house feel unsafe. You didn't know what she might do when she finally got up, and what kind of day she might make it be. Sometimes she sat in the kitchen with Clementine's mum, or did things around the house; sometimes she sat on the back veranda by herself, smoking cigarettes and turning the pages of an old newspaper with small, yellow-fingered hands. Those days were all right.

But there were other, awful days when a sudden fearful energy would take hold of her; when she'd wrench all the curtains down and boil them in the old copper, or go out the back and chop wood so fiercely that sparks flew from the axe and chips sprayed everywhere. Or she might go after Fan. She might suddenly decide to wash Fan's hair, unbraiding the long plaits with fierce little tugs so the hair came tumbling down her back in heavy ripples and curls, right down past her waist. It was a dark, streaky gold like the wild honey they spread on their toast at breakfast time, so silky that it looked precious, like something you might find in a pharaoh's tomb.

Aunty Rene didn't think it was precious, she called it "a filthy mop" and treated it like string, dragging the comb through the wet tangles until Fan screamed out loud and Aunty Rene hit her legs with the back of the hairbrush, and

Fan screamed louder and called Aunty Rene a witch, and then Aunty Rene would hit her again and shriek, "What did you say? What did you call me?" Clementine's mum would come running, crying, "Rene! Rene!" And Clementine would put her hands over her ears and more than anything she'd want to run out the back and hide until it was all over. But she didn't run; she had to stay with Fan.

"And don't tell your mum either," said Fan now, climbing into her bed and pulling the thin gray blanket right up to her chin. "Because she might tell mine. You know how they are, always whispering."

"They're sisters," said Clementine, and she thought again how peculiar it was that someone nice like Mum could have a sister like Aunty Rene.

There was a little silence. Perhaps Fan was thinking about her sister, Caroline. "Don't tell your mum," she said again, her voice muffled by the blanket.

"I won't."

"Cross your heart and hope to die?"

Clementine sketched a quick cross on the top of her pajamas, then she got up and went to switch out the light.

"No, leave it on," called Fan. "I like it on."

Clementine went back to her bed. She lay down beneath the prickly blanket and closed her eyes and listened to the sounds from the lounge room, where her mother and Aunty Rene sat talking by the fire. Though the summer days were burning hot, the nights at Lake Conapaira could be icy cold beneath that wide black sky. Mum and Aunty Rene spoke softly, so softly you could hardly hear, and sometimes they giggled, like the big girls did in the playground when they talked about boys. But every now and again Aunty Rene's voice would turn all hard and hissy, and there were swear-words in it. "Bloody swine," Clementine heard her say now, and she knew Aunty Rene was talking about Fan's dad, Uncle Len. "His Lordship," she called him, which wasn't a swear-word but sounded like it because the words were full of hate.

Clementine's mother asked a question in a low, soft voice; you could tell it was a question because of the way her voice went up a little at the end.

"Gunnesweare," hissed Aunty Rene in reply. "I told you before, Cissie."

Gunnesweare was the place where Uncle Len had gone off shearing months and months ago, and when Clementine heard it she pictured one of those small stations they'd passed in the train, the single sandy platform, the signs with the long, strange names: Stockinbingal, Narriah, Goolgowi. Gunnesweare would be like that, she thought: a thin wedge of bare platform with no houses or shops behind it, only a narrow dirt road winding over the plains.

"Gunnesweare!" Aunty Rene shouted suddenly, and for the first time Clementine heard the word properly, and real-ized that Gunnesweare wasn't a little town, a real place you might find on a map. What Aunty Rene was shouting, what she'd always been shouting, was "God knows where!" Uncle Len had gone God knows where. "And I don't care!" cried Aunty Rene in a voice like a chair scraping back. A rough sob-bing came through the wall, and Mum's voice saying "There, there, there," as if Aunty Rene wasn't a nasty, cruel old witch but a little kid who'd fallen over and grazed her knee. Clemen-tine glanced toward Fan's bed and saw her cousin's fair head burrowing beneath the pillow.

There was silence from the lounge room now, a silence

so complete you could hear the dry wood popping and crack-ling in the grate, and then there was the creak of someone getting up from one of the old wicker chairs and footsteps coming down the hall. Clementine sucked in her breath, but when the door opened it was only her mum come to kiss her good night. She kissed Fan, too, easing the pillow from her grasp. "Good night, lovie," she whispered, and Fan whispered "Good night" back to her.

"Do you want the light out?" asked Mrs. Southey, and Fan said "no," but she didn't tell her that she liked the light on all the time, and Mum smiled at them both and went out of the room and down the hall toward the bathroom.

Clementine waited. She waited for Aunty Rene's steps coming from the lounge room, coming to kiss her daughter good night. She waited and waited, like she did every night, hoping that this night, this once, Aunty Rene would come.

Aunty Rene didn't come. She never did. She never would, thought Clementine angrily, stealing a quick, furtive glance across the room. Fan was sitting up again, the covers thrown back, picking idly at the hard, stained soles of her feet.

How awful to have a mum who never bothered to kiss you good night! And a sister who'd run away and a dad who went off shearing God knows where. And how odd it seemed to feel sorry for Fan, who was a whole year older, and beautiful, and hardly scared of anything.

Fan sensed her gaze and looked up. "What are you star-ing at?" she demanded.

"Nothing," said Clementine quickly, and Fan lay down again and pulled the gray blanket and the raggy old sheet right up past her face.

Late in the night Clementine woke up. Someone had switched off the light, and the house was silent, the kind of silence where you know at once that everyone else is asleep. She twisted and turned beneath the rough blanket, then she knelt up at the window and pulled the curtain across so the big stars couldn't look in at them. The curtains didn't meet properly: there was a big gap where the stars could still see inside, and Clementine gave up and lay down again.

Oh, how different from home all this was! How different from 33 Willow Street! You could even smell the difference: a mixture of sun and dust, wild honey and the smoky tang from the old kerosene fridge on the back veranda. And you could smell feelings, too—Clementine was sure of it: you could smell anger and hatred and disappointment and jagged little fears. The anger smelled like iron and the disappointment smelled like mud. When she thought of Mum's thick linen tablecloth with the red cross-stitched border and how she'd set the table every evening before Dad came home from work, it all seemed silly up here. The little sense of happiness she used to have, smoothing the creases from the cloth, laying it on the table, getting the edges exactly even, was like a toy given to a baby who had nothing to do but play.

Everything had gone different. Like a changeling, this little room she shared with Fan had stolen the place of her own room back home, where when you looked out the window you saw the park across the road and the lights of the Brothers' house shining through the trees. This old house had taken the place of their house in Willow Street: instead of Willow Street there were the red unpaved streets of Lake Conapaira with the tiny pieces of glass she'd thought were diamonds until Fan had told her, laughing, that they were only bits of old broken bottles crushed into the ground. And the heat of the day and the cold of the night, a different heat and a different cold, and the strange winds that Fan called "the winds of heaven," which sprang up suddenly out of nowhere and blew about the vast empty spaces of the sky. Even the sky was different from the one at home.

And the frightening thing was that all of this, so strange in the first few days, was now after only two weeks so familiar that it seemed more real than the home she'd left behind, as if that home had only been a kind of dream. Even her dad seemed like a dream now: when she tried to picture his face she couldn't remember it clearly.

It wasn't Dad who had forgotten her, it was she who'd forgotten him. Clementine flung herself back down on the bed.

"Oh," she sobbed. "Oh, oh!"

"What is it?" Fan woke quickly like a cat and sat up straight. "Are you crying, Clemmie?"

"No!"

"Yes you are."

"No I'm not."

"You were so." Fan jumped out of bed and padded across the old linoleum. "Are you sad?" she whispered.

"No."

"Is it the cold? Are you cold?" She glanced toward the window, where the stars in the gap between the curtains seemed even bigger now, as if they had come down closer to the earth. "You can have my blanket if you like." She dragged it from her bed and tucked it around her cousin.

"No, you have it!" Clementine tugged it out and threw it back across the room.

Fan picked it up. "'Sokay, I don't want it. I'm used to the cold." She looked down at Clementine. "Want me to come in with you?"

"No!" cried Clementine. And then she changed her mind and whispered, "All right then." She drew the covers back and Fan slipped in beside her. They lay close together, so close they were all tangled up, and Clementine could feel the grains of gritty red dust on her cousin's legs and arms.

"Soon I'll take you to see my friend," promised Fan.

In a little while they were both asleep, a single hump beneath the thin sheet and worn gray blankets. The old house creaked in the cold, and outside the window the big stars grew closer and closer, until they were like cold faces peering through the glass. And the winds of heaven sprang up and blew above the paddocks and rocked in the great spaces of the sky.

CHAPTER

3

F an marched out through the back gate and began to walk away quickly down the lane, so fast that Clementine had to run to keep up with her.

"Wait! Wait for me!"

At the end of the lane Fan stopped and turned around. Her beautiful face, which was always so bright and lively, had gone pale and still. Her eyes gleamed with unshed tears.

At breakfast that morning something bad had happened. In Clementine's house at Willow Street it wouldn't have been bad, only a little accident that could happen to anyone and didn't matter in the least.

Fan had knocked over her cup of milk. Clementine's mum had been sitting next to her, and some of the milk, only a little bit of it, had spilled onto Mrs. Southey's skirt.

Aunty Rene had jumped up from her chair. She was like a match being struck. "Get the cloth!" she'd screamed at Fan. "Get the cloth!"

Her scream flew into every little nook and cranny, exactly as Clementine had imagined when she was coming up in the train. It got into things and made them weak: you felt that if you picked up your cup it would shatter, a spoon might give off an electric shock.

"Get the cloth!"

Fan got to her feet. Usually sure-footed, she stumbled now, as if the scream had sucked her balance away.

She brought the wrong cloth, the dirty dish one from the sink instead of the clean tea towel, and it made greasy streaks all down Mrs. Southey's skirt. "It doesn't matter, Rene," Clementine's mum had protested when Aunty Rene began shrieking some more at Fan, telling her she was a dummy and a retard, a thing that should never have been born. "It's only an old skirt, no harm done. And Fan didn't mean to—it was an accident, Rene."

"Nothing's an accident with that little madam!" Aunty Rene's eyes had glittered. "They say she's backward up the school."

Backward. There'd been a kind of triumph in the way she'd spoken that word; she'd licked her lips on it as if it were chocolate, rich and sweet. A wave of bright crimson had flooded Fan's cheeks, so quick and sudden you barely caught it before it was gone again and her face turned pale as milk. She'd dropped the cloth on the floor and run out of the room, and Clementine had run after her, out of the house, across the yard, and out into the lane.

"Wh-where are you going?" Clementine asked this silent, angry Fan.

Her cousin said nothing for a moment. With the big toe of one bare foot she drew a curved shape in the red dirt of the lane. Then she drew lines around it, like the rays of the sun.

"I'm going to see my friend."

"Can I come?"

Fan took a long time making up her mind. Clementine could have said, "You promised!" but she knew today was different, the kind of day when you didn't remind people of the promises they'd made.

Fan raised her eyes and looked at her cousin. She studied her.

Clementine stood very still.

"All right," said Fan at last. "You can come."

The house in Palm Street was on the very edge of town. At the end of the lane real country began. On their left lay blazing paddocks, to their right a narrow red road that led toward the steely sheet of water that gave the town its name. Lake Conapaira.

"This way." Fan turned onto the red road. It was hot. There was a sky like a brass band. From here the lake seemed far away, yet glittered so fiercely you had to narrow your eyes to look. It was so bright the sun might have fallen down beneath the water and been lying on the muddy bottom with the leeches and little fishes, the rusty old tins and jagged stones. The lake was dangerous; however hot the day was, you could never swim in there.

A dust-filled shimmer hid the farther side. "What's over there?" asked Clementine. She wanted her cousin to talk; she wanted her to be the Fan she knew again.

"The *land*," replied Fan, and her voice lingered on the word, so that it seemed to come out in two falling syllables, la-and, like part of some mysterious song.

"Oh," said Clementine.

They turned off the red road onto a clay track between tall banks of reeds. Water gurgled in among them, and

Clementine heard small, quick scurrying sounds, and then a single, heavy *plop*. A line of black ants crawled in single file along the dry edge of the track.

Clementine stooped to pick up a small white pebble. It felt warm and smoothly perfect in her hand. "Look," she said to Fan. "Look what I found."

Fan took the pebble and examined it closely, turning it this way and that, holding it up to the light. "Reckon it might be one of those teeth them bad spirits lost," she said at last.

Clementine dropped the pebble onto the track. She shuddered.

"Hey!" Fan touched her arm. "It's all right, I was only kidding." She picked up the pebble and began tossing it from hand to hand. "Those teeth didn't fall down here. It was some other place, honest, miles and miles away." She held out the small white stone and Clementine took it and thrust it deep into the pocket of her shorts.

Fan was kind, reflected Clementine. And she was clever, too, no matter what Aunty Rene said, or those kids who sang stupid songs in the street. It didn't matter that she read badly and had to repeat at school; you could tell from her face and the things she said that she was clever. She knew all the secret tracks and places around the lake, and words from another language, and stories other people didn't know. And she was clever with thoughts and feelings, too: she grasped things no one else could see. When Clementine had told her about the Griffiths Tea signs, Fan had understood exactly how Clementine had imagined the jeweled palace and the tea that tasted like ambrosia, and the way she'd felt when she'd missed the place and begun bawling like a little kid.

Even Mum hadn't understood about Griffiths Tea. She'd

told Clementine it was just an ordinary old tea you bought in an ordinary grocer's shop, and the signs along the railway line were only advertising. "You haven't missed a thing, sweetheart," she'd said. "There's nothing to cry about."

But Clementine thought there was, and Fan had agreed with her.

"You were crying for *gadhaang*," she'd said.

Gadhaang. It was the kind of word you just knew meant something important.

"That's happiness," Fan had explained. "Proper happiness. Serious happiness. That's what you thought Griffiths Tea might be."

Serious happiness. Even Clementine's best friend, Allie, wouldn't have understood so well, and as for girls like Lizzie Owens and Christa Jorgensen, if Clementine had so much as breathed a word to them about Griffiths Tea, they'd have said she was barmy and the green cart would be coming to her house that very night to take her to the loony bin for ever and ever, amen.

They walked and walked, and there was no other sound except their footsteps and the rustle of the reeds and the steady lapping of the lake water against the crusty mud of the shore—*lap, lap, lap,* like an old dog licking at a sore. The sun was right up high in the brassy sky, blaring like trumpets and drums, and Clementine could feel the heat of the earth beating up through the thin soles of her canvas shoes. "Don't your feet get burned?" she asked Fan, and Fan stopped and lifted one bare foot in her hand and examined its bright stained sole. "Nah," she said, dropping the foot and walking on again. "Guess I'm used to it."

"Are we nearly at your friend's place?"

"It's just up here." Fan pointed to a steep stony slope that rose away from the shore. "C'mon!" She grabbed Clementine's hand and pulled her up the hill.

At the top was a small plateau surrounded by a hedge of dusty bushes; sheets of rusty corrugated iron and a curtain of old sacking formed a makeshift shelter between two spindly gums. A few battered tins lay beside a circle of blackened stones, and the bits of glass that looked like diamonds were crushed into the ground.

"Does your friend live here?"

"Sometimes. And sometimes he goes away."

"Where to?"

Fan stretched her arms out wide. *"Birrima,"* she answered dreamily. "A place far, far away." She went up to the shelter and drew the curtain aside. She beckoned to Clementine. "See?" she whispered.

Behind the sacking an old black man was lying on a bed of flattened reeds. He was old as the hills, just like Fan had said: the deep grooves and wrinkles on his face were gray against the dark skin, as if they were filled with ash. He lay so still he didn't seem alive; one of the small black ants they'd seen on the track was crawling along his arm.

Clementine swallowed. "Is he dead?" she whispered fearfully.

"Of course he's not. Can't you see his chest going up and down? He's asleep, that's all. And we mustn't wake him up."

"Why?"

"Because he might be away from here," said Fan.

Clementine stared at her cousin. "But he isn't away. He's there. He's lying there."

Fan shook her head gravely. "He's a magic man. Sometimes when he's asleep his spirit goes out walking."

"Walking?"

"Over the land. It might be a long, long way from here, and if you wake him up, then his spirit mightn't be able to get back, see?"

"And if it can't get back, then what happens?"

Fan didn't answer. She slipped through the sacking curtain and crouched down beside the sleeping man, placing one hand softly over his, light as a moth settling on a crumpled leaf. She closed her eyes.

The quiet inside the shelter was like peace. Clementine remembered the shape Fan had made with her hands when she'd been trying to describe her friend, the shape that showed strength and calm. And when Fan got to her feet and came back out to Clementine, her face had lost its sadness and anger and become brave and sweet again, as if some kind of strength and comfort had been passed from the old man to her, and the harsh scene at breakfast had faded from her mind. She was smiling. "Let's go!" she cried, skipping lightly across the clearing, disappearing through the thicket of dusty bushes at its edge.

Clementine hurried after her, pushing her way through the bushes where sharp little twigs snatched at her legs and arms. On the other side of the thicket a rutted track snaked between gray-gold paddocks, and Fan was running along it, little puffs of red dust rising like smoke about her feet. "Hurry up!" she called when she saw Clementine.

"Where are we going?"

"My hidey. Well, it's not a hidey, really, it's just my special place. You'll like it, there's shade. It stays really cool there."

Cool. Out here, coolness seemed an impossibility; the air was so hot that simple breathing was like sucking in a flame. Above the paddocks the sky had turned a strange color, a dull reddish gray, and a little wind was stirring in the bristly grass. Clementine caught at her cousin's arm. "Is there going to be a storm?"

Fan glanced up at the peculiar sky. "No," she said. "It's just dust." Her gaze swerved over the rustling grasses, and then out to the horizon. "Reckon there's a willy-willy not far off, though."

"A willy-willy?"

"Yeah. See? Over there!" She pointed over the paddocks, and Clementine saw a tall, hazy figure in a long brown robe moving rapidly over the dry grass, rushing first one way and then another as if some invisible demon were chasing after him. Where he ran the grass bowed down before him, and twigs and straw rose up around his brown skirts in a flurry: it was as if someone immensely strong and angry were stalking over the land and everything that wasn't rooted firmly in the earth was gathered into his whirling robe. As she watched, a whole branch from a dead tree was plucked up into the air.

Clementine clutched tighter at her cousin's arm. "Is that his spirit coming back?"

"What?"

"The old black man's spirit?"

Fan gazed at her in astonishment. "Of course it isn't."

"Who is it, then?"

"Who? No one. I told you, it's a willy-willy, that's all. A sort of whirlwind, with all dust and stuff in it. It's not a person, it's not anything alive." Fan took Clementine's hand from her arm and grasped it firmly. "Don't be scared. It won't hurt us. It'll come close but not right here."

How did she know? Clementine wanted to run, only how could you know which way to run? The whirling brown column seethed this way and that, first in one direction, then another—it could get you whichever way you ran. There was a rushing sound, dust swirled in the air. "Close your eyes," ordered Fan, and Clementine closed them and stood there, trembling, holding tight to her cousin's hand while heat and dust surged around her and the air itself seemed to boom. The booming passed them and the air went still. "It's going now," she heard Fan say calmly. "See?"

Clementine opened her eyes. The willy-willy was far away over the paddocks, a long, thin figure in a brown robe again. And though it was tall and looked like a man, the strange thing was that it reminded Clementine of Aunty Rene. It was the way the thing seethed, the way it veered from place to place, the way it sucked things inside it like Aunty Rene sucked in griefs and spite until she was made of them.

They walked on. The track curved back toward the lake, to a hollow in the bank above the water, a shady place between two she-oak trees. They lay down on grass, which was still soft and green, and watched the clouds racing across the sky. The lake lay spread beneath them, making its sad old dog lapping sound. A flock of black cockatoos wheeled out over the water, shrieking.

"*Bilirr*," murmured Fan dreamily.

"Does that mean 'cockatoo'?"

"Course it does. Fan reached across and laid a finger on Clementine's lips. "Now you say it, Clemmie."

Clementine felt shy. "I can't."

"Yes you can. It's easy. Go on."

"*Bilirr,*" said Clementine, very slowly and carefully, in the way you might carry someone else's precious object across a slippery floor.

"That's it." Fan's delighted laughter flew up into the air.

"*Bilirr,*" said Clementine more confidently, and a single gleaming black feather floated down onto the grass beside her, just like the pigeon's feather had floated down at Central Station, only now Mum wasn't here to snatch it away. She picked it up and studied its color—if you held it one way, it wasn't black at all, but a deep, deep blue, and the blue sheen stirred a long-ago memory of Fan's big sister. Caroline's hair had had that same blue sheen. "You know your sister?" she blurted. "The one who ran away?"

She'd forgotten how Fan never talked of Caroline. Beside her on the grassy bank she felt her cousin tense and draw in her breath.

"Who told you that?" Fan demanded angrily. "Who told you she ran away?"

"N-no one," stammered Clementine. "I just thought . . ." she tailed off, because how could she explain the desolate feeling the old house in Palm Street stirred in her, or the picture she'd imagined so clearly in the train, of the black-haired girl running away across the paddocks. "Mum said she went away because she found a job," she mumbled.

"That's right," said Fan sharply. "That's what she did. She found this job in Temora and went down there. That's all. She didn't run away, and anyone who says that's a liar!"

There was a silence. Clementine didn't know how to break it. She'd never seen Fan get angry before, except with Aunty Rene, and she was afraid she might say the wrong thing again and make everything worse. So she stayed quiet, and it was Fan who finally spoke. "She visits us sometimes," she said in a low, grudging tone. "Only"—now her voice trembled—"only she doesn't stay long. Temora's a long way, and Caro doesn't get many holidays, see?" Fan puckered her lips and her next words were spoken in a voice that didn't sound like hers at all, and which Clementine guessed was an imitation of Caroline's. "By the time she gets here, it's practically time to go home again." Fan tore up a handful of grass, studied each blade carefully, and then scattered them over the ground. "Anyway, I don't care!" She lifted her chin defiantly, and Clementine saw she was angry with Caro for going away and leaving her alone.

"You're lucky having a sister; I wish I did, even if she lived a long way away."

"You think so?"

Clementine nodded. "I've always wanted a sister. Always."

"I could be your sister." Fan smiled and her lips became soft and generous again. She grasped the ends of her plaits and twisted them up on her head. "If—if you wanted me to be, that is."

"I do."

"But you might like a different kind of sister. Someone more sort of . . ."

"More sort of what?"

Around went the plaits again, twisting.

"I dunno. More like other girls. Like your friends down in Sydney."

"Oh, no! I'd like you."

"Honest?" Fan's face shone with delight. She tossed the plaits gaily over her shoulders.

"All right, then," she said, and leaned forward to place a soft kiss on Clementine's lips. "Now we're sisters, see."

"Sisters," echoed Clementine.

"That's *gindaymaidhaany.* Say it."

"*Gingaymaid—*"

"*Gindaymaidhaany.* It's hard, I know."

"*Gin-gindaymaidhaany.*"

"Got it! And now I'll tell you a secret, eh? A special, serious secret, like you told me yours about the Griffiths Tea. But you mustn't tell anyone. Promise?"

"Promise."

"Okay. It's this: Caro didn't run away, but I'm going to, one day."

"Honest?" But Clementine knew she'd run away if she had a mum like Aunty Rene.

"Honest! And guess where I'm going."

"*Birrima?*"

Fan laughed. "Sort of." She turned from the lake and pointed in the other direction. "I'm going there!"

"Where?" All Clementine could see was the country that lay outside their bedroom window back at Palm Street: the endless paddocks, the rounded hills, the great aching arch of sky.

"Where?" she asked again.

"I'm going to the blue hills," said Fan. "See those hills over there? They're not blue today, but sometimes they are."

"I know."

"They look close, don't they? They look like you could walk there in a single morning. Only you can't. I tried it once, one day when I bunked off school—"

"Do you bunk off school?"

"What do you think?" Fan's voice was full of scorn. "Anyway, there was this morning last winter when I didn't want to go because everyone was cranky with me, so I packed my schoolbag with some stuff to eat and I pretended I was going to school, same as ever, only I sneaked off down at the crossing and took the other road, and then—" Fan paused to take a breath.

"And then what?"

"I walked and walked and walked all morning, and those hills didn't get the least little bit closer. No matter how far I went, they just seemed the same distance away." Her gaze drifted away toward the horizon, where the hills crouched, mysterious in the haze, their round, humped shapes blurred in heat and dust. "You know what? Next time I'm gunna go on Dad's old bike. It's still out in the shed; only needs the tires pumping up."

"But what's there?" asked Clementine. She thought the hills had an empty look about them.

"Oh, anything! That's the secret!" Fan's eyes were shining. "I reckon there could be just about anything up there, anyplace you'd ever dream about—jungles and deserts and forests—"

"And the sea?"

"And the sea." Fan spread her arms out wide. "Seas and seas and seas. And snow—"

"Snow!"

"Yes! Anything you wanted might be up there. That's what I reckon, anyway. And"—she gazed around her, at the shining lake and the gray-gold paddocks and the blue sky blazing over them—"and this place too, it could be up there, only without school in it or—or anything bad."

Bad. Clementine thought of Aunty Rene's fierce black eyes, her sharp little teeth like a bad child's, that scream in her voice that made you feel weak and afraid.

Fan reached out a dusty foot and nudged at her cousin's leg. "And there'll be a palace made of jewels for you, with peacocks in the gardens, and swans on the lake, and a gold table and chairs where we can drink your Griffiths Tea, and it'll taste like, like—what was it?"

"Ambrosia," whispered Clementine.

"That's right. There'll be ambrosia just for you."

A great wave of tenderness flooded Clementine's heart: she felt that in her whole life, even when she was grown up and married and had children of her own, even when she was a grandmother and very, very old, there would never be anyone she loved so much as Fan.

They lay back on the grass and watched the clouds take on amazing shapes: three ducklings in a wobbly line, a kangaroo with a long curved tail like the one on the back of the two-shilling piece Clementine's dad gave her for her pocket money, and a bride with a long floating veil. The winds of heaven sailed them across the sky and changed their shapes so tenderly that the ducklings found a mother, and the kangaroo grew wings, and the bride picked up her floaty veil and danced for them, and they felt that everything beautiful was possible in the world.

CHAPTER

4

There were certain evenings when Aunty Rene would leave the house after tea, returning a few hours later, flushed-faced and strangely excited, to fall asleep almost at once in her chair beside the fire.

"Where does she go?" Clementine asked her mother, but all Mrs. Southey said was, "It's none of your business, Clementine."

She didn't ask Fan, because on those evenings when Aunty Rene went out, Fan's face would close as fast as the door behind her mother, and she'd run to her room and lie down beneath her blanket, even if it was only seven o'clock and still light outside. If Clementine went in to talk, Fan would pretend to be asleep, and then Clementine would take one of her books and sit with her mother in the lounge room.

"Mum?" she asked on one such night, speaking softly so that Fan wouldn't hear them through the wall. "Mum, can Fan come and stay at our place next holidays?"

Her mother didn't look up from her knitting.

"Can she, Mum? In the May holidays? It's only two weeks," begged Clementine.

Mrs. Southey gave a sharp little tug to her gray wool, and then an even sharper one, as if it had refused to do what she wanted and answered back quite rudely.

"Can she?" persisted Clementine, and watched the skin between her mother's eyebrows pleat up in a frown. "We'll see," she murmured. It was the answer she'd given in the train when Clementine had asked if she'd be able to swim in Lake Conapaira. "We'll see," Mrs. Southey had said, when all along she'd known the lake was too deep and there were big leeches that fastened to your legs and grew fat and brown with sucking on your blood. "We'll see" was what her mother answered when she wanted to say no but didn't want to say it yet; when she was hoping you'd forget all about the awkward thing you wanted. Clementine stomped off to bed.

It was hours later when Aunty Rene returned, and the bang of the door as she came in was so loud that the whole house shook and rattled and Clementine woke with a fright in her bed.

"It's all over town and of course I'm the last one to know!" Aunty Rene was shouting from the lounge room.

"Calm down, Rene," she heard her mother say in a frightened voice. "I don't know what you're talking about. What's all over town?"

Aunty Rene didn't answer her sister's question; she went on yelling as if she hadn't heard. "I hate this bloody place! I hate it, hate it!"

"Rene, what's the matter? What's happened?"

"Happened! As if we hadn't sunk low enough! His Lordship off to Gunnesweare and that little madam in trouble up the school more than she's out of it. And now she's hangin' 'round with boongs!"

"What?"

"You heard me! Hangin' 'round with boongs!"

"Are you talking about Fan?"

"Who else?"

"But—but I thought the Aboriginal people lived out of town, at the camp."

"Not him! Not that old bugger got a humpy the other side of the lake!"

"The old black man? Rene, what on earth do you mean? What's the harm there? Mrs. Ryland at the baker's was telling me about him only yesterday when I went down to get the bread. She said he's some kind of storyteller—"

"Storyteller!"

"That's what Mrs. Ryland said. Her brother's staying with her at the moment. He's a historian from the university, and he goes to talk to that old man."

"The university! Don't talk to me about bloody universities!"

"If people saw Fan out there, that's what she'd have been doing: getting the old man to tell her stories. You know how she loves that sort of thing. What harm can it do?"

"What harm?" Aunty Rene's voice was incredulous. "You don't know what you're talkin' about, Cissie! I'll tell you what bloody harm! He might be old, and he might be some kind of storyteller, like you say—but he's a boong, isn't he? He's got mates, young mates, take my word for it."

"What?" Clementine felt the ring of shock in her mother's voice.

"You heard!" There was a small sharp *bang* followed by a broken tinkling, as if Aunty Rene had thrown a cup or plate against the wall and it had fallen in a shatter on the floor.

"She'll be out the bloody river camp, next! She'll be hangin' 'round there! And you know what they say about girls who hang 'round the river camp!"

"Rene, you've got it all wrong, I'm sure you have."

"Got it wrong, have I?"

"This is your own child you're talking about, and Fan *is* a child—she's hardly ten."

"Hardly ten, eh? Well, ten's near enough to twelve, isn't it? And twelve to fourteen? They start early up here, Cissie."

"Start early? Rene, I can't believe you're saying all this. How can you? Fan's a good girl."

"A good girl? You tried talkin' to her teachers?"

"That's only because she doesn't do well at school. It's got nothing to do with—with the sort of thing you—you mean."

"You sayin' if she's bad it's my fault?"

"No! Of course not! And she's not bad. Listen, what I'm saying is that Fan—" Mrs. Southey's next words were drowned out because Aunty Rene had started screaming.

"It's gunna happen!" she shrieked. "I know it is! Look what happened to me!"

The silence that followed seemed to tremble with some kind of grief. Beyond it, Clementine could make out a muffled thumping sound, like dust being beaten from a dirty old mat, and a picture rose up of Aunty Rene's small clenched fist thudding on her bony chest, over and over again. Was it that? Could it be? Clementine cast a quick, furtive glance across the room toward her cousin's bed. The rigid stillness beneath the blanket told her Fan was awake and listening too.

Aunty Rene was crying now. "I was a girl once, wasn't I?" she sobbed. "A pretty girl?" Her voice lost its savagery and took on an imploring sound. "You remember, don't you, Cissie?"

"Of course I do."

"Remember that Tangee lipstick I used to wear?"

"Yes." Mrs. Southey's voice was the barest breath.

"And the Coty powder? Evenin' in Paris scent?"

"Oh, Reenie!"

"Jeez, I was a fool!" Another piece of china crashed and tinkled to the floor. "Dressed in me flimflams, off to the Roxy . . ." Aunty Rene's voice descended to a hiss. "And that's where I met him, wasn't it? That's where I met His Lordship. And before I knew what hit me, there's a bun in the oven, and—"

"Rene!"

"Oh, leave me alone, Cissie! I'll say what I like, now it's too late for me. A bun in the oven and me hardly more than a girl, and what was I to do? Then he carts me off up here! To this dump! This place! Bloody end of the world and I'm stuck in it!" Aunty Rene paused to gulp in breath and when she spoke again her voice was hoarse with loathing. "And I'm tellin' you, Cissie, what happens down there in the city happens sooner up here! And that little madam—"

"But she's only ten," repeated Clementine's mother helplessly.

"Only ten and she's gunna learn now before it's too bloody late! She's gunna learn something she won't forget in a hurry!" Aunty Rene's voice soared up again. "And that's to stay away from bloody boongs!"

Clementine sneaked another glance across the room. Fan was kneeling up on her bed now, straining for every word.

And now there came the sound of footsteps running to the kitchen, and a queer little noise from there, a small metallic chatter followed by a brief swishing sound. When she heard this, Fan gave a little cry and leaped from her bed. She ran to the door, but she was too late, Aunty Rene was already halfway up the hall. Rushing. You could hear her, like the willy-willy, seething.

"The window, quick!" Clementine began to wrestle with the catch and Fan scrambled up beside her. Stiff with rust and ancient paint, the window wouldn't budge. There was nowhere to go.

A small, furious figure burst through the doorway, swinging a wide brown belt.

Clementine had noticed this belt in the kitchen, hanging from a hook beside the gas stove. She'd noticed, too, how her cousin's eyes would sometimes swing toward it and then swerve away. Once Fan had seen Clementine looking at it and whispered to her, "She uses the buckle end." Clementine hadn't quite realized what her cousin had meant. Now, as Aunty Rene came seething across the room, one hand outstretched to grab her daughter, she knew.

Fan jumped from the bed and slid under it, but with the same single swift movement she used to gut a rabbit, Aunty Rene seized Fan's ankle and pulled her out again. She dragged her to her feet and brought the belt down hard across her daughter's legs. There was a fat fleshy sound and a bright red stripe appeared across Fan's calves, beaded with drops of blood. Fan screamed, she strained like a dog on a leash, but Aunty Rene's strong fingers held her fast.

She ran in a tight circle around her mother, who turned with her, bringing the strap down and down and down. Buckle end. "You'll learn!" Aunty Rene was screaming, over and over and over again. "You'll learn!"

"That's enough, Rene! That's enough!" Clementine's mother was in the room now, pulling at her sister, struggling to get her away from Fan, but small as she was, Aunty Rene was strong. She flicked her sister off like a bothersome fly. Her black eyes glittered, her lips were pulled back from her bad child's teeth, her chin was flecked with foam. Around and around they went—like a maypole or a hurdy-gurdy or something dreadful at a fair.

Clementine rushed past them, down the hallway, through the kitchen, out the door, down to the back of the yard, where she crouched behind the woodpile and clamped her hands over her ears. She thought of home, the quiet house in Willow Street, the small park across the road, the lights from the Brothers' house burning comfortingly all night. She thought of her father sitting in his chair in the lounge room, the lamp turned on beside it while he read through the *Daily Mirror*. And when he'd finished reading he'd unclip his pen from his shirt pocket, turn to the second-last page, fold the paper over, and begin the crossword.

He wouldn't have gone away, of course he wouldn't—how silly she'd been to worry that he would! What a baby she'd been on that train! Though the journey was only a few weeks back, it seemed like years and years; she felt like a different person now. Dad would never leave them. He wasn't like Uncle Len, who'd run away to Gunnesweare. In her mind Clementine still thought of her uncle's destination in this way: a small railway siding with nothing but a lonely road behind it, winding away into the dusty plains. Her dad would never go somewhere where you couldn't find him; he'd keep on coming home in the evenings at five thirty, the chain of his bicycle purring up the path beneath the kitchen windows while Clementine set the table for tea. She took her hands from her ears. From the house she could hear her mum and Aunty Rene fighting: their voices rose and fell, full of anger and pain and tears. There was no sound from Fan, not even crying. Was she all right?

Clementine knew she should go inside and find out. She shouldn't have run away in the first place, because wasn't she Fan's sister now? But when she tried to get up from her hiding place, she found she couldn't move, her limbs had turned into some soft, heavy substance like clay. She was afraid. "I want to go home!" she sobbed treacherously, disloyally—because wasn't she Fan's *gindaymaidhaany*? "Fan can come home with us," she whispered to some silent, invisible accuser. She knew this wasn't possible; they couldn't take Fan away from her mum.

"Oh, I want, I want . . . ," she cried to the big bright watching stars, and then she stopped, because she didn't know what she wanted, except that Fan could be safe and the world be different from the way it was tonight.

It was barely dawn when she woke the next morning. A pale gray light filled the room, and if Clementine had looked out through the window, she would have seen a band of bright, unearthly pink along the horizon—the color of the candy floss her dad always bought for her at the Easter Show. "Red sky at night, shepherds' delight," her mum would have recited if she'd seen it. "Red sky at morning, shepherds' warning." But Mrs. Southey was fast asleep and Clementine didn't look through the window anyway; she looked across at Fan's bed to see what would be there.

The bed was empty, and it frightened Clementine, for in some way she couldn't quite understand—was it the way the tangled sheet looked cold as ice? And the pillow tossed

sideways to the wall as if it would never again be needed?—
she knew that the bed had been empty for a long, long time.
Perhaps it had been empty since Clementine had finally fallen
asleep last night.

If only she'd spoken to Fan then, if only she had! But
when Clementine's mum had called her from the back door
and told her to come to bed, and she'd tiptoed down the silent
hall into the bedroom, Fan had been lying with the blanket
pulled right over her face, like she always did when she
didn't want to talk to anyone. And so even though the room
seemed full to bursting with her cousin's sorrow, and Clementine's own heart was full of it as well, she'd slid down beneath her own blanket without a single word.

Now Fan had gone, and Clementine could tell she wasn't
in the house: the old green petticoat lay abandoned on the
floor; the big drawer where most of Fan's daytime clothes
were kept hung open, trailing hems and sleeves.

She'd have gone to her hidey, decided Clementine, her
special place in the grassy hollow by the lake. She jumped out
of bed, pulled on her shorts and T-shirt, thrust her feet into
her sneakers, crept from the house and hurried across the
backyard, out the gate, and up the lane toward the narrow red
road that led to the lake. Then she ran.

The hidey was empty. Clementine walked around and
around it, unable to believe her cousin wasn't there. Where
was she, then, if she wasn't here?

A terrible thought seized hold of her: perhaps, like the
people in her stories, Fan had gone to climb up into the sky.
Where would you go if you wanted to climb into the sky? How
would you find the ladder if you didn't know where it was and
it didn't come down to you by itself? Perhaps you needed a

magic word, like Ali Baba's "Open Sesame!" And then Clementine remembered the old black man: they were his, those stories, so perhaps Fan had gone to him.

She ran out from the hidey and into the paddocks. A crowd of cockatoos, busy at their breakfast in the dry tussocky grass, rose up at her approach and whirled off in a raucous cloud. *Bilirr.*

"Where's Fan?" she called after them. "Where's Fan?" But even if cockatoos could speak, she was certain it would be in the language of the old black man, and she wouldn't be able to understand them.

When she reached the place where he had his shelter, she saw at once that the old man had gone. The sheets of iron lay flat on the ground, the sacking curtain on top of them, folded neatly as a piece of her mother's fresh ironing on a Tuesday afternoon. The rusty tins had vanished, the pile of rushes had been swept away. There was nothing but the prickly bushes and the spindly gums, the bare earth and the circle of blackened stones.

"Fan!" she called. "Fan!" The only sounds that returned to her were the faint rattle of dry gum leaves and the old-dog lapping of the lake upon the shore. A wind had risen, and she became aware that the light had changed. When she'd been running along the track to Fan's hidey, the sun had come up; now it had gone dark again. The sky had clouded over, but not with the shapely white clouds she and Fan often watched beside the lake: this cloud was like a dingy blanket thrown across the whole of the sky, the color of washing-up water, flecked at its edges with livid dirty foam. Thunder rumbled distantly.

She hurried from the old man's camp and began to run

across the paddock where the willy-willy had come seething across the land. What if another one was coming? She didn't know how to judge its direction like Fan. What if she got swirled up into its brown skirts like an old tree branch, and whirled away over the plains? Where was Fan? Where? Had she gone away with her friend? To Birrima, the place far, far away? Had they both climbed up into the sky? A sob caught in her throat; she ran and ran and she didn't know where she was going, she didn't know anything.

It was all Aunty Rene's fault. Oh, how she hated her, hated her, hated her! She wished Aunty Rene would die; surely she deserved to die. Yet even as she thought this, Clementine re-membered an afternoon last week when there'd been a sud-den shower of rain, and Aunty Rene had run out into the yard and stood there with her face lifted to the raindrops: a face that looked unexpectedly young and even gentle, so you could see how once she'd been a different person. The person who'd chosen the beautiful name Francesca for her baby girl.

A great branch of lightning tore across the sky, and in its livid light she saw a strange creature hurtling down the narrow road that led away to the hills—a thin, dark, rigid thing that carried some softer, paler shape upon its back.

Clementine didn't move. Let it get her, then! She didn't care anymore. She didn't care if it was a Hobyah carrying a great big bag, she didn't care if it leaped on her and stuffed her in the bag and took her home to gobble; because if Fan was gone, then nothing really mattered anymore.

Only Mum and Dad. Especially Dad. How would Dad feel if she went away?

It was raining now. Big, heavy drops fell like coins onto the dust at her feet. She dashed the tears from her eyes, looked up, and saw that the strange dark creature was only a rusty old bicycle, and the shape on its back was Fan.

Fan on her dad's old bike! How could she have forgotten? Hadn't Fan told her she'd run away to those hills one day? Hadn't she planned to go on her dad's old bike?

Fan skidded to a stop in the middle of the track, a few yards from her cousin. She threw the old bike down, and it lay on its side in the mud, wheels spinning, while Fan stood beside it, head down, crying. Clementine ran to put her arms around her. Fan's hair, escaped from its plaits, felt cold, and it was darker, too, the color of treacle instead of wild honey, and her face was streaked with red stripes where the dust had muddled with the rain and tears. Even in the gloomy light, Clementine could see the marks from Aunty Rene's strap on her cousin's legs, and they made her feel sick. They shouldn't be there—they made you feel the world had gone all wrong.

"I couldn't get there," Fan sobbed. "I couldn't get there, Clemmie! I rode and rode, and they were still as far away as ever, just like the other time. And then I started thinking how I hadn't left you a note or anything, and you wouldn't know where I'd gone, and how you'd worry, like you do, and so"—she gave a long, shuddering sigh—"so I came back again." She pressed her face down into Clementine's thin shoulder and they stood together silently, while the thick, cold rain poured down.

"She shouldn't hit me," Fan whispered.

"I know she shouldn't."

"Because I'm *Yirigaa*. I'm the morning star, see? And that means I'm—I'm a kind of princess. My friend said so."

"I know."

Fan lifted her head and stared back hopelessly at the elusive hills. "I just can't seem to get there."

"You will."

"No I won't."

"Yes you will. Why do you think you won't? When you're grown up, what's going to stop you then? You'll drink Griffiths Tea up there one day, I bet. You'll taste ambrosia."

Fan didn't say anything. On the ground beside them one wheel of the old bicycle still spun, a faint sibilant whisper beneath the rain. Fan put out a hand and stilled the wheel with a single fingertip, and then there was only the rain.

"And when you go there, I'll come too," said Clementine.

"Would you? Even when we're grown up?"

"Of course."

"Promise?"

"Cross my heart."

Fan stepped back and beamed at Clementine. She gave a little skip, grabbed two handfuls of her cold wet hair, and flung them over her shoulders triumphantly. "When we grow up!" she shouted, and her laughter flew up in the air.

The very next morning Clementine and her mother left for Sydney on the diesel train. They were going home a whole week earlier than they'd planned because Mum and Aunty Rene had quarreled. "Can Fan come with us?" Clementine longed to ask. She didn't, though, because she knew what the answer would be. They were leaving so fast there wasn't even time for Mum to say "we'll see."

It would be almost five years before Clementine saw her cousin again.

PART TWO

1957–1958

CHAPTER

5

When she was thirteen and in her second year at Chisholm College, Clementine had a geometry teacher called Mr. Meague. He was a slight, gray-haired man, soft as a whisper. You wouldn't think he could frighten anyone.

Mr. Meague liked silence. Silence was the element he breathed, he told his class, with that strange little twitch at the corner of his mouth that might have been a smile and might have been something else you couldn't put a name to: he breathed silence as they breathed air, or fish breathed water down beneath the sea.

Mr. Meague caned boys for talking. There were plenty of teachers at Chisholm who used the cane. Boys were always getting whacked—for fighting or giving cheek or smoking in the toilets and around the back of the canteen. No one except Mr. Meague caned for talking. The penalties for talking were writing lines, or detention, or the hollow rap of a blackboard duster on the very center of your skull.

Teachers weren't allowed to cane girls, but Mr. Meague had found his way around this restriction. When he caught a girl talking in his class, he told her to stand up, and then he ordered her to pick a boy. And when she did this, when she chose a name and spoke it out, then Mr. Meague would cane the boy she chose.

Most girls picked a Home Boy. The Home Boys came from St. Swithin's, which everyone knew was a terrible place. They were awkward, bony-looking boys, rough and pasty-faced, whose skin and clothing looked like it might be damp to the touch. They were always in trouble for fighting and swearing, always being caned, at Chisholm and at St. Swithin's, where there were far worse things than canes.

So Jilly Norris said, anyway.

Jilly Norris sat next to Clementine in geometry, and she should know because her mother had a part-time job in the kitchens of St. Swithin's. The kitchen was disgusting, Mrs. Norris had told Jilly: cockroaches floated in the soup like big brown shiny dates with legs, and the smell from the fridge when you opened it would knock a strong man down. They used whips at St. Swithin's, Jilly Norris claimed, and special straps with little bits of metal worked into them. And there was a dark cellar like a dungeon where they kept the worst boys chained up to the wall.

Clementine's mum said Jilly Norris was making it up, but Jilly said you only had to look at the palms of the Home Boys' hands—they were as hard and callused as normal people's feet. Jilly Norris and her friends said it didn't matter if you picked a Home Boy for Mr. Meague to cane; they were used to it, weren't they? And they were orphans, so there wouldn't be any bother with mums or dads coming around to your house to complain you'd picked on their son. And they would come around to your place, you could bet on it. They wouldn't go up to the school and complain to Mr. Meague or the headmaster, because most of the parents considered that their kids were lucky to get into Chisholm. It was a school for clever kids and had good teachers and opportunities to get on in the world.

And the teachers were forbidding, with their aloof, stern faces and their long black gowns. You'd never think those faces could once have belonged to children who'd grown up in the very same suburbs the students came from: the drab flat clusters of small fibro houses strung out along the western railway line, suburbs where you baked in summer and froze in winter, and where the grass in the vacant lots burned brown or turned icy white and beautiful, like fields of frost, in the cold heart of July. Yet dignified Miss Evelyn, who taught Latin, had grown up in the very same street as Clementine's mum. "Eight children in the family and not a penny to bless themselves with," Mum had told her. And everyone knew that Dr. Rawson, the headmaster, had been a Home Boy from St. Swithin's.

It wasn't only the academic gowns and stern faces that made some of the Chisholm parents hesitate to bring a problem to the school. It was more than that, it was hope—they believed Chisholm College offered their children the chance to have better lives than their own. Clementine's dad always said you made your own chances in life, but she could see that he and Mum had shy hopes of their own for her. She'd noticed how, on Sunday visits to the city, bus rides through the waterside suburbs, the harbor glittering on one side, the beautiful houses in their long gardens on the other—her parents would grow wistful, even a little sad. It wasn't for themselves—Mum and Dad didn't want to live in grand houses, they didn't want to be rich. They were happy with the house in Willow

Street, but if their daughter wanted something grander, they wouldn't stand in her way. When she was older, Clementine realized that they were modest even in that. She remembered how, as the bus idled around the tree-lined streets, her mother would point—not to the dazzling white mansions on the harbor shore, but to some small, plain weatherboard, half hidden in its garden, and say, "Imagine, Clementine! One day you might live in a house like that! If you do well at school," she would add. "If you study hard, and get into the university." Her voice would go dreamy on that last word.

All the same, Clementine knew that if she'd been a boy and got whacked by Mr. Meague because some girl had been talking in his class, Dad would have been up at the school like a shot. He wasn't scared of teachers who wore long black gowns. Even if you begged and pleaded with him because the other kids would sneer at you for running to your dad, he'd have gone there just the same.

Clementine was scared of Mr. Meague. His brown dustcoat was exactly the same color as the willy-willy she'd seen that time up at Lake Conapaira, tearing senselessly across the paddocks, gathering every weak, unrooted thing into its boiling heart. And though Mr. Meague was so quiet, Clementine sensed in him the same kind of seething she'd felt in Aunty Rene; as if deep inside them was something urgent and un-nameable and furious, desperate to get out. She never talked in his class—of course she didn't—but what if, one day, despite herself, she did? What if Jilly Norris asked her a question she really had to answer? Or if she got so nervous that words suddenly spilled out from her lips and she said, "I hate geometry!" or "Only five minutes to the bell!" right out loud in that deathly silent class? And then Mr. Meague would make her stand up and pick a boy.

She didn't want to pick a Home Boy. The Home Boys reminded her of something else she'd seen up at Lake Conapaira: a group of calves being herded down Palm Street to the saleyards, blundering, ungainly creatures with the same long legs and knobbly knees the Home Boys had, and the same big heads, and large soft eyes that slid this way and that, as if they were looking for their mothers. No, if Mr. Meague ever caught her talking, she wasn't picking out a Home Boy.

But who could she pick, then? Because you had to choose a boy once Mr. Meague caught you, there was no getting out of it. If you refused, a worse thing happened: Mr Meague picked one for you. And he picked a boy you liked, just as he'd chosen Andrew Milton for Annie Boland when she'd refused. Andrew was Annie's boyfriend, and Mr. Meague had known that. It wasn't difficult to know because they always stood together in the playground at recess and lunchtime, holding hands and smiling into each other's faces: they were easy to see.

But Mattie Gaskin and John Larsen hadn't been so easy; no one had ever seen them together; even Jilly Norris and her gang hadn't known about Mattie and John. Only Mr. Meague had known. He'd worked it out; a single stray glance, a smile— that was enough for him. He'd spotted it and marked them down. When Mattie Gaskin was caught whispering to Kay Dimsey in the seat behind her; when she'd begun to cry so much she couldn't pick a boy, then Mr. Meague had gone and chosen John Larsen.

What would happen if Clementine refused? Would Mr. Meague know about Simon Falls?

Simon Falls shared Clementine's math and English classes. He was a tall, quiet boy with thick dark hair and a serious expression in his long-lashed eyes. "He's got bedroom eyes," Jilly Norris had whispered to Clementine when Simon Falls had handed back the English tests for Mrs. Larkin. And then she'd added, with a knowing gaze into Clementine's face, "You like him, don't you?"

"Of course not," Clementine had replied.

Except she did. She wasn't sure if he liked her. Once in history class, she'd glanced up from her work and caught him staring at her from his seat across the aisle, but she didn't know if that meant he was interested in her. She never knew things like that, which seemed to come so naturally to other girls. Perhaps he'd really been looking at Kay Dimsey, who sat next to Clementine. A week ago she'd passed him in the corridor outside the staff room and she'd felt a blush spreading right across her cheeks. She hated the way she blushed so easily; it meant everyone could see the feelings she struggled desperately to hide. The door had been open; what if Mr. Meague had been in there and spotted her blush when she saw Simon Falls? He'd have marked it down, and if ever he caught her talking—if Jilly Norris asked her that question she really had to answer—he'd know who to choose if Clementine refused to pick a boy.

She didn't think Simon Falls had noticed her that day outside the staff room. He'd been gazing off in another direction, through the window that looked out onto the playground; he probably hadn't even seen her passing by.

She knew she wasn't the sort of girl boys noticed. She wasn't like Mattie Gaskin or Annie Boland, or even Jilly and her gang—girls who hung around the oval when the boys had football practice and stayed late after school to watch the cadets march in uniform. She'd remained small for her age; she could easily have passed for a kid in sixth class, still at primary school. Though she was thirteen, she hadn't started her periods and her chest was as flat as Mum's old wooden washing board.

Only one boy had ever approached her, and that was David Lowell.

David Lowell was a Home Boy. Clementine had been amazed when, crossing the lower quadrangle one morning, she'd felt a tap on her shoulder, turned around, and found David Lowell. He'd asked her if she'd like to be his guest at St. Swithin's Easter Fete.

His guest!

A Home Boy's guest!

At a home!

Clementine had stood there, paralyzed with shock. For almost a minute she simply couldn't speak. No one went out with Home Boys. She hadn't even known they were allowed out, except for school. Jilly Norris's mum said they were kept locked up at weekends. "And a good thing too," she'd declared, "or we'd never sleep safe in our beds!"

Even at school you didn't talk to them, not like you talked to other kids. And Home Boys didn't speak to girls. Not normally. So how come David Lowell thought he could speak to her? Why did he think it was all right to ask her out? What was wrong with her?

She hadn't been able to stop herself from staring at him: at his long, gangly legs, too long for his Home Boy trousers, which were school uniform trousers but of a distinctive darker gray, the cloth so coarse and stiff it would surely chafe and burn. His socks were thick and hairy, the kind of socks a gorilla might have knitted, Clementine had thought nastily, if someone had taught it how. They slumped clumsily above his ugly boots, and between their tops and the bottoms of his awful trousers a narrow strip of pallid shank showed, stippled with fine black hairs. Yuck!

And yet his voice was mild and gentle, which was confusing because you didn't associate gentleness with Home Boys.

"I could come and pick you up," he'd said unexpectedly. "At your place."

At her place! Would he just! Clementine had barely suppressed a gasp of outrage. At her place! Every stickybeak in the street would be hanging over their gates to goggle, the minute they saw a Home Boy at her door. It would be the talk of the neighborhood.

"Do you know Clementine Southey's going out with a Home Boy?"

"She's never! She'll be murdered in her bed!"

"Or something . . ."

"Some people must be hard up for a boyfriend, that's all I can say!"

"Right hard up!"

"Comes of going to that fancy school. They get ideas."

"She's a funny little thing. Very small for her age, isn't she?"

"Chest like a washing board!"

"He could have a grand game of marbles on it, heh, heh, heh!"

Clementine's gaze had darted frantically across the playground. What if Jilly and the others saw her with a Home Boy? There'd been kids everywhere, shouting and running and jostling, but she'd seen no sign of Jilly and her gang, or anyone else in her class. Only there, leaning on the railing of the upper quad, his pale blank face intent, she'd spotted Mr. Meague.

"Clementine?"

The Home Boy was still waiting for an answer. He wouldn't go away.

"Clementine?" He'd used her whole name; he hadn't called her Clem, or Clemmie, like the other kids.

Clementine thought her name was ridiculous. Her mother had chosen it; she said it was from her father's favorite song. Clementine wished heartily that Grandpa Clements had been struck dumb before he'd sung a word.

The Home Boy had spoken the hated name softly, slowly, as if he loved saying it and didn't want the word to end, and when it did he said it over again. "Clementine?"

"I can't go to the fete with you," she'd said coldly. "I'm not allowed to go out with"—she'd stared at his uniform, that dark, unhappy gray—"with boys."

"Oh," he'd said, and gazed for a long while at her face, as if he were learning it for some peculiar, solitary exam. "I'm sorry, Clementine."

As if, she thought furiously, it was she who'd been refused, she who'd missed out on something.

She'd run away then, leaving the Home Boy standing there. She'd run down the steps to the library, where she often spent her lunchtimes, and grabbed a book of poetry from the shelves. It was called *A Shropshire Lad*, and no one had taken it out since 1944. "What are those blue remembered hills?" she'd read, and thought of her cousin and those low, rounded hills at Lake Conapaira where Fan said everything beautiful might be.

As she'd sat there reading, a shadow had fallen sharply across the page. She'd glanced up and seen a face looking in through the window at her. Clementine's vision had blurred with terror. Who was it? Had the Home Boy followed her? She'd blinked, and as her sight cleared she saw the face belonged to Jilly Norris, who'd paused to stickybeak into the library as she passed by on her way to better things. Jilly had pressed her lips against the glass in a pure round shape that obviously said "swot."

That was the only time a boy had asked Clementine out. And Mr. Meague had seen them talking, but it didn't matter because Clementine knew that if she got caught and wouldn't pick a boy, Mr. Meague would never choose David Lowell. He'd sense she didn't like the Home Boy. Mr. Meague only went after boys you liked.

Jilly Norris and her gang started picking on Vinnie Sloane. Vinnie Sloane wasn't tough like the Home Boys. He didn't give cheek or get into fights, and he'd never been caned in his life. He was small and weak-looking and his eyes were pink like a white rabbit's, and Clementine knew this was why Jilly and the other girls had picked him out. They'd chosen him because of his looks, because he was pale and skinny and wore his hair combed flat, hair so dull a brown that in some lights it seemed gray. And this gray color made you notice how Vinnie Sloane looked a little like Mr. Meague, especially in those tense and airless moments when the pair of them were standing face to face before the class and Mr. Meague was steadying Vinnie's hand to get the cane.

Vinnie Sloane got the cane every week, because every week Jilly or Kay Dimsey or Ba Purcell would whisper on purpose, and then Mr. Meague would ask them to stand up and pick a boy, and they'd choose Vinnie Sloane. Clementine couldn't make sense of it. Mr. Meague was a teacher, a grown-up. Surely he could see that Jilly and the others were doing it on purpose? Of course he could! So why did he keep on letting them do it? Why didn't he tell them to pick on someone else? Why didn't he say, "I think this boy has been chosen quite enough"? Why did he make girls pick out boys anyway? Why didn't he just give them detention or lines like all the other teachers? And why, when he'd finished caning Vinnie, or any other boy, did he recite, in a low, soft voice you had to strain to hear, "I wasted time, and now doth time waste me"? Why did he sometimes say "look what this girl has made you suffer," pointing with his cane to the girl who'd picked the boy? You couldn't work it out. You only knew it made the ground feel soft and tricky beneath your feet, made you want to cry out, like a tiny little kid who could hardly talk might do, "Bad! Bad! Bad!"

Clementine's work began to falter, her marks got lower in each of Mr. Meague's weekly tests. The sight of the diagrams in her textbook, the terms *right angle, obtuse angle, hypotenuse* gave her a sickish feeling deep down in her stomach. When she tried to do a homework exercise, she couldn't concentrate, her mind went veering off in all directions, like a willy-willy, senselessly. She hid her geometry textbook down at the bottom of her school case beneath her gym bag and shoes, so she wouldn't see it when she took out her books for other lessons. She hated geometry now. It was as if she were scared of it, and this feeling made her think of Fan again—how Fan had hated reading and snatched Clementine's books away from her, saying loudly, "Let's go out and play!"

She hadn't seen Fan since that last visit. Her mother and Aunty Rene had made up their quarrel, and every year Mum talked about going to Lake Conapaira. But nothing ever came of it, and when Clementine asked if Fan could come down to spend the summer holidays with them, all her mother said was "we'll see." Mum was working part-time at the bank now and she got only two weeks holiday, and in those two special weeks Dad rented a house for them down the coast at Stanwell Park. "We'll go up to Lake Conapaira again one of these days," Mum kept on promising, but somehow they never did.

On the nights before Mr. Meague's classes, Clementine took a long, long time to get to sleep. She lay awake hour after hour, thoughts whirling in her head, fears pinching like cruel fingers, her chest so tight that it was difficult to breathe. Would Vinnie Sloane get the cane again tomorrow? Or on Thursday, two days away? She'd come to hate Vinnie Sloane. She knew none of it was his fault, because how could he help being thin and weak and ugly, the exact kind of boy that girls like Jilly Norris picked on? But although she knew this, she couldn't stop herself from hating him; she hated him for looking like a silly white rabbit and she hated the squealy blubbery sounds he made when he was caned, and the hunched way he walked back to his desk, head bowed, hands thrust into his armpits, shameful tears running down his pallid cheeks.

Clementine tossed and turned beneath her bedclothes on those sleepless nights. Could tomorrow be the very day when Jilly somehow pushed her into talking? When she would have to stand up and pick a boy? And when she refused, because she wouldn't, just wouldn't pick a Home Boy, would Mr. Meague call Simon Falls out to the front of the class? And if he did, what would she do then? When he'd picked Andrew Milton, Annie had given a small sharp cry and then begun sobbing. Mr. Meague had ignored her so completely you'd think Annie hadn't been there.

What if you stood up to him? What if you said "I don't think it's right"? What would Mr. Meague do? Clementine pictured his still, pale face, white as a blank sheet of paper no one would dare to write upon. Not one of them had ever confronted him; the very thought of such a thing was somehow shocking.

Fan would stand up to him, Clementine thought suddenly. If Fan lived down here and went to their school, she'd stand up to Mr. Meague, and she'd stand up for Vinnie Sloane. Fan was strong. For a reason she couldn't fathom, and never would until she was very, very old, Clementine had a sudden image of her cousin's old black bicycle, flung down on the track that stormy morning when Fan had tried to run away to the blue hills: the wheel still spinning, hissing in the rain. She saw Fan's slim finger reach out and touch it, saw the spinning stop, the wheel go still. When she thought of her cousin, it wasn't the girl in the back bedroom struggling to get away from Aunty Rene's strap that she remembered, but the calm girl who'd held her hand when the willy-willy came seething across the paddocks, who'd said with utter certainty, "It won't hurt us. It'll come close but not right here." That was the real Fan, she thought, that was how Fan would be all the time, when she was grown up.

Clementine knew she wasn't strong like her cousin. She

wasn't whole—she was all bits and pieces. One moment she would think one way, the next moment in quite another, as if inside her there was a scattering of girls, all with different thoughts and feelings, instead of a single girl who was sure. She was like a tiny candle whose flame flickered and wobbled and faltered at the slightest breath of air. She wasn't even sure if she really liked Simon Falls, or if she'd made the feeling up from longing, and all the books and poetry she'd read, and the films she saw at the pictures on Saturday afternoons. She was thirteen and no braver or wiser than she'd been on that night when Aunty Rene had gone after Fan, when she'd run out and hidden behind the woodpile with her hands over her ears to escape the sight and sounds of her cousin's thrashing.

Clementine kicked the bedclothes off onto the floor. Why did some grown-up people have to be cruel? And why did they pick on kids?

She sat up on her bed and pressed her cold nose against the window. It was a very dark night outside: the moon had set and the stars were far away and tiny in the heavens, like a sprinkle of silver glitter on a Christmas card. And as she gazed up at that high cold sky, Clementine had a sense of something huge and grand and scary, and knew it was the shadow of the world into which she'd have to go when she grew up. The warm safety of the little house in Willow Street, and even Mum and Dad, who loved her, weren't for always, or enough.

She peered out over the front garden and the empty park across the road, through the trees to the Brothers' house, where lighted windows shone out into the dark.

"Why do the Brothers keep their lights on all night?" she'd once asked Mum.

"Catholics," her mother had sniffed. "Who knows what they do?"

Clementine had asked Brian Keenan up the road. He went to the Catholic school. "Daffy Brian," the kids in the street called him, but his mother said he was simply a little slow. "He'll catch up," she told everyone cheerfully. "There's a day coming when our Brian will surprise us all."

When Clementine had asked him why the Brothers kept their lights on all night, Brian's brown eyes had grown serious and round.

"They say prayers."

"All night?"

"They pray the Hours," he'd replied mysteriously. Clementine didn't know what he meant but she liked the sound of the phrase: it made her think of Fan telling the old black man's stories, the way her face had looked when she'd explained how the magic child had sung the tree.

"And the prayers keep the sun up, and the moon, and the stars," Brian had gone on, "and if they stopped, everything would fall down."

"Would it?"

He'd nodded solemnly. "They keep the world in place."

It seemed a strange idea to Clementine that the Brothers—ordinary homely red-faced men despite their long black robes, whom you could hear shouting at the rowdy Catholic boys whenever you passed the school, or meet any day in Jimmy Lee's shop buying tobacco and packets of Minties—could ever do anything so grand as keep the world in place. And yet their steady lighted windows were so consoling in the awful reaches of the night that Clementine almost felt it might be true: that inside the old house the Brothers were watching over the world, keeping it safe, seeing that everything would be all right. And then Mr. Meague would go away and Vinnie Sloane wouldn't be caned ever again; she'd never have to pick a boy, and Simon Falls would never be called to the front of the room. And that Home Boy, that David Lowell, he'd forget about her and never ask her out again. Everyone would be rescued, even Jilly Norris and her gang. And all the little bits and pieces that fluttered around inside her would become whole. And soon she'd see Fan again.

One night Clementine dreamed of Fan. She dreamed she'd crossed the park and gone into the Brothers' house and found them sitting silently in a circle in a big high-ceilinged room. They weren't saying prayers; they were sewing with big, thick needles and long lengths of heavy thread, making a big net, a kind of safety net like the one Clementine had seen at the circus, stretched beneath the trapezes and the high wire. And in the very center of the net, in a red dress and soft red shoes, was Fan, dancing.

Then Clementine noticed that the Brothers hadn't quite finished sewing: there was a big hole in the net, right beside Fan's dancing feet. "Fan, watch out!" she cried. "Fan, stop! Jump off!" But though she heard her cousin, Fan didn't stop dancing; she only waved and smiled. She was so happy that every little bit of her was shining, as if a million bright candles were lit beneath her skin. "Hello, Clementine!" she called in that laughing voice that was like water thrown up in the air. "Hello, little sister! Hello, *gindaymaidhaany!*"

Gindaymaidhaany. Clementine had quite forgotten this word and how it meant "sister," and now, when she woke from the dream, here it was again in her possession, to keep, like the small white pebble she'd found beside Lake Conapaira. She still had that pebble. She kept it in a little blue box in her dressing table drawer, and sometimes she took it out to look at, and hold in the palm of her hand. Like the Brothers' lighted windows, it gave her a fleeting sense that everything would be all right.

CHAPTER

6

In Clementine's English class there was a girl called Daria, who reminded her of Fan. Perhaps it was Daria's long corn-colored hair, which she wore plaited and pinned up on her head like a crown, or her high cheekbones and long almond-shaped blue eyes—or a certain way she had of standing, with her chin lifted defiantly and her head held very high. Or it might have been because Daria was strong.

Her family had come from overseas. The kids at school called her "The Balt," but this didn't seem to worry Daria; she would look them in the eye and say in her slow, proud voice, "I am not from the Baltic, I am Hungarian." Nothing about Chisholm College seemed to worry Daria; it was as if she were outside it, already grown up, a person from some older, more experienced world.

"He should stand up for himself, that boy," she observed coldly when Clementine told her about Mr. Meague and how Jilly Norris and her gang kept picking on Vinnie Sloane. "And he should not cry." Daria's voice was stern. "I will tell you this, Clementine: never, never should one cry." She leaned closer, and it seemed to Clementine that the Hungarian girl's clear blue eyes grew darker as they fixed upon her listener's face. "And now let me tell you something else—" She paused, and her broad face took on the considering expression of a person making up her mind.

"What?" whispered Clementine.

Daria sighed. Slowly, neatly, she began to fold the square of brown waxed paper in which her unfamiliar sandwiches had been wrapped.

"What?" asked Clementine again.

Daria leaned down and placed the neatly folded paper in the school case that she never left in the locker room like other kids, but carried with her all the time. She clicked the shiny brass catches shut, smiled at Clementine, and began her story.

"I come from Hungary. You know this, of course."

Clementine nodded.

"Back there my grandparents had been landowners, you see, quite rich." She frowned again. "Do you believe this— that we were rich?"

Clementine swallowed. Her eyes fixed on Daria's long fingers pinching at the faded cloth of her shabby tunic. "Yes," she said, because somehow, despite the secondhand tunic, it wasn't hard to imagine Daria being rich.

"Good," said the Hungarian girl. "And so when my father grew up, when he finished school, then my grandfather sent him away to Budapest, to the university, to become a lawyer."

"And did he?"

"Of course he did. An important lawyer, a big—big-time man, as you might say here. Budapest is where I grew up, in a beautiful house, beside the river, the kind of place you have never seen, Clementine. Only then—" Daria's face clouded, the almond eyes went still.

"Then what?"

"Trouble came. We lost everything. We were driven—we had to—" Daria looked up and gazed around her, at the gray asphalt of the courtyard, the benches around the wall, the slender young gum trees in the park outside the fence. She closed her eyes.

"Daria? Daria, are you all right?"

The blue eyes snapped open. "Of course I am all right. So—where was I?"

"Um. Um, you said 'trouble came.'"

"And so it did." The Hungarian girl sighed softly and went on with her story. "We had to come here. And here, my father mends the roads. Can you imagine this, Clementine? This man who had been, in his own country, like a—like a prince? And here, he has the pick and shovel, and the roads. When he comes home in the evenings, he is—" Daria sprang up suddenly from the bench where they were sitting and in a single violent movement twisted her back sideways and drooped her head, so that she looked, for a moment, tired and even old. "You see?" she asked Clementine.

"Yes."

Daria sat down again. "At weekends," she continued, "he lies in his bed very much, and is silent, as he never used to be back home. But I tell you one thing, Clementine, one single thing, the most important—he never, never cried. When we left our country, when we were in the camp, my mother cried, and I cried too, because I was young and knew nothing, but my father, never once did he cry." Daria tossed her head back proudly. "I am going to do well in this school, you know, Clementine. And when I leave it I will go to university, and become a lawyer like my father was." She tossed her head again. "You will see."

Clementine didn't doubt it for a moment. She could see this future as if it had already happened. It was there in the determined tilt of Daria's chin, the bright, tearless shine of her eyes. Nothing and no one would stop her.

It was a bright winter's day, warm as springtime. The grass in the park was a deep, dense green, the sun shone down from a flawless sky. On the other side of the courtyard Clementine could see Annie Boland and Andrew Milton; they stood very close together, close yet not quite touching, and the thin line of light in the space between them was bright as a blade. They gazed into each other's faces, wordlessly.

Daria glanced across at them and smiled. "In my country, in my grandmother's time," she said, "the peasant boys would chase the girls in the fields—fields of sunflowers, little Clementine, can you picture this? And when a boy caught a girl, he would pull up her skirts, so that she was quite naked, down here"—Daria brushed at the lap of the faded tunic—"and then they would tie those skirts up over her head, and then they would, you know—"

Clementine did know. You couldn't get through two years at Chisholm College, not to mention primary school at Merrylands State, without learning the basic facts of life, though there were many little mysteries she still didn't understand.

"Why did they tie their skirts over their heads?"

"So as not to get in the way, of course. And you know what they called it, this tying up of the skirts, and what would happen then?"

"What?"

Daria laughed. "They called it 'turning her into a flower.'"

"Turning her into a flower," repeated Clementine.

"That's right. Do you see?"

"Yes, but—didn't they mind, those girls?"

"Mind?" Daria's voice was scornful. "They were peasants, I tell you. For them, that was life." And abruptly, turning her golden head, Daria spat down onto the asphalt at her feet. "Peasants!" she repeated. And then she added softly and quite sadly, as if she had forgotten all about Clementine and was talking to herself, "They took everything from us."

Clementine was crossing the quad toward the library steps when David Lowell came right up to her. One minute there'd been no one, the next minute the Home Boy was there. He asked her to the school dance, which was almost six weeks away, in the middle of July. She saw with a kind of horror that he'd combed his spiky hair flat, with water, so you could see the comb marks in it, like dark wet tracks across his scalp. Clementine turned her head quickly, desperate to get away from the sight of David Lowell. She wanted to run.

"July the fourteenth," he said in his gentle voice. "Saturday."

"I know." Her own voice rose up shrilly on the second word.

He gazed at her. "Clementine," he said, and his voice lingered on each small syllable, so that Clementine, with some instinct she hadn't been aware she possessed, knew that he thought about her as he lay in bed at night, and whispered her name to himself, over and over and over.

His narrow Home Boy's bed. A smelly bed. "They wet their beds," Jilly Norris had told her. "Mum says the whole place stinks of piss."

Lying there. Thinking of her. The simple idea of it made her cringe, as if he'd touched her with his scabby Home Boy hands. Only they weren't scabby, she saw, simply ink-stained—slender, elegant hands that could have belonged to some other person hidden beneath that drab gray uniform.

"I can't go," she told him coldly. "My grandma's sick. She's in an old people's hospital, we always visit her on Saturdays." Her mouth twitched on the lie, but David Lowell didn't seem to notice.

"Oh," he said. "I'm sorry." There was such genuine sympathy in his voice that she wondered if he, unlike her, really did have a sick grandmother. Did orphans have grandmothers? If they did, thought Clementine irrelevantly, then those grandmothers, whose children must have died, would be sort of orphans too.

"The dance doesn't start till eight, Clementine. Do you think—"

"Stop saying my name!" she hissed.

His pale face flushed. "What?"

"Stop saying my name! I don't like it! And I can't go to the dance with you! I told you I'm not allowed to go out with boys! And I don't want to go anywhere with you! Leave me alone!" Tears spurted brazenly from her eyes. She turned and fled.

This time she ran to the toilets, hid in a cubicle, and went on crying. She thought of his hair, combed flat, for her, and a jolt of wild anger coursed through her, like savagery. She hated him for liking her. Oh, it wasn't fair. Why did it have to be him who liked her, instead of Simon Falls, who barely knew that a person called Clementine Southey existed on the earth?

She dried her eyes. The bell sounded. It was Thursday afternoon. Double-period geometry with Mr. Meague.

The class was halfway through, and there was silence, utter silence, when Clementine felt a small sly nudge at her arm.

She glanced sideways, where Jilly Norris sat beside her. With her right hand Jilly was copying a theorem from the board; her left, beneath the desk, held a slip of paper, a note for Clementine.

Clementine shook her head—getting caught with a note in Mr. Meague's class was almost as dangerous as talking. Jilly rolled her eyes and loosed her fingers; the scrap of paper fluttered onto Clementine's lap and threatened to drift to the floor. Clementine snatched at it.

Mr. Meague had his back to them, writing on the board. Kids said he had a thousand eyes all over his head, like a fly. Invisible eyes. Beneath the desk Clementine unfolded the note, silently.

"I know who you love."

Everything inside her seemed to jump, to squirm.

"I know who you love."

The "o"s were drawn in the shape of a heart.

Had Jilly Norris seen her with David Lowell? Had Jilly seen her run away, crying, and thought, as Jilly and girls like her always thought, that Clementine was the one who'd been turned down? That she'd asked a Home Boy to go out with her and he'd said no? That even a Home Boy didn't want her?

Or was it even worse than that? Did Jilly mean Simon Falls? Hadn't she once said, "You like him, don't you?" What if she'd said something to Simon Falls? Jilly and her friends were always telling boys that girls liked them, just to see what would happen next. A hot wave of shame flowed through her, she could hardly breathe; it was as if she'd been thrust headfirst into some small, hot, suffocating space. She had to know.

Clementine did something that even an hour back she'd

have thought impossible—she forgot they were sitting in Mr. Meague's class and hissed at Jilly, "Who do I love?"

Mr. Meague turned around from the board.

"Miss Southey?"

Clementine looked up.

"Miss Southey, would you stand, please?" He always said "please" to them.

Clementine stood. The seat rattled loudly behind her knees.

She looked away from him, toward the window. Outside in the park an old man was throwing a stick to his dog in the wonderful calm blue day. "Good boy," he said. "Good old fella!" You could hear every word, almost hear the dry, raspy sound of the old man's hand patting the dog's rough brown fur.

"Miss Southey," said Mr. Meague, "Miss Southey, would you kindly pick a boy?"

Clementine said nothing. There was an odd flapping sensation in the top of her skull, as if her soul were trying to get out and fly away.

Mr. Meague's gaze wandered across the room and settled lazily on Simon Falls.

"Miss Southey?" he said again.

She glanced over the rows of boys to the desk in the second front row where David Lowell was sitting. She'd vowed she'd never choose a Home Boy, but David Lowell was different, wasn't he? David Lowell had come after her when she didn't want him to, he'd stared at her, he'd said her name in that slow, lingering way that made you know he thought about her in bed. He'd made her cry.

Out in front Mr. Meague was still waiting, his flat gaze fixed on Simon Falls.

"Da—" she began, and then stopped before the name was

spoken. David Lowell's head was bent, she could see the nape of his neck above the collar of his coarse gray shirt: it was white and tender as a beloved child's.

"Miss Southey?"

He always called them that. Miss and Master, and the formal titles contained a secret mockery, for who, in his stifling little kingdom, was the master or mistress of anything, least of all themselves?

The blood roared in her ears, she felt hunted, hounded. There was a sudden sensation of falling from a great height, all grace and kindness rushing out from her.

Her lips parted for the name.

"Vinnie Sloane," she said.

CHAPTER

7

A nd then it began to rain. It rained for four days straight, and on the fourth day Clementine got soaking wet on the long walk from the station to the school. She sat all day in her wet, heavy tunic, and when she reached home that afternoon she had a cough so small and dry that it didn't sound human. It was like the cough of some small sick animal hidden beneath the floorboards of their house.

"You've caught a chill," said her mother. "Fancy sitting all day in those wet clothes! I sometimes wonder about you, Clementine, I really do. You don't seem to have the sense you were born with, for all you go to that clever school. Why didn't you ask the teachers to send you home?"

"Everybody got wet," answered Clementine. "If they let one person go home, they'd have had to let all of us, the whole school. And no one would come back."

Which was what Mrs. Larkin had said when Jilly Norris asked if she could go home and change her clothes.

Mrs. Southey banged the frying pan down on the stove.

"What's for tea?" asked Clementine, though she didn't feel

at all hungry. She couldn't imagine any kind of food she would actually like to eat.

"Liver and bacon."

"Ugh!"

"Liver's good for you."

Clementine gave another small dry cough, and her mother swirled the onions angrily in the pan. "Those teachers! Oh, it's all right for them! They don't have to do the looking-after when you get sick! They don't have to do the worrying! Oh no, not them. High and mighty!" Mrs. Southey slid the pan to the back burner, crossed the kitchen, and placed a cool hand on her daughter's forehead. Clementine shuddered: the smell of cooked onions on her mother's fingers was so overpowering it made her want to be sick. All afternoon her sense of smell had gathered sharpness: the reek of sweat and wet wool in the classroom, of mud and rain outside, even her soaking, squelchy shoes had a smell, and the exhaust fumes from a bus outside the station had almost made her faint.

Mrs. Southey drew back when she felt her daughter shudder. "What's wrong? Surely that didn't hurt?" She peered anxiously into Clementine's face. "Did it?"

"No." Clementine wiped at her forehead. "It wasn't you. I was just—just thinking of something." Which was true in a way, because she had only that moment remembered that tomorrow was Thursday, when they would have Mr. Meague for a double period again. How could she have forgotten? Why did Thursdays come around so quickly?

"What kind of thoughts could they be?" wondered Mrs. Southey, astounded.

"Oh, nothing."

"Well, at least you haven't got a fever." Mrs. Southey winced as Clementine coughed again, and added, "Touch wood."

"Can I stay home from school tomorrow?"

"We'll see how you are in the morning."

Clementine went to bed early, straight after dinner, and she didn't eat any of the liver and bacon that her mother had said would be so good for her. She didn't feel like eating anything ever again. The tomato sauce bottle in the center of the table seemed suddenly to belong to a different world, one she could no longer get the sense of. She drank two sips of tea and then thrust the cup and saucer aside. Even the dread of double geometry began to fade: it was as if Mr. Meague and Vinnie Sloane and Jilly Norris and David Lowell—even handsome Simon Falls—were far away in that strange world where the tomato sauce bottle had gone, and the milk jug, and the pot that poured out tea. She fell asleep as soon as she got into bed: a sleep that was really like falling, going down and down and down, through the hole in the net she'd dreamed the Brothers had been making, where Fan had danced and her happiness had shone out into the room.

When she woke it was the middle of the night. "Huf," came the small dry cough in her throat, like a little animal caught in there, struggling to get out. "Huf, huf, huf!" The blankets were heavy on her body and yet they had no warmth in them: they felt damp and shivery as a Home Boy's skin. She climbed out of bed and crept down the hall to the lounge room, where she switched on the small electric fire and lay down on the floor beside it, studying the shadows on the ceiling and the faint red glow the heater cast between them. Her chest had gone hard, as if it were made from some ungiving substance that had nothing to do with breath. "Like the tomato sauce bottle," thought Clementine dazedly, and then she fell asleep so suddenly it was as if someone had turned out a light.

When she woke again she thought she saw three tiny, ugly goblins crouching on the heater's glowing bars, but they couldn't be goblins, could they? There were no such things as goblins, or fairies, and Santa Claus was only a man dressed up in a red suit and a fat false beard. Or might there be such things, in that world where the tomato sauce bottle and everything else had disappeared? She blinked and the goblins vanished but when she sat up her head felt swimmy and she was hot now, so very hot—"Mum!" she called. "Dad! Daddy!" but her voice wouldn't come out properly, only the little cough that went "Huf! Huf! Huf!"

Slowly, very slowly, because her whole body felt heavy and strange, a body that might have belonged to someone else instead of her, Clementine crawled back to her room and fell across the bed. She struggled to sit up so she could look out through the window and see the lights of the Brothers' house. She wanted to tell Fan that the Brothers hadn't finished their net and there was a hole in it right near where she was dancing—but her back felt all crumbly and her legs wouldn't move at all. She couldn't get up to the window, she couldn't even sit up. "Huf!" went the little cough again, and then something stabbed deep and hard inside her chest and there was a pain so bright she could almost see the color of it: a fierce, wild crimson like a big amazing flower.

Clementine didn't remember anything more until she woke up in the hospital. Inflammation of the lungs, they called it, and she had to stay in hospital for days and days and days. As she lay there she remembered how her friend Allie had once been in the hospital. It had happened when Allie was very small, only three years old, and she'd needed to have her appendix out, only Allie hadn't known that because her parents had told her she was going on a holiday. Although she was so little, Allie had felt it was strange how when they got to the place they told her was a holiday hotel, her mum had undressed her and put her into bed in a long room that was full of other children. Then they'd left. "We're just going to get you an ice cream," they'd told her, "and then we'll be straight back."

Except they didn't come back. Allie had got out of bed and waited at the window while the afternoon faded and the evening came on—waited and waited and waited for her parents and the ice cream that never arrived. And even though they'd come next day at the visiting hour, "I've never trusted them since then," Allie had confided.

Allie was gone now. She and her family had moved to New Zealand at the end of primary school, and Clementine had never found a new best friend. She had her cousin, a cousin who'd promised to be her sister, her *gindaymaidhaany.* Only she never saw her. Fan wouldn't know she was sick, not for a long time, and if she were to die she would never see Fan again.

Clementine stayed in hospital for ten whole days and her parents visited every evening. Then she was allowed to go home, where she had to stay in bed for three weeks more. She didn't remember much about the first week except for one morning when she woke just after sunrise, knelt up at her window to look out at the world again, and there in the park she saw David Lowell. He was standing quite still, gazing across the road at her house, and despite the distance between them she could swear he saw her at the window. She could feel his eyes lock on hers.

He still liked her, then. She'd got Vinnie Sloane caned, she was as bad as Jilly and the rest of them, and yet he still liked her. How tall he looked, standing there, almost as big as a man. He must be nearly fourteen, and Home Boys always left school when they turned fourteen. David Lowell was clever, but all the same he'd leave because he had to get a job and then she wouldn't have to see him anymore.

He wouldn't come to the park again either, she knew. This was the only time.

"Go away," she whispered, and as if he'd heard her, the Home Boy snatched his eyes from hers and began to walk away. As he crossed the park, sunlight flashed suddenly from the windows of the Brothers' house and glinted on his spiky hair so it looked for a moment as if his head were rimmed with fire.

When she was starting to get better, Jilly Norris came to visit her. Clementine was surprised. Jilly wasn't really a friend.

"You look awful," said Jilly, plonking herself down on the edge of the bed, staring at Clementine's thin white face.

Clementine didn't reply. There wasn't all that much you could say to a remark like that.

"Honest you do," said Jilly. "You look like something the cat dragged in." She moved farther up the bed, until she was sitting right next to Clementine's sore flat chest. "Guess what?" she said.

"What?"

"Mr. Meague's left."

"He has?" Clementine should have been overjoyed, but

Mr. Meague and everything else at Chisholm College still seemed very far away. Even her glimpse of David Lowell in the park might well have been a dream.

"Aren't you glad?" urged Jilly. "Aren't you glad that old creep's gone?"

"Of course I'm glad."

"You don't look it."

"That's because my chest still hurts."

"Does it?" Jilly stared down at the striped top of Clementine's winter pajamas and shifted a little farther back down the bed.

"It's not catching," said Clementine.

There was a small silence and then Jilly burst out, "But don't you want to know what happened? I thought you'd want to know! I thought you hated Mr. Meague!"

Clementine shrugged. "What happened, then? Did Vinnie Sloane's dad come up to the school because we'd all been picking on him?"

Jilly flushed. "Course not. Mr. Meague just left, no one knows why. It was really sudden." She snapped her fingers. "Like that, he was gone. The teachers say he went to another school, but none of us believe them. Some kids reckon the green cart might have come and taken him away to the loony bin. He was crazy, you know." Jilly sucked her breath in and pushed her chest out proudly, so Clementine could see how she'd grown. "Mad as a meat axe, don't you think?"

"Probably," agreed Clementine listlessly, though she thought that Mr. Meague was the kind of person who showed his craziness only to kids. He'd be careful with adults and they'd think he was okay.

"You know what I reckon?"

Clementine shook her heavy head. She wished that Jilly would go.

"I reckon he's got a job at St. Swithin's, a secret job, you know, in the dungeons. My mum hasn't seen him, but then she doesn't go down the cellars, does she? She says she wouldn't go down there for all the tea in China. The Home Boys swear he isn't there, but then Home Boys never tell the truth, do they? Mum says they're born with crooked tongues. What do you think?"

"I think if you were born with a crooked tongue you wouldn't be able to talk at all."

Jilly stared. "I meant about Mr. Meague, stupid! Don't you reckon he's at St. Swithin's? He'd like it there, don't you think? He'd fit right in with all those chains and whips and stuff."

Clementine remembered how her mum said Jilly had a nasty mind. "Jilly, there aren't any dungeons at St. Swithin's, or any chains and whips and stuff."

"Yes there are—you should ask my mum."

"You just said she'd never been down the cellars. Anyway, I reckon your mum doesn't know what she's talking about." Clementine hoisted herself up against the pillows. "Or you don't."

Jilly bridled. Clementine had always wondered what that word meant, and one free period she'd looked it up in the big dictionary in the school library. To throw up the head and draw in the chin (as a horse does when reined in), she'd read, expressing pride, vanity, or resentment. Now she saw the word in action: Jilly's head went up and her chin drew in, her eyes slewed inward, resentfully, toward her nose. She sniffed. "All right, so you don't believe me. But"—she lowered her voice to a thrilling whisper—"have you ever seen a Home Boy's back?"

"No," said Clementine. "Have you?"

"My mum has. She says they're all over scars."

Clementine thought of David Lowell's bowed head, the frail white neck above his stiff gray collar. She flinched.

"What's the matter?" demanded Jilly.

"Nothing." Clementine closed her eyes and wondered again why Jilly had come to visit her; she didn't believe it was simply to tell her that Mr. Meague had left the school. There had to be some other reason. Most likely Jilly wanted to find out what it had been like to nearly die. Because Clementine had nearly died, that's what Dr. Macpherson had told Mum and Dad. And Mum had told Mrs. Sheedy up the road, who was a friend of Jilly's aunt Rose, and then Aunty Rose would have told Jilly's mum, and Jilly's mum would have told Jilly.

"Are you all right?"

Clementine opened her eyes. "Just a bit tired," she said, but Jilly didn't take the hint.

"Guess who else has left?"

"What?"

"Guess who else has left the school?"

"Vinnie Sloane?"

"Nah." Jilly pulled a face. "Not him. He's still there, worse luck, the little blubber. Didn't you hate the way he used to squeal?"

"But if you and the others had left him alone, then—"

"You picked on him too."

"I know I did."

A silence fell. Jilly interrupted it. "It's Simon Falls who's left."

Clementine could feel the heat of her visitor's avid gaze. So this was why she'd come. "I know who you love," she'd written on that note, and it was Simon Falls she'd meant, not David Lowell. She'd probably told Simon Falls that Clementine Southey loved him.

"His dad's sent him to the King's School."

"Good."

"Good? Is that all you can say?"

Clementine shrugged. The small movement hurt her chest.

"His dad's a doctor." Jilly smiled slyly. "Bet you wish he was your doctor."

"Why?"

For a moment, Jilly was disconcerted. Then she rallied. "Oh, come on, everyone knows you've got a crush on Simon Falls."

Everyone. So Jilly had been telling. Clementine felt the blood rise to her cheeks; she was never going back to that school. She took a deep painful breath and said carelessly, "Do they?"

"Oh, don't be like that, Clementine. Think how beautiful he'll look in that King's School uniform. Like a soldier."

It was true, he would. The khaki jacket and trousers, the scarlet sash looped around the gallant slouched hat; they could have been made for him.

"Oh, and David Lowell's left too."

"What?"

"You know, that Home Boy with the spiky hair." There was no malice in Jilly's voice, which meant she hadn't noticed David Lowell talking to Clementine in the playground, had never seen the way the Home Boy looked at her.

"Oh, yeah, him," said Clementine. She'd been right. David

Lowell had turned fourteen and left to get a job—over at the flour mills or the brake-lining factory, or out digging up the roads. She thought of his inky, elegant hands.

"He won a scholarship to Fort Street," said Jilly. "You know, that place for really brainy boys. That's where he's gone."

Fort Street was far away on the other side of the city. Good!

"Fort Street!" crowed Jilly. "It's miles! Way off in Sydney." She spoke as if they, living on the city's outskirts, were in some distant galaxy. "He'll have to get up so early! He'll have to get up in the dark to go to school."

Get up in the dark. A memory stirred in Clementine: a big, raggy old moon above the dark backyard, a rattling train carrying her through lightless suburbs. She closed her mind to it. She didn't want to feel she had something in common with David Lowell. For a second she saw him, tall and gangly, waiting on a still-dark platform, a bulging old briefcase tucked beneath one arm. There were raindrops in his spiky hair.

"What was it like to nearly die?" asked Jilly suddenly.

Clementine's mother appeared like magic in the doorway of the room. "Jilly," she said, "Clementine isn't quite better yet. She gets tired easily. This might be a good time to go."

She'd been out in the hall listening in to every word, you could bet on it, but for once Clementine was grateful, because now Jilly would have to leave.

"Oh," said Jilly, getting up from her chair. Clementine heard her talking to Mum on the front veranda. "She looks awful, doesn't she, Mrs. Southey?"

"Well, she's been very ill, Jilly. But now she's on the mend."

"Is she? She doesn't look it. She looks like—have you seen that film called *The Specter of Hensbane Hall*, Mrs. Southey? It's a Hammer Horror."

"No, I don't think I have, Jilly. But I'll look out for it, if you say it's good."

"Oh, it is, Mrs. Southey. It's great. There's this specter in it looks just like—"

"Off you go, Jilly dear. I'm sure your mother will be wanting to get on with the tea."

When Dr. Macpherson said she was better, Clementine's mum and dad didn't send her back to school right away. There were only a few weeks to go before the August holidays, and they decided it wasn't worth it. Instead, she was going up to Lake Conapaira. Dr. Macpherson said a spell in the dry, cold air up there would be just the thing for Clementine's lungs, it would have them better than new. And Aunty Rene had written that she and Fan would be happy to have her. There was no mention of Uncle Len, who was obviously still at Gunnesweare.

"But Mum, what about your job?"

"You'll be going on your own," said Mum.

Clementine's eyes widened. "On my own in the train?"

"Your dad and I decided," said Mum. "Seeing as you're better and Dr. Macpherson says the trip will be good for you."

"You're a big girl now," said Dad. "Second year at high school, getting on for fourteen. The guard will look after you, and Aunty Rene will meet you at the other end. You'll be right as rain."

Aunty Rene. For a moment, Clementine's happiness clouded. She thought of her aunty's fierce black glittering eyes, the bad child's little pointed teeth. The seething. The strap.

Mrs. Southey must have noticed the shadow cross her daughter's face because she came forward and hugged her close. "Things are better up there now," she said softly, stroking a damp strand of hair back from Clementine's forehead.

Clementine's happiness broke through in a rush. "Oh, I can see Fan again!" she cried. She could hardly believe it.

"Oh, you and your precious Fan!" said Mrs. Southey, but not unkindly. "You just concentrate on getting strong again, that's all."

CHAPTER

8

Fan had left school the minute she'd turned fourteen. "The very minute!" she'd told Clementine triumphantly on the night that she'd arrived. "I checked up with Mum, see? I asked her what time I was born, exactly, and she said it was around two o'clock in the afternoon. So that day I went to school, and I waited till exactly two—it was right in the middle of old droopy-drawers' bookkeeping lesson—and I just got up and marched straight out of there! She couldn't do a thing!"

Their room was the same back bedroom they'd shared on Clementine's last visit, with Caroline's old bed pushed up beneath the window and the view of endless moonstruck paddocks stretching away to the hills.

"None of them could do a thing! I just walked out the gate and then I ran and ran and ran!" Fan had flung herself across her bed in the same old way, shining hair hanging over the edge of it, narrow brown feet walking up the grubby wall, just like she'd done when she was ten. She was bigger now, of course, a whole head taller than Clementine, and beautiful as ever. More beautiful—her lips were fuller, sweeter; her eyes a deeper blue; and her hair had darker tones in it, streaks of rich treacle swirled into that color of wild honey. Her legs and arms seemed burnished, as if they'd been polished by the red dust—like the big copper fruit bowl back home that Mrs. Southey would shine with a gritty black powder and then hold up to gleam against the light.

Fan was grown up. She was working. She was down serving in Mr. Chiltern's hardware store at the bottom of Main Street, five days a week and half a day on Saturdays. She loved it, she said; yet whenever Clementine thought of the dark little cave of Mr. Chiltern's cluttered store, and the way her cousin's golden head seemed to shine there like a lamp, a feeling would rise up inside her like a sorrow to which she couldn't give a name.

Left to herself all through the weekdays, Clementine grew bored—bored with the books she'd brought with her, bored with idling around the lake and wandering the narrow tracks that meandered over the empty common and never seemed to get to anywhere except the paddocks and back to the lake again. The little waves still made their old-dog lapping sound among the reeds, the winds of heaven blew, and the clouds in their fantastic shapes still sailed majestically across the sky. On a lonely day that wide sky and those grand sailing clouds could make you feel unreal.

She did messages for her aunty, helped her hang out the washing, and even sat companionably beside her at the kitchen table, peeling potatoes or slicing beans or shelling sweet green pods of peas. "You're a good kid," Aunty Rene said unexpectedly one morning—though then she'd gone and spoiled it by adding, "Not like that little madam of mine."

"Things have changed up there," Mum had told her, and the biggest change was in Aunty Rene. She wasn't so scary now; the seething had gone out of her, her voice had lost the little scream inside it, and the leather strap no longer hung beside the kitchen door. Uncle Len's name remained unspoken; and somehow you knew now he'd never come back from Gunnesweare. But one thing had stayed the same about Aunty Rene: most nights she went out after tea.

"Where does she go?" Clementine asked her cousin.

"Down the club to try her luck."

A picture of the church fete swam into Clementine's mind, and her dad saying, "Think I'll try my luck."

"You mean they've got a chocolate wheel down there?"

Fan burst out laughing. "I mean, she's looking for a fancy man."

"Ah." Clementine knew about fancy men: Mrs. Garrick in their street had one; it was what you called a boyfriend when you were middle-aged.

"Can you imagine?" Fan giggled. "At her age?" And then she'd stood on her toes and spun around like a dancer, and her full blue skirt had flared out perfectly around her slender dancer's legs.

Fan wore beautiful clothes now, clothes she chose from the mail-order catalogue and paid for with her own money from the job at Mr. Chiltern's store: rope petticoats and tiered skirts in brilliant colors, blouses in fabrics so soft and silky they made you want to touch. Her long hair was gathered in a ponytail or twisted in a thick plait braided with narrow satin ribbons and pinned up on her head.

Sometimes Fan went out at nights too. Secretly. Clementine would be woken by the soft tap of the bedroom door closing, a drift of sweet perfume in the air, and she would look across the room and see Fan's bed empty, the sheet trailing on the floor. When she got back it might be almost light. "Don't tell," she'd whisper, putting a finger to her lips.

"Don't tell" was because Aunty Rene didn't like Fan's boyfriend, Geoff. Clementine had never seen Geoff because Aunty Rene wouldn't have him in the house. Before Geoff there'd been a boy called John, and one called Charlie when Fan was still at school.

"No-hopers every one of 'em," Aunty Rene told Clementine. "Boy-mad, that's what she is. And we all know where it's gunna end." Aunty Rene tossed her head and her new frizzy perm crackled with electricity. "But she's too big to be told, isn't she?"

"I don't know," Clementine mumbled miserably.

"Well, she'll get what's comin' to her one day, mark my words," declared Aunty Rene, adding mysteriously, "We make our bed and then we have to lie in it."

Boy-mad. Back at Chisholm, Mrs. Larkin called Jilly Norris and her gang boy-mad, but Clementine could see they were different from her cousin. Jilly and her friends didn't have boys of their own like Fan did, or Annie Boland or Mattie Gaskin, and Clementine understood that this was why Jilly's gang talked about boys all the time and hung around boys' places, like football games and cricket matches and cadet parades. It was why they read the boring sports pages of the *Telegraph* and the *Daily Mirror*, so they would have something to talk about with boys. They were searching for boys of their own and they wouldn't stop searching until they found one. And when one of them did, then that girl would peel off from the gang, like Annie Boland had done when she started going around with Andrew Milton. It was a bit like "The Farmer in the Dell," thought Clementine. Everyone got taken, one by one by one.

With Fan it was different. She didn't have to do any search-ing; it was the boys who were looking for her, one by one by one.

It was the tail end of Saturday morning and Clementine's very last day. By this time tomorrow she'd be on the diesel train, halfway to Cootamundra and the Riverina Express; by this time the day after tomorrow she'd be home in Willow Street. This time Tuesday she'd be back at school. School seemed unbelievable.

Clementine turned the corner into Main Street: she was on her way to meet Fan after work. At the baker's she stopped to buy some bread for Aunty Rene. "Two loaves," Aunty Rene had told her. "One white and one brown. Can you remember that?"

"Of course."

"Good." Aunty Rene had opened her purse and dropped a clutch of coins into Clementine's hand. "And no pickin' the crust off to eat on the way home, eh?" She'd smiled at Clemen-tine, a rusty sort of smile that showed her teeth, still small and pointy but somehow no longer those of a bad child.

Though it was a cold day, inside the baker's shop there was a smell of dust and summer beneath the scent of baking bread. It was the same in all the shops of Lake Conapaira, even Mr. Chiltern's dark little hardware store, as if, despite the frosty paddocks and the ice on puddles in the morning, summer never truly went away. It was hiding, seeped into the walls and floorboards of the shops and houses and the chilled red earth, waiting for the winds of heaven to bring the sun around again. "Two loaves of bread, please," she asked Mrs. Ryland behind the counter. "One white and one brown."

"Righty-o." Cheerful Mrs. Ryland took two loaves from

the rack and slipped them into a big brown bag. "How's your aunty today?"

"She's fine."

"Fan's doin' good down the hardware store, I hear. Old Mr. Chiltern thinks the world of her."

"I know," said Clementine.

"She's a lovely girl, your cousin. It's a pity that—" Mrs. Ryland broke off, twirling the ends of the bag into neat little brown paper ears.

"That what?"

"Oh, nothin'." She handed the bag across the counter. "It's none of my business, old busybody that I am. You just tell her to mind that Geoff Peterson, right? He's the type who's only after one thing, and we all know what that is, eh?"

Clementine blushed.

"Oops! Sorry, love," said Mrs. Ryland. "Never know when to keep me big gob shut, do I?"

As Clementine reached the front of Mr. Chiltern's store, Fan came bursting out of it, her face lit with such happiness you'd think that in the gloomy depths among the hardware some miracle had occurred.

"Guess what?" She grabbed hold of Clementine's hand and danced her up the street.

"Watch out! The bread!"

"Bread!" Fan reached into the bag and tore off a chunk of warm brown crust.

Clementine snatched the bag away. "Stop it! Your mum said not to!"

"Who cares!" Fan let out a joyful whoop. "Don't you want to know what happened?"

"What?"

"Geoff came into the shop this morning, and—" She whooped again, bouncing up and down on the balls of her feet.

"And what?"

"He's got a loan of his mate's car! Just for tonight."

Clementine knew what was coming. "But it's my last night!" she protested.

"I know. I know it's your last night and I know I said I'd be staying home, and I was, honest, Clemmie, I really meant to. Don't be mad at me."

"I'm not mad."

"Yes you are, and I don't blame you. But I love him, Clemmie, I really, really do. I think he might be the one."

Clementine rolled her eyes. "One what?"

"The one I'm gunna marry, that's who."

Clementine remembered what Mrs. Ryland had said in the baker's shop. "But—" she began, and then stopped, like Mrs. Ryland had done, because how could she tell Fan something like that? "You're still only fourteen," she muttered.

"So what? When I wear makeup and put my hair up, I look at least sixteen. Eighteen, even." Her voice went soft and wheedling. "Clemmie?"

"What?"

"If I don't go tonight, just for a bit, Geoffie's going to think I've gone off him, and there's this girl called Jeannie Harper fancies him like anything and he knows it too. He'll go over her place and—" Fan's blue eyes were suddenly glossy with unshed tears, and Clementine had an uneasy perception that even if you were as beautiful and strong as her cousin, love might let you down. The thought was like a cold puddle she'd stepped into, expecting dry, safe ground. Love with the wrong person, she corrected herself, anxious to keep her own dreams. Love with the wrong person might have menace at the back of it, like Aunty Rene's old strap hanging behind the kitchen door. She looked at Fan's dancing feet and sighed.

"It's okay," she said. "You go. I'll be all right."

"Oh, dearest, darling Clemmie!" Fan flung her arms around her cousin and gave her a quick, fierce hug. "It'll only be for a little while. It's just because he's got the car, see? I'll be back early, promise. We're only going for a ride 'round the common, just an hour or so, that's all."

"An hour or so," mocked Clementine.

"No, honest! Cross my heart."

Clementine giggled.

"Tell you what," said Fan. "Later we'll go down the lake, eh? Straight after lunch. We'll go to the old hidey and we'll lie in the grass and look up at the clouds like we used to do. We'll see lions and dragons and castles, and—and perhaps we'll see one shaped like a guitar, or even one that looks like *his* face."

This didn't mean God's face, or even Geoff's. It meant Johnny Cash's. Fan loved Johnny Cash with a passion: the walls of her room were covered with pictures she'd sent away for or cut out from newspapers and old magazines. When she was home the radio played constantly, just in case one of his songs should come on, and when one did, Fan would stand very still and quiet, one hand to the small of her back as if she could feel the music running down her spine.

"Want to? Go to the hidey?"

"Course I do."

"Okay then." Fan let go of Clementine's hand and skipped around the corner into Palm Street. Halfway up she stopped and waited for her cousin to catch up, and when Clementine did, Fan gazed into her cousin's face and said earnestly, "You should have got that boy to ask you out."

"What boy?" But Clementine knew Fan was talking about Simon Falls. She wished she had never told her about him, but they'd been telling secrets in the bedroom, and Simon Falls was the only secret she had. The only good one, that is—she hadn't Fan told about the Home Boy, or about Vinnie Sloane and how she'd let him get caned. She didn't want Fan to think her mean and cowardly: Chisholm College was a different world; to her cousin its customs might sound like those of a strange and brutal country where she was lucky not to live.

"You know what boy I mean!" cried Fan. "Look how you're blushing!"

"I'm not blushing."

"Hah! Honestly, Clemmie, you should have asked him, before he went off to that King's School place."

"Well, I didn't, and I didn't want to."

"Didn't want to? Course you did."

"No. I didn't."

"Okay, no need to get mad at me, I was only kidding." She grinned and murmured in a small coaxing voice, "Don't get mad at me again, little Clementine."

"I'm not little. I'm only a year younger than you are!"

Fan was looking at her slyly, and the corners of her mouth twitched as she began to sing, *"Oh my darling, oh my darling, oh my darling Clementine—"*

"Don't!" Clementine pushed at her. "You know I hate that song!"

"Thou art lost and gone forever, dreadful sorry, Clementine."

"No, stop!" Clementine grabbed at her cousin's sleeve.

Laughing, Fan twisted free, spinning out into the middle of the street.

"In a cavern, in a canyon—"

"Stop!" Idiotic tears suddenly filled Clementine's eyes.

Fan saw them and stopped at once. "Sorry," she said. "I didn't mean to—"

"It's a stupid name!" Clementine burst out. "A—a cowgirl's name."

"I think it's beautiful, like bells ringing."

"Bells ringing!" But Clementine was smiling.

"If you really hate it so much you could change it to Tina."

"Tina!" Clementine knew she wasn't a Tina—Tinas were big girls, blond and small-eyed, all lush curves and rounded languid limbs.

"If you could choose any name in the world," asked Fan, "what name would you have?"

"Madeleine," said Clementine firmly. She had loved that name ever since she'd come across it in a book about knights and their ladies. Often she longed to be Lady Madeleine, in a long crimson gown, crossing the greensward with her greyhound on a golden leash.

"Madeleine!" crowed Fan.

"Yes, Madeleine."

"Okay, tell you what. When I have my first little girl, I'll call her Madeleine for you."

"Will you?"

"Cross my heart. And guess what?"

"What?"

Fan threw her a teasing glance. "Promise you won't get mad at me?"

"I won't."

"Cross your heart."

Clementine crossed it.

"Well, one day, in about, mmm, can't tell how many years, but one day, for sure, there'll be this girl, see? This girl about thirteen called Madeleine, and she'll be hating her name and saying it's a cowgirl's name and wishing she could be called Anne, or Jean, or even plain old Fan—"

"Get you for that!" cried Clementine, lunging toward her.

But Fan was too quick. Dodging her cousin's outstretched arm, she ran away up Palm Street, and as she ran her blue skirt flared out and the ribbon fell from her ponytail and her hair came tumbling down, curling and falling all down her dress. She was laughing, and the sun was shining, and Clementine thought that Fan, in the bright day, was like some sweet and everlasting song.

CHAPTER

9

"Which do you like best?" Barefoot, in her white rope petticoat and silky black top, Fan held up a deep green skirt with frilly tiers, and then a full black one with a pattern of tiny red flowers.

"That one. The one with the flowers. It goes better with your top."

Fan slipped it over her head and fastened the zip at her waist. Then she took a narrow red ribbon from her drawer and skipped over to the big wardrobe with the speckled mirror on its door. She gazed into it for a second, smiled at her reflection, and then began to braid the ribbon into her hair, all the while singing happily to herself.

A Johnny Cash song, of course, noted Clementine sourly.

She leaned her forehead against the cold windowpane. It was dark out there, but a big rising moon silvered the paddocks and the far-off hills. "Hey, did you ever get to go to the blue hills?" she asked idly. Her cousin turned from the mirror and Clementine saw a strange little flicker pass across her face, as if the child Fan had been five years ago had suddenly come running after her, tugging at the hem of her skirt.

"Nah," she said. "Guess I grew out of that, eh?"

Like Clementine had grown out of the imagined splendors of Griffiths Tea; of the palaces and peacocks, and the princesses and grand ladies drinking ambrosia from cups so fine the light shone through. She'd meant to watch out for those signs on the way up in the train, but she'd been so excited to be traveling on her own that she'd forgotten all about them.

"And did the old man ever come back? You know, that old black man who was your friend?"

"No, he didn't. I waited and waited. I used to sneak off to his camp all the time to see if he'd be there. But he never came."

"Oh."

"It was ages ago. I was a kid then." Fan's words were careless but her voice sounded sad. "I missed him," she said tremulously. "I missed him like anything. More than—more than anyone."

"Oh! I'm sorry," whispered Clementine.

"'Sokay. Nothing to be sorry about. I'm still here, aren't I? Still around!" She turned back to the mirror, lifted the ribboned braid, and pinned it across the crown of her head. "There!" She danced across to Clementine. "How do I look?"

She was shining, everything about her was shining: the lovely clothes, her golden hair, her clear open face, her burnished skin—she looked just as she had in Clementine's dream where she'd danced on the great net the Brothers hadn't finished making.

"Like—like an angel," said Clementine.

Fan laughed. "An angel! Come off it! I don't think Geoff would have much use for an angel! Not him! Oh, Clementine, he's so sexy." She stooped and took a pair of soft red shoes from the bottom of the wardrobe.

Like the shoes in the dream, thought Clementine with a little shiver of fear. They'd been exactly like that. Coincidence, she told herself. Hadn't their math teacher, Mrs. Campbell, told them that coincidence was more common than most people supposed? "Mathematically, more likely than not," she'd said. "Nothing spooky about it."

"Do you know what French kisses are?" Fan asked suddenly.

"Of course I do." Clementine's voice was sharp. She felt stung by the way Fan seemed to think she mightn't.

"Bet you don't."

"I do so!" Hadn't she been forced to listen while Jilly Norris told her, over and over again? "And what's more—"

"Well, go on!"

"I bet I know something you don't know."

"What?"

And Clementine told Fan the story Daria had told her in the playground at Chisholm: how the peasant boys in her grandmother's time had chased the girls over the fields of sunflowers and then pulled their skirts up, tying them over their heads, making them into flowers.

"Making them into flowers," echoed Fan dreamily, and you could almost see the images from Daria's story floating across the shining blue of her eyes.

And then she did something astonishing. In that narrow space between their beds, in her rope petticoat and black skirt with the pattern of red flowers, Fan threw her hands up in the air and her whole body flowed into one single, perfect cartwheel. And as she rose out of it, bare feet slapping on the floor, she stretched one arm toward Clementine, hand held out, palm open, as if she were presenting to her cousin on that uplifted palm everything marvelous she might ever do in the world.

Outside, farther down the street, a car horn sounded. Fan's eyes blazed. "It's Geoff," she said joyfully, and without a backward glance, she ran out of the room.

The front door banged. Clementine was left on her own. She stared down at the floor. The linoleum was a grayish-blue color, the pattern long worn away, and so thin that in patches it was no more than a blackish net of threadwork above the wooden floor. But beneath Fan's bed, where Clementine had once crawled to retrieve a kicked-off shoe, the lino was as good as new, and you could see its pattern: gray fluted columns and urn-shaped stone vases spilling out great branches of purple flowers. Clementine tried to imagine a younger Aunty Rene choosing this pattern in a store, perhaps accompanied by Uncle Len, before he'd gone to Gunnesweare. She couldn't picture it. She had never seen her uncle, not even in a photograph, and Aunty Rene didn't seem like the kind of person you'd find in a shop that sold home improvements.

Fan's pictures of Johnny Cash stared down mournfully from the walls all around her. Some showed him full-length, in concert or posed against a wall with his guitar, but most of them were only of his face—a face that made Clementine uneasy, with its girlishly curved lips and dark, unsettling eyes. And on lonely nights like this one, when Fan was out and Aunty Rene was trying her luck down at the club and the house was empty except for her, those eyes seemed to follow her about the room.

There was something about Johnny Cash that reminded her of the Home Boys; you felt his skin would be damp to the touch. You could see the comb marks in his hair, like she'd seen them in David Lowell's that awful time he'd asked her to the dance. An image of David flashed into her mind, standing in the park that day when she'd been ill, staring across the road at the window of her room. Had that been real, or a dream? She remembered how their eyes had caught, and how he'd walked away. "Good riddance, then," muttered Clementine now, and she jumped up from her bed and went to the chest of drawers where her handbag lay ready for tomorrow and the journey home. She pressed open the catch, took out her ticket, and stared at it. How grown-up she'd felt on the journey to Lake Conapaira, traveling all on her own, with only the guard to peep into her compartment now and then to check she was all right. She'd kept taking the ticket out to look at her name on it: Miss Clementine Southey, Sydney Central–Lake Conapaira. It was like a certificate, a certificate that she was an adult at last. As long as you avoided those two small words stamped across the bottom: *Half Fare.*

Half fare was right for her, thought Clementine angrily, because she wasn't grown up in the least. How could she be, sitting here and sulking like a baby just because Fan had left her behind? She couldn't take her little cousin along when she went out with her boyfriend, could she? How stupid could you be? She didn't know things like Fan did: she lived in a world of lessons and homework and exams and daydreams and stuff that wasn't real. She was growing up so slowly she hardly seemed to be moving at all, like a dawdling old train in a dark tunnel where you saw nothing except sudden inexplicable flashes of light that revealed no more than the walls of the tunnel and the shadow of the train going on and on as if it would never reach the bright new country outside.

"Don't know whether I'm comin' or goin'," Granny Southey

used to say in the year before she died, and that was how Clementine felt now. And she was only thirteen, and had a whole long life to go! Oh, it was so awful to be thirteen!

She thrust the ticket back into her purse, crossed the room, wrenched the curtains back from the window, and looked out into the night. The full moon hung in the center of the sky now; beyond the back gate the silver sea of paddocks stretched endlessly away. How strange it seemed that there was this little house, on that empty land under that vast black sky, a little house with a little room full of pictures of Johnny Cash and with Clementine all by herself at the window. It made her think of the address she used to write in her exercise books back in primary school: Clementine Jane Southey, 33 Willow St., Merrylands, Sydney, NSW, Australia, Southern Hemisphere, the World, the Milky Way, the Universe, Infinity. . . .

Soon she wouldn't be here. She'd be far away, back in her own room in the house in Willow Street with the lights from the Brothers' house shining across the park. There'd be no trace of her in this room; Fan would take the spare bed back out to the veranda, and you wouldn't be able to tell Clementine had ever been in this place. And one day Fan would also be gone. She'd get married, to Geoff or some other boy, perhaps a boy whose name she didn't know yet, a boy who at this very moment might be sleeping dreamlessly in a house Fan had never seen. How strange it all was! How mysterious when you really thought about it. . . .

You knew there'd be someone for Fan. He was promised already in her beautiful face, her soft rounded body and slender brown feet; in the way she danced around the room, her arms spread wide, in her laughter and the sound of her voice when she sang one of her Johnny Cash songs. You knew it in the same way you knew that Daria would one day be a lawyer like her father had been when they'd been rich and lived in Budapest.

Clementine didn't know if there'd ever be anyone for her. She leaned on the windowsill and gazed up at the sky, and there seemed nothing she could grasp or hold. She wasn't sure of anything. "You haven't got your feet planted on the ground, Clementine," Mum was always saying. Except where on the ground were you supposed to put your feet? Where was a firm, safe place? With a funny little blink of memory, she recalled the swamp she'd seen from the train window on that earlier trip to Lake Conapaira. "If you walked there," she'd asked her mum, "would you sink? Over your head?" And all that Mum had answered was, "Oh, Clementine!"

Clementine turned from the window, reached under the pillow for her pajamas, and began to dress for bed. Yawning, she wandered down the hallway to the bathroom to clean her teeth. When she opened the door, she found a little kid in there, a skinny little kid with mousey tousled hair and a small freckled face almost wholly taken up by an expression of great surprise. "Hey!" she cried. "What do you think you're doing? Get out of here!"

A full fifteen seconds passed before she realized the startled little kid was her own reflection in the mirror. It was the pajamas that alerted her: pale green with a pattern of the gumnut babies, Snugglepot and Cuddlepie. Granny Southey had bought those pajamas for Clementine's eleventh birthday. "As soon as I saw them," Granny had told her delightedly, "I said to myself, I said, 'That's little Clementine all over!' Because I know you just love Snugglepot and Cuddlepie!"

"But that was years ago!" Clementine had complained later to Mum and Dad. "I had that Snugglepot and Cuddlepie book when I was five."

"I know, love, but your granny's getting a bit forgetful these days," Mum had consoled her. "They look like they'll be nice and warm in winter, and anyway, who's going to see you in them?"

Who indeed?

"Just thank your lucky stars she got the size right," chuckled Dad, and then Mum had started chuckling too and Clementine had hated the pair of them. She was grateful for small mercies, though; at least she hadn't been wearing them when Jilly Norris had come to visit.

"Don't be in too much of a hurry to grow up," Dad was always saying, but this was beyond a joke. Clementine strode into the bathroom and faced the scrawny kid in the mirror: her freckles had got darker in the winter sun of Lake Conapaira, they speckled her cheeks like threepenny bits dipped in chocolate syrup. Her hair, which she'd been trying to grow longer, had been dried out by the winds that Fan still called "the winds of heaven" and it stood out from her head like an echidna's spines. With a trembling hand she undid the buttons on her pajama top—her flat chest seemed even flatter now, almost concave, like a dish of mashed potatoes from which some greedy person had taken an enormous scoop. Oh, it wasn't fair! A sudden tear rolled down her cheek and she brushed it angrily away.

Outside the house a car door slammed. "Luv ya!" a male voice shouted. The motor revved and screamed off down Palm Street—so Fan had come back early after all! The front gate jingled, high heels clattered up the path. Clementine drew in her breath: those soft red shoes Fan had taken from the wardrobe didn't have high heels. It was Aunty Rene.

She ran back to the bedroom. Aunty Rene rarely came in to check on them, but this seemed the kind of electric night when almost anything might happen. The strap no longer hung on the back of the kitchen door but Aunty Rene could still screech gamely when the mood was on her and Fan got her going; it was better nothing should upset her. Hastily Clementine snatched her dressing gown and an abandoned towel, and molded them into a rough body shape beneath her cousin's blankets. A key turned in the lock of the front door. "Hi-de-ho!" a voice trilled out into the hall.

It was the strangest thing how Aunty Rene always sang this out whenever she entered the quiet house after an evening down at the club. Clementine jumped back into bed and listened to her aunty's footsteps dithering in the hall. They paused at the bathroom door; a moment later the toilet flushed, taps ran, and the footsteps came on again, this way, that way, meandering into silence outside the room where Clementine lay holding her breath in the dark.

"Hi-de-ho?" The door creaked open, and Clementine's gray eyes met her aunty's black ones in a bright shaft of light from the hall.

Aunty Rene's blithe permed curls encircled her sharp face like teddy-bear wrapping paper around a dangerous toy. She wore tall high-heeled boots and a tiny little dress with leather fringes along the shoulders and the hem.

"Hi-de-ho!" she exclaimed again. "Still awake, eh?"

"Um, yes."

Aunty Rene's eyes drifted toward the other bed, flickering over the clumsy shape beneath the blanket, which Clementine now saw looked nothing like a human being. She waited tensely for the shriek of rage, but Aunty Rene's gaze seemed hazy, unfocused. "Home for a change, eh?" she murmured to the shape, and then turned back to Clementine.

"Can't get to sleep?"

"No." Clementine wished she'd go away.

Aunty Rene lingered, holding on to the doorknob, gazing sadly at her niece. In her tiny cowgirl's dress and shiny boots she soughed and sighed, and then said softly, "I was like you when I was young."

"Oh!" gasped Clementine, horrified, stifling an urge to cry out, Oh no, no! You couldn't have been!

"Well, nighty-night!" With another vague glance in the direction of Fan's bed, Aunty Rene let go of the door and retreated down the hall, warbling her favorite old song, "Irene, good ni-i-ight, Irene good night, good night Irene, good night Irene, I'll see you in my dreams!" The door of her bedroom slammed. Clementine wriggled down beneath the blankets and closed her eyes.

It was much later when Fan came home. "Are you asleep?" she whispered, leaning over Clementine's bed, a tall silver girl in the moonlight flooding through the gap in the curtains, her hair all loose and tumbled, the pair of red shoes swinging from one hand.

Clementine didn't reply; she kept her eyes shut tightly and gave the kind of tiny sigh people make when they are asleep.

Fan stepped back. The shoes dropped from her hand. There was a rustle and slither as she took off her clothes and left them lying in a silky puddle on the floor.

"Sorry," she said softly. "Sorry I'm late, Clemmie."

Her bed creaked as she climbed into it. Clementine opened her eyes the smallest fraction and peered across the room. Fan was lying on her side, watching her.

"I knew you were awake," she said.

"No, I'm not."

Fan laughed. Who wouldn't? She lay down and pulled the blanket up and stretched her arms out straight above her head.

"Oh, Clemmie," she whispered.

"What?" said Clementine sulkily. But she knew what had happened to her cousin that night. Of course she did.

"Oh, Clemmie, I'm so happy, so happy! And I'm always going to be! For sure! And you, too—" Fan turned on her side again, and through the darkness Clementine could see the liquid shining of her eyes, could almost feel the warmth of her gaze across the space between them. "You'll have, have—" Fan's voice stumbled sleepily.

"Have what?" whispered Clementine.

"*Gadhaang,*" answered Fan.

"*Gadhaang?* What's that? Why can't you talk properly?" she demanded.

"I was. That is talking properly."

Clementine didn't reply.

"All right, if you're so cranky, I'm not going to tell you." There was another small rustling sound as Fan pulled the blanket up over her head and then there was silence in the room.

The silence went on and on.

Clementine couldn't bear it. "What's *gadhaang?*" she whispered. She knew Fan had told her that word before, but she'd forgotten.

"Happiness," answered Fan, who had the kind of sweetness

in her that made it impossible to keep up a fight. "Serious happiness. Happiness for you." Then she leaped from her bed and danced across the floor to Clementine's. *"Oh, my darling,"* she was singing, *"oh, my darling Clementine! Thou art lost and gone forever, dreadful sorry, Clementine!"*

CHAPTER

10

E very day she looked for a letter.
    The minute she came in from school she would ask her mother, "Any letters for me?"

As the weeks passed by with no reply, Clementine became embarrassed, as much for the silent Fan as for herself. She stopped asking her mother and tried not to let her eyes stray too eagerly toward the kitchen sideboard, where the day's post was kept. She would go into her room and unpack the books she needed for her homework, then she would come out to the kitchen again and sift carelessly, nonchalantly, through the mail, as if it didn't matter whether there was anything for her or not.

She made up explanations. Excuses. Perhaps her letter had been lost and Fan had never received it. Letters did occasionally go astray. Kay Dimsey at school was always telling this story about how she mightn't even have been born because her dad's marriage proposal to her mum had been lost in the mail and he'd thought she couldn't even be bothered to answer it. "Pity it wasn't lost," Jilly Norris had sneered.

The first time Jilly said this, Kay Dimsey had cried for

ages, because it was always awful to hear that someone thought you were useless on the earth, even if that someone was Jilly Norris. But after the first time Kay had simply tossed her head and taken no notice of Jilly.

Clementine wrote again and still there was no reply.

And yet Fan had wanted her to write. As Clementine's train pulled away from the station Fan had run along the platform beside it, hair flying, her smoky warm breath plainly visible in the freezing morning air as she called out, over and over again, "Don't forget to write to me! Don't forget me, Clemmie."

As if she ever could!

Fan was busy—that was it, of course. She had her work down at Mr. Chiltern's hardware store all week and Saturday mornings too, and when she wasn't working, there was Geoff, and jobs to do around the house for Aunty Rene. She didn't have time to sit down and write letters like Clementine did, to muck about with writing pads and envelopes and leaky pens—Fan wasn't a schoolgirl anymore. She would answer, one day when she had the time, Clementine was sure of it; and meanwhile she herself would keep on writing, faithfully.

And she did. She wrote and told Fan about the dancing lessons they'd begun in Thursday gym periods; and how Mr. Andrews, the boys' PE teacher, had to whack the boys to make them ask the girls to dance. And how awful it was dancing with them: how their hands felt hot and clammy, how they trod on you with their heavy feet, and how even the cleanest boy seemed to smell of mud and sweat and something strange and sharp that Clementine couldn't identify.

She told her how Mr. Simkin, the geography teacher, had taken a fancy to Ba Purcell and kept calling her out to the front to sit beside him at the teacher's table while he went through her homework. And how when Mrs. Larkin had sent Ba to the staff room with a message, Mr. Simkin had come out and said, "A little bird told me it's your birthday today. How old are you?"

"Sixteen," Ba had innocently answered. She was older than the other kids in her class because she'd once missed two whole years of school.

"Sweet sixteen and never been kissed!" Mr. Simkin had exclaimed, and then his big red face had swooped down toward Ba's little one—only then Mr. Leyland had come up behind him and said, "Can I have a word with you, please, Wally?"

Wally!

Ba had come back to the classroom with her eyes all red from crying. "What's wrong, dear?" Mrs. Larkin had asked, but Ba hadn't told her. It was too embarrassing to tell a teacher. Mr. Simkin (Wally!) was old and balding, with a big stomach which wobbled over his trouser belt; there was absolutely no glamour in such a person having a crush on you. But she told her friends; she couldn't help it, she was too upset to keep quiet.

"How did he know it was my birthday?" she kept asking them over and over. "How?"

"He must have looked it up in the records," said Kay Dimsey, and then they'd all gone quiet, thinking about this.

"He could find out all about you there," said Jilly Norris. "Anything he wanted, your telephone number—"

"We don't have a telephone."

"Where you live—"

"Oh, no," Ba had whispered. "Oh, no, no!"

Then Jilly Norris had begun singing. "Baa, baa, blond

sheep," she'd crooned to fair-haired Ba, "have you seen your Wally? Creeping up your own street, looking for his dolly—"

"Shut up, Jilly," said Kay Dimsey. People were always telling Jilly to shut up.

Last of all—because it seemed most important to her, and most secret, the kind of secret she would never tell the girls at school—Clementine told Fan how at least once a week she walked past the King's School, taking the long way to the station, hoping to catch a glimpse of Simon Falls in his dashing soldier's uniform, out in the schoolyard or walking home with his mates. Not once had she seen him, and she began to wonder if Jilly Norris had got it wrong and Simon Falls's family had moved away to Queensland, or even overseas. When Jilly wasn't sure of things she simply made them up. There was no way Clementine could ask her anything about Simon Falls. "What do you think?" she wrote to her cousin, but even though she knew she sounded desperate, there was still no reply from Fan.

Months passed, and the summer holidays arrived and all that came in the mail from Lake Conapaira at Christmas was a card for Mum from Aunty Rene. Clementine lost heart. Fan probably thought her letters were childish and boring—why on earth would she be interested in what went on at her cousin's snobby school? They'd all seem like babies to Fan, little kids playing silly games. She'd think it stupid that Clementine walked past the King's School like a lovelorn girl from a *True Romance* comic when she'd hardly known Simon Falls and it was over six months since he'd left their school.

"Grow up, why don't you!" she imagined her cousin thinking, her clear blue eyes scanning the breathless pages of Clementine's letters, her small nose crinkling with distaste.

Only she knew Fan wasn't really like that. Fan might call her "Little Clementine" and tease her with that silly old song of Grandpa's, but she wasn't the kind of girl who'd sneer at you, however childishly you behaved. Fan was kind. She'd never say "Grow up, why don't you?" like other girls might do.

Growing up was something that still wasn't happening to Clementine. She hadn't grown a fraction of an inch since she'd been at Lake Conapaira in August, and now it was the end of February. Six whole months! Her chest was so flat she couldn't wear a two-piece cossie, and she was probably the only fourteen-year-old girl in Australia who hadn't got her periods. At bad moments Clementine thought it was just possible she was some kind of biological freak. No one would ever want to marry her. She'd be an old-maid schoolteacher like Miss Evelyn, who took them for Latin, who wore lisle stockings when she didn't have to, when she could have worn nylon or silk; and whose glasses were rimless and looked like smoky pebbles from the bottom of a riverbed. Anything was better than being an old maid.

A few weeks back Jilly Norris had sent Miss Evelyn a Valentine card, with "Love and Kisses from St. Jude" written inside beneath the printed verse.

"St. Jude's the patron saint of hopeless cases," Clementine informed her mother.

Mrs. Southey wasn't impressed.

"It's true," said Clementine. "Jilly Norris read it in this magazine."

The magazine had been in the doctor's surgery, where Jilly had accompanied her mother when she'd gone to have a wart burned off her thumb. Mrs. Norris claimed she'd caught the wart from the kitchen of St. Swithin's, from the family of toads she said lived behind the fridge. Jilly had intended to watch the operation but Dr. Macpherson had made her go outside and sit in the waiting room, where you couldn't hear even the loudest scream. That's where she'd stumbled on the information about St. Jude.

"I didn't say it wasn't true," said Clementine's mother. "But, sweetheart, don't you see how cruel it is? Sending the poor woman a card that makes fun of her—that practically says no one except a saint in heaven would ever love her?"

"You should see Miss Evelyn! She looks like a—"

"That's enough, Clementine. It's cruel."

Clementine looked down at the floor. She knew it was cruel. She'd giggled with the other girls when Jilly had told them what she'd done, because you wanted to think it was funny instead of sad, and somehow all Miss Evelyn's fault. If you thought it was sad and not her fault, then you might start feeling scared.

"Jilly Norris and her lot are a bunch of nasty, cruel girls," declared Mrs. Southey flatly.

Oh, they were nasty and cruel all right, thought Clementine, but at least they could wear two-piece cossies without the top half coming down, and little old ladies didn't stop them in the street at Christmastime to ask them what they were getting from Santa Claus.

Anything was better than being an old maid.

"Can you be a nun if you're not a Catholic?" she asked her mother one afternoon when she came home from school and of course there was no letter from Fan, and she had six pages of French translation for homework, and as she'd turned the corner into their street there'd been this boy in the park who'd looked like David Lowell. When she'd first spotted him Clementine had felt a little surge of anger. But when the boy came closer and she'd realized it wasn't the Home Boy after all, only some ordinary kid on his way home from school, the anger had drained out of her and a feeling surprisingly like loss had taken its place.

Clementine's mother didn't answer when her daughter asked about being a nun. She was doing the ironing. It was boiling hot, but she was ironing because today was Tuesday and Tuesday was ironing day, just like Monday was washing day even if it poured with rain.

I won't be like that when I'm grown up, vowed Clementine. If it's hot I'll leave the ironing until Wednesday and go off to the beach. At least if you were an old maid there wouldn't be so much ironing to do. She wondered if nuns did ironing. And were they allowed to go to the beach?

"Can you be a nun if you're not a Catholic?" she repeated, because it was obvious her mother wasn't listening.

Mrs. Southey woke from her ironing daze and looked around her. She seemed surprised to find herself in her own kitchen; she'd been miles away, at Luna Park on a Saturday night in 1938, riding the ghost train with a boy called Harry Cane. When she saw her skinny daughter standing there in front of her, Mrs. Southey made a little sighing sound, like a breeze gathering in the garden just before a storm. "What?"

"Can you be a nun if you're not a Catholic?" Now Clementine sighed. How many times did she have to ask?

"A nun, eh?" said Mrs. Southey, trying not to smile.

"Well, can you?"

"No." Mrs. Southey turned back to the frilly apron her iron had been dreamily negotiating.

No. So that way out was closed.

Mrs. Southey put the iron down and looked at Clementine as if her daughter's question had just registered. "Why do you want to know?"

"It's just this girl at school," said Clementine, her eyes avoiding her mother's. "She wants to. Be a nun, I mean."

"Ah," breathed her mother, watching the tide of pink coloring her daughter's face. And then, "Tell her they'll shave all her hair off."

"What?" Clementine gazed at her mother in horror. "Do they do that?"

"First thing," said Mrs. Southey. "The minute they've got them through the door." She folded the apron and bent down to the laundry basket to take out a shirt.

Clementine saw a great wooden door with iron studs in it, dropping down upon a floor of stone. "Oh," she said.

Yes, that way out was definitely closed.

"Five," said Raymond Fisk.

"Four," countered Clementine.

"Five." Raymond's voice was as sharp as his wedge-shaped face and narrow sneaky eyes. Though he was three years younger than Clementine and still in primary school, Raymond Fisk was the meanest kid in the street and normally Clementine wouldn't have had anything to do with him. But Raymond had something Clementine wanted: a razor blade so sharp it could slice through a thick sheet of cardboard with the merest whisper of a touch, and with a flat steel edge so you could hold it firmly without cutting your fingers off.

Wanting Raymond Fisk's razor had a lot to do with wanting to hear from Fan.

The screen door on the Fisks' back veranda squealed open. Clementine looked up and smiled. "Hullo, Tom," she said.

Tom was the Fisks' foster child—which meant there was something wrong with his parents and the government paid the Fisks for having Tom in their house, for giving him food to eat and a bed to sleep in and sending him off to school. He was the same age as Raymond, but smaller and thinner, and so beautiful he made you draw in your breath. He had curly brown hair and the large tender eyes of a fawn—he was like Bambi, decided Clementine. Tom was the Fisks' servant: he did housework and chopped wood and ran errands and helped Mr. Fisk in the garden, and if anything got lost or broken Tom always got the blame. There were marks on Tom's legs that made Clementine's heart do a funny little tap dance every time she saw them; she didn't know whether it was the memory of that long-ago night when Aunty Rene had gone for Fan, or the closer one of Mr. Meague and Vinnie Sloane, but she knew no matter how old she grew to be, she would never be able to bear the sight of those sorts of mark on anyone.

There wasn't a single person in their neighborhood who didn't think it was a crying shame the way the Fisks treated poor little Tom, but what could anyone do about it? There was no use calling the Welfare, because they were even worse. Around where they lived, no one ever called the Welfare.

Raymond's pointy head swung around when he saw Clementine smiling at his foster brother. His narrow eyes gleamed and fixed on Tom.

"You chopped that wood for Mum?"

Tom's eyes jumped when Raymond spoke. His whole body juddered. He nodded silently.

"Answer when you're spoken to," said Raymond, lordly. "You chopped that wood?"

"Yes," said Tom.

"Yes, who?"

"Yes, sir."

Raymond darted a challenging glance in Clementine's direction. When she said nothing he turned back to Tom.

"Well, go and split some kindling then," he ordered. "Don't just stand there doin' nothing. What do you think we feed you for? And make sure you split it right, or you'll get what's comin' to you." He snapped his fingers, and Tom ran round the veranda and down the side of the house. A moment later Clementine heard the sound of an axe from the backyard and shivered, thinking of Tom's skinny arms and delicate frame—the axe would be nearly as big as him.

"Lazy little bugger," observed Raymond, turning his attention back to the haggling with Clementine. "I want five," he said. "Five *Phantom* comics for that razor. It's special, that is; my cousin give it to me before he joined the army."

Before he got nicked, you mean, thought Clementine, but she didn't speak the thought aloud.

If Clementine's English teacher had known she read comics, Mrs. Larkin would have had a major fit. But all the kids in Willow Street read comics, and they were always good for swapping. And every payday since Clementine could remember Dad had come home with two blocks of chocolate— Peppermint Cream for Clementine and Old Jamaica for Mum—and there'd be a *Women's Weekly* for Mum too, and a comic for Clementine: her favorite *Phantom* or *Superman*, and sometimes *Archie and Friends*. Only a few weeks ago Dad had asked her shyly if she'd like a change of comics now she was growing up. "I saw one down the shop last week called *Girls' Crystal*, looked like it might be in your line." Clementine couldn't help smiling, thinking of Dad down the newsagents, checking the girls' stuff out. "It's okay," she'd told him. "I like the ones you get."

"Five," said Raymond Fisk again, and Clementine knew he wouldn't budge; he was like her granny's granite doorstop once he'd made up his mind. Immovable. She handed the comics over, and Raymond gave her the blade.

He smirked. "Gunna cut someone's throat, eh?"

She knew he thought she wasn't game to do anything. "Pity someone doesn't cut yours," she retorted and took off down the path. Half a flying housebrick followed her, bouncing on the pavement at her heels.

That Christmas Clementine's parents had given her a new bicycle—a scarlet Malvern Star with a stripe and trimmings in brownish gold, colors that made her think for a sad moment of the King's School and Simon Falls in his soldier's uniform. The bicycle had a basket on the front, and a big leather saddlebag on the back, and Dad had talked Mum into letting Clementine ride it to school. "She won't have to carry that heavy old case anymore," he said, patting the leather saddlebag proudly. "She can put all her books in here." He turned to Mum with a little air of triumph. "See, Cissie? Plenty of room!"

"That school case is heavy," Mum agreed. "Some days it bends her right to one side."

"There you are, then," crowed Dad, and he'd winked at Clementine. "We don't want her waking up one morning with one arm longer than the other, do we?"

Mum looked doubtfully at Dad, and then at Clementine, and then at the bicycle, gleaming against the wall. Mrs. Southey had a dimple in her cheek, and suddenly it showed. "Oh, all right," she said, and Mr. Southey put his arm around her waist and gave her a little squeeze.

"I know you both think I'm an old fusspot," said Mrs. Southey, with a sudden tearful sound in her voice.

"No, no! We don't!"

"Yes you do. You think I don't realize she's growing up, but I do. I know it." Mrs. Southey dabbed at her eyes. "You don't have to keep reminding me."

Clementine rushed at her mother and hugged her tight. "Thanks, Mum!"

"But only on the back roads, mind, Clementine. Take the back way, up the hill. I don't want you getting skittled riding down Villawood Road."

"I won't go anywhere near Villawood Road," promised Clementine.

These days Clementine sometimes went to the library after school. She was in third year now, the year of the Intermediate Certificate, and had even more homework to do. "Ring me if you're going to be late," her mother said every morning, because now they had a telephone, a shiny cream one, which sat beside the thick white telephone book on a new little table in the hall. "Otherwise I'll worry. You know how I am."

"Sure do."

"What was that?"

"Nothing. I'll ring."

And so she did, and when she said she'd be late, Mrs. Southey assumed she'd be at the library, which meant that

Clementine didn't actually have to tell a lie. And this was fortunate, because she wasn't much good at lying: her eyes darted all over the place and her head would feel suddenly too heavy on her neck, and even a little transparent, as if the person she was lying to could actually see the thoughts inside. She was like the mouse she'd discovered in the kitchen late one night—so startled when the light snapped on that he didn't have the sense to run away but simply crouched there, staring at her with tiny, beady, frightened eyes.

For Clementine wasn't always going to the library after school. On some of those warm, hazy evenings of late summer, she sailed along the back roads of the surrounding suburbs on her scarlet bicycle, Raymond Fisk's razor blade concealed inside her glove. In her prim Chisholm College uniform, the bright blue pinafore and blazer, black gloves and stockings, the creamy panama with the pale blue stripe around its navy brim, Clementine sought out newsagents and stationers and those milk bars that sold magazines. Inside, she browsed and lingered, turning pages carelessly, but when she came on a picture of Johnny Cash, her blade flicked out and sliced the picture clean, and then Clementine whisked it deftly inside her blazer. She was good at this; quick and calm and soundless as Raymond Fisk's razor. She'd practiced at home in her room.

The newsagents paid her no attention. They knew the uniform. She was a Chisholm College girl, and girls from Chisholm could be trusted. "Just looking," she murmured, and they smiled at her. And then she would ride away under the great arch of sky where the winds of heaven billowed and the city clouds dissolved into the evening haze. Standing on the pedals, she coasted down the small hills and sailed over the long flat stretches toward home. Elation filled her, she felt brave and strong and free; a totally different kind of person to the mousey little goody-goody she'd always been.

And then one evening, pedaling along Railway Parade, later than usual because she'd ridden almost out to Greystanes, Clementine saw her father. It was Wednesday, payday, and he was coming out of their own newsagent's shop (which Clementine had always avoided) with the two blocks of chocolate in a brown paper bag, Mum's copy of *Women's Weekly* and Clementine's new comic tucked beneath his arm. A gray film of asbestos dust from the factory clung to the front of his shirt and the ruddy skin of his arms.

He looked up and saw her. A smile lit up his tired face. "Clementine!"

She stopped. All at once the scarlet bicycle felt heavy and clumsy beneath her; it would have toppled over if Dad hadn't reached out a hand. "Steady, there," he said. "Are you all right?"

"Yes," said Clementine.

"Been to the library? Working late?"

"Yes," she whispered again, turning her head aside.

"You're a good girl, Clementine," he said.

She looked up and caught his eyes; he was gazing at her with such tenderness, such trust, that her own eyes filled suddenly with tears. Imagine if he ever found out what she was doing. Stealing, that's what it was. She'd been stealing things from shops, and if one of those newsagents had caught her and come to their house—imagine Dad's face then! She couldn't bear to think about it. Why had she done such a thing, when she could easily have bought the magazines with her pocket money? It was as if she'd slipped through some strange hidden crack in the real world and fallen into a dangerous waking dream. The elation of the afternoon, and all the afternoons before it, drained out of her in a long, slow sigh.

"Tired?" asked Dad.

"Just a bit."

That night she wrapped Raymond Fisk's razor in newspaper with the day's wet tea leaves and took it out to the bin. She was a goody-goody after all.

But she kept the stolen pictures of Johnny Cash. She folded them into a big brown envelope she'd bought from Woolworth's (she thought it just possible she might never enter a newsagent's shop again) and sent it up to Lake Conapaira. Writing out the address—Miss Francesca Lancie, Palm Street, Lake Conapaira, NSW—brought the place to mind with a painful clarity that was almost like grief: she saw the red earth of the unsealed streets, the old houses with their steep roofs and wide verandas, the gray-gold paddocks, the rough clay track around the lake. And the memory of the grand night sky seen from the window of Fan's room made her want to keep on writing, to continue the address in the old childish way: Australia, Southern Hemisphere, the World, the Milky Way, the Universe, Infinity. . . . She didn't, of course, because then the people at the post office might think it was some kind of little kid's joke, and not a proper letter at all. They might send it to the dead letter office instead of on to Fan at Lake Conapaira.

And then she waited. And eventually, though it was a long time, halfway through the autumn term, a letter from her cousin finally arrived. It was written on a single sheet of lined paper torn from a pad, the sort of paper Aunty Rene had once used for her messages. Fan's handwriting was big and rounded and careful like a child's, and the words sloped backward on the page. "Backward," she remembered hearing Aunty Rene tell Mum. "They say she's backward up the school."

Dear Clementine,

Thank you for the pictchers of Johnny Cash which you sent. I stuck them up on my wall, in the space next to the window where your bed used to be. Geoff and me had a row and now he's gone up north— good ridence! I have a new boyfriend his name is Gary. He has a sweat mouth, the same shape as Johhny Cash.

Love and kisses, Fan

p.s. Mum has got herself a fancy man at last. Reckon he must be blind eh?

Clementine turned the letter over and over in her hands. Sweat lips, what were they? Then she realized: Fan meant sweet—sweet lips—it was just that she couldn't spell. Apart from the PS, the letter didn't sound a bit like her; its short, awkward sentences and bald, stiff tone seemed more like a little kid who'd been asked a question and was afraid she'd get it wrong. She remembered how Fan had hated reading. Probably she hated writing, too; this might even be the reason she hadn't answered any letters before.

This letter Clementine held in her hands was that Fan: the little kid who'd been scared of reading, hidden way down inside the confident, beautiful girl she'd become when Clementine had last seen her. And Clementine herself had another girl hidden inside her—the one who'd ridden around the suburbs with a razor inside the glove of her Chisholm College uniform.

It was strange how Fan's awkward words could bring that little room they'd shared so vividly to life: the two beds so close together you could hold hands, the old wardrobe and the chair and the battered chest of drawers, the faded linoleum with the bright piece under Fan's bed. And Johnny Cash's face, illumined by moonlight, peering down from the walls; and the big stars, like faces at the window, peering in. The memory squeezed at Clementine's heart so fiercely that anyone would think she'd lost not just her cousin, but a world.

That was the only letter. Fan didn't write again, and neither did Clementine, because third year was a busy, anxious year at Chisholm College, with the Intermediate Certificate looming in November. It wasn't until after Christmas that they heard again from Lake Conapaira, and the letter was from Aunty Rene to Mum.

"Your cousin's gone and got herself married!" her mother greeted Clementine one evening as she came home, all hot and tired and sweaty from her summer job down at the bakery. The letter fluttered in her mother's hand; on it she could see her Aunty Rene's small, spidery black scrawl.

"What?"

"Fan's got married. Some boy called Gerry, is it? Rene's handwriting always was shocking."

Clementine glanced over her shoulder at her aunty's inky scrawl. "Gary."

Mrs. Southey peered at the name. "You're right. It's Gary."

Clementine stood there. The kitchen furniture receded and then came back again. She felt like she'd run into something solid and immovable and had all the breath knocked out of her. Fan was married. Clementine recalled a rainy afternoon from that early visit to Lake Conapaira: she and Fan lying on the old rug on the floor of the lounge room, a big sheet of white butcher's paper spread on the floor between them, crayons scattered everywhere. They'd been drawing pictures of their wedding dresses. Clementine had drawn a long dress with puffed sleeves and a heart-shaped neckline; Fan's dress had been a crinoline. "I'm going to have a lace veil," she'd said. "And we'll be each other's bridesmaids because we're like sisters, okay? Because you're my *gindaymaidhaany*!"

Her *gindaymaidhaany*! And now Fan was married and she hadn't even bothered to write and tell her. Clementine swallowed. "Did she have a lace veil?"

"A lace veil? I don't think so, darling. It wasn't that sort of wedding."

"How do you mean?"

Her mother flushed. "Just—it wasn't a church wedding."

"Shotgun," said Dad.

"What?"

"A shotgun wedding," explained her father, unembarrassed. "You know, a case of have to"—he jerked his head toward the front door—"like Susie Nesbitt up the road."

"Oh." Clementine had an image of Aunty Rene in her little cowgirl's dress, a rifle held against her shoulder, its barrel black and glittering as her eyes. She'd have been seething again.

"Poor little devil," her father went on. "And she's hardly older than you are." He glanced at Mum. "How old is Fan, Cissie?"

"Fifteen," replied Clementine's mother, tight-lipped.

"Fifteen, then," said Dad. "A kid." He shook his head sadly. "What a way to start a life!"

"Oh, I don't know," said Mum, suddenly defensive. "Sometimes those marriages work out—if there's love somewhere."

"It didn't work out for your sister, did it?" said Dad. "Poor old Rene!"

Mrs. Southey's cheeks turned from pink to scarlet. She pushed her chair back from the table and stalked out of the room.

"Put my foot in it again," sighed Dad. "Me and my big mouth."

A few months later Aunty Rene wrote to tell Mum that Fan had a baby son.

Cash, she'd called him.

PART THREE

1961

CHAPTER

11

Fan was waking in the old house in Palm Street, all by herself in the bed in the big front room that had once been her mum's, and before that, in a time so distant she could barely remember it, her dad's as well. All she could remember of her dad from those days when he'd lived with them was a smell of tobacco and wool grease, and the marvelous sensation of being lifted up and held against something big and warm, solid as a thick plank of red gum baked out in the sun. Then there was the time when he went off shearing and still came back home, and the rows and shouting and the pounding on the doors when Mum wouldn't let him in. Then he was gone for keeps.

And good riddance to bad rubbish, murmured Fan sleepily, because that was what you said when they went away.

She lay in that comfortable space between sleep and waking, drifting in and out of memories, snatching at bits of dreams. And then a shaft of brilliant light, diamond hard in that first hour of the summer dawn, pierced a crooked slat in the blind and fell relentlessly across her face. She didn't stir. She didn't want to get up and straighten the slat because if she did then she'd be properly awake, properly awake at five o'clock in the morning with the whole long day ahead. She wanted to get back to sleep. Sleep was safe, it was like another country, a place where she felt strong and certain, where she wasn't confused and always knew what to do. Fan closed her eyes and turned her face into the pillow, but though she couldn't see the shaft of light now she could feel it, like a warm hand laid firmly across the back of her head. "Go away," she whispered.

A dull sickish feeling began to swim about behind her eyes, a little like the beginning of a headache, only she knew it wasn't that.

It was waking; it was fear.

Fear!

Who'd have thought it? When she was little she'd hardly been scared of anything. She hadn't been scared of storms or the dark or ghosts like other kids. Even the sounds of Mum and Dad fighting hadn't frightened her all that much, or the teachers shouting at her up the school. The only thing that really scared her was those times when Mum lost her block and went for the belt, or when Mum—but no, she didn't want to think about that; it was something that would have frightened anyone. Now she's all grown up—a mum with a little kid of her own, and she's afraid of a slit in the blind that shows the day. Francesca Jameson, who had once been Francesca Lancie, was afraid of the day.

The trouble with the day was there were all these things to do in it, like washing and cooking and going down the shops, and she knew these things were important because how else could she and Cash keep living? And yet in her heart she had another feeling altogether: that those things weren't worth doing, were joke stuff that took the place of something important she'd never managed to find. The old black man who'd been her friend, her *miyan*, he would have shown her how to find it, if he hadn't gone away. He would have known what it was you really needed to live your life. Sometimes she thought that if he'd stayed around, if he'd told her that thing she was sure he knew, then no matter what happened she'd have kept on being strong.

But now, as each day crawled along, a feeling would grow in her like a kind of anguished disappointment. It was the kind of disappointment you'd feel if you were in the desert and had this single flask of water you'd been saving and saving for the moment you got so thirsty you couldn't stand it anymore—and then the moment came and you took the flask out and found the precious water had trickled away through a hole you hadn't known was there.

Fan rolled over onto her back and stared up at the ceiling. It didn't matter about the light stabbing through the blind now. It didn't matter because she'd started thinking, and once she started thinking, that was it—she was awake for good. She sighed and stretched her legs out, sinking deeper into the long hollow that made up her side of the bed. The other side, Gary's side, was hard and cold and springy, almost as good as new. He was hardly ever there, that was why.

"Never marry a shearer," Mum had warned her, but Fan had taken no notice. She'd thought that was, well, just Mum. Okay, Dad had been a shearer, and he'd run off, but who wouldn't run off from Mum? The temper she had, and the way her voice rose up in a shriek that would scare the crows off, like a blunted chain saw hacking at a gum. The way she

used to lock him out when he came back from the sheds—
Caro used to let him in, she remembered suddenly. Caro
would wait until Mum was asleep and then she'd creep to
the back door and let Dad inside, and he'd doss down in the
lounge room, rolling out his blanket on the floor beside the
fire. In the morning he might be gone, or he might be in
the big bedroom with Mum—you never knew. You crept about
until you could be sure. Shearing had nothing to do with Dad
pissing off; that's what Fan had thought, anyway.

Except Trev Lawson had stuck with Mum, hadn't he? It
was more than two years now they'd been together, and Fan
still found it hard to believe that Mum—Mum!—was actually
living happily with this bloke down at Coota. Good as married,
and they would be married, said Mum, once they found out
where Dad had gone and she could get a proper divorce. "The
fancy man," Fan had called him, but there was nothing fancy
about Trev. He was an accountant, of all things, and solid all
the way through. You could have knocked her down with a
feather the first time she'd set eyes on him in his suit and tie,
holding on to Mum's scrawny little hand like it was the one
thing on earth he prized. "This is Trevor Lawson," Mum had
said in a soft voice Fan had barely recognized. "Trevor, my
younger daughter, Francesca." Francesca! She'd never used
that name before; Fan had almost forgotten it was hers.

You had to laugh sometimes. Mum and Trev had gone in
for ballroom dancing now; they'd actually won a cup in last
year's state finals. They were happy, Trev and Mum. Who'd
have thought it, eh? Serious happiness they had. *Gadhaang.*

Everyone had gone. First Dad, and then Caro down to
Temora as soon as she'd got that job, and the old man, her
miyan, the one she'd thought would always be there. And then

Mum off to Coota with Trev. Fan was the only one who'd stayed, and yet when she was little she'd been sure that when she grew up she'd be living in one of those magical countries she'd imagined was out there in the hills. The blue hills, she'd called them back then.

She'd been there. Not with her cousin Clementine like they'd planned when they were kids, but with Gary—in the beginning, when he was still keen on her, before Cash had come along. They'd gone in his old ute, rattling along to the end of the narrow road where there was only a little town as ordinary as Lake Conapaira. Close up, the blue hills were gray-green, forested with eucalyptus. From the lookout by the roadway the thick-leaved treetops had seemed all soft and billowy, like fat green pillows swayed gently by the winds of heaven.

"It snows in this dump," Gary had told her. "Would you believe? Once in a blue moon." And Fan had imagined those treetops covered in snow, like pillows in pillowslips, or a fat white quilt you could jump into like a little kid, pull over your head, and cuddle down to sleep.

"Cold enough to freeze the balls off a brass monkey, anyhow," Gary had complained.

They'd parked the ute and walked the short length of the main street. There was nowhere to have a cuppa except for the service station; the single tea shop had been boarded up a long time ago. Fan had stood in front of it, gazing through the fly-specked glass at the shadowy spaces where chairs and tables must once have been.

"C'mon," Gary had kept nagging, pulling at her arm. "What's there to see?"

But Fan's attention had been caught by a faded sign in the

corner of the window, "Griffiths Tea Served Here," and she'd smiled to herself, remembering how Clementine had imagined jeweled palaces and peacocks, and princesses and grand ladies sipping—what was it? Oh yes, ambrosia—sipping ambrosia from cups so fine you could see right through. Fan had put out a hand and slowly traced the faded letters, thinking about Clementine and what she might be doing down in Sydney and how they'd lost touch because Fan was no good at answering letters. She hadn't even got around to telling Clementine about the baby that was coming, or even that she'd got married. She'd left it all to Mum. And yet the two of them had been close as sisters when Clemmie was here those times. My *gindaymaidhaany*, she thought, and then nearly jumped out of her skin when Gary said, "What?" She'd forgotten all about him standing there beside her; she hadn't even realized she'd spoken the word aloud. "Nothing," she'd answered, and then Gary had grabbed her arm. "Let's get out of here!" Even when he was in a good mood, Gary had a way of talking that was like a snarl. Big man. "Place gives me the creeps," he'd growled. "There's bloody nothin' here!"

"Satisfied?" he'd asked her as they drove away, unable to leave it alone because she'd wasted a whole Saturday afternoon when he could have been down the pub with his mates. "Yes," she'd answered. "Yes, I am."

She'd thought about writing a letter to Clementine when she got home, just sitting right down and doing it, telling her about the old tea shop and the sign for Griffiths Tea, but by the time they got back to the house, the energy had drained out of her and the idea had begun to seem silly, anyway. Down there in the city, Clementine had probably forgotten all about Griffiths Tea.

Fan stared up at the ceiling, at the old damp stain in the very center of it, shaped like a map of Tasmania. It had been there when she was little, and probably long before that, when other people had lived in the house and then moved on. People did move on from Lake Conapaira, which made it even more strange that she was still here when everyone else had gone.

And still in the house on Palm Street. "Friggin' waste a dough, paying rent on this dump," Gary had grumbled, aiming a kick at the scarred kitchen door of the furnished house they'd rented over near the common. "Now your mum's hopped it down to Coota with Trev and your old man's house is sittin' empty, I reckon we should move in there."

And so they had: moved themselves, the baby, and all their bits and pieces, and hardly had they settled in than Gary was off out west, just like Dad. Shearing, it had been that first time, and then it was the cane cutting up north. He'd be coming back and then some other job would crop up; always farther away, it seemed, farther west and farther north, and even south, one time, for the apple picking down in Tassie. "We need the dough," he'd say if she complained about always being by herself. And when he said this, he'd squint hard at Cash lying in his cot or cuddled up in her arms, as if poor little Cash, and she as well, were responsible for every blister on his hands.

Oh, he came back sometimes, but never for more than a few days, and after those few days you could practically hear him chafing at the bit. He'd go into a sulk and wouldn't meet her eyes when she tried to talk to him. Once, when she'd put her hand on his arm, he'd taken it off and let it drop, like you'd pick something off your shoe. The time when he'd have given everything he had for one single glance from her seemed unimaginable, as unreal as those magical countries she'd once believed were up there in the hills.

Last time he'd come back had been one time too many. She hadn't been over to the cottage hospital to check, but she knew she was up the spout again. Like a fool she'd gone and told Caro, and Caro had got cranky with her, gone on and on about how she shouldn't have let Gary touch her when he was hardly ever there. "Poor little Cash doesn't even know who he is!" she'd scolded.

It was all right for Caro to talk; she didn't have a clue. What did she know? She'd been lucky; she had her lovely Frank, who was no oil painting and years older than her, but kindness shone out of him. He loved Caro. Really loved her. He would never, never ever, take her hand from his arm and drop it down.

Fan pulled the sheet up over her head. She knew it was better not to think about all this, because there was no way out of it, not now, not with a baby coming, anyway. Thinking only made it worse.

"Mummy?"

Fan took the sheet from her face. Cash was standing beside the bed, his hands behind his back, staring at her solemnly. How long had he been there? She hadn't heard him come into the room, but sometimes the thoughts inside her head could be like a storm, shutting out any sound from the ordinary world. He was wearing his pajama top but no bottoms, which meant he'd been on his little potty chair by himself; he knew how to pull his pants down, though he couldn't manage to get them up again. Fan smiled at him and moved farther back into the hollow of the mattress, patting the place beside her for him to climb up and have a cuddle.

"Up?" he asked, and she struggled out from the hollow and reached toward him, thinking he wanted to be lifted, but he shook his head and stepped back from her arms. "Up?" he repeated, and she knew that what he wanted was for her to get up from bed.

"In a little while," she told him. "Mummy's having a little lie-in. Are you hungry, sweetie?"

He shook his head.

"Thirsty?"

He took one hand from behind his back and waved his feeding bottle, beaming at her; it was still half full of the apple juice she left beside his small bed every night. "Tell you what, sweetie," she said, leaning toward him so she could kiss the top of his head, the blond hair that was still downy as a baby's. "Why don't you go and play with your cars for a little while, and then when Mummy gets up, she'll make you pancakes for breakfast, eh? How's that, then? Pancakes—your very favorite!"

"With gowden syrup?"

"With golden syrup."

He beamed again, showing tiny pearly teeth. "When?" he asked.

He wanted to know how long.

The yearning for more sleep rose in her like a flood.

"When, Mummy?" His dear little fingers touched her arm.

"I'll show you," she said, picking up the small clock from the bedside table. It was later than she'd thought: it was eight fifteen. Nine, then. She'd get up at nine. Sometimes it was nearly afternoon before she could get herself going properly. She gathered Cash closer to the bed and showed him the hands of the clock. "See these? The hands?"

"Arrows," he said.

"Okay, arrows. Well, when this one, the big arrow, is up here on twelve, and the little one down here, on nine, you come and get me, all right?"

"Asleep?" he said doubtfully.

"Even if I'm asleep. Wake me up."

He gazed at her, frowning. "Twelve?" he said. "Nine?"

He didn't understand. She'd forgotten he didn't know numbers. When she'd been his age, Caro had taught her how to tell the time in this way, long before she went to school. Caro had taught her numbers, and the letters of the alphabet, so school should have been easy for her when she started— only it hadn't been, and Caro had left home by then.

Fan took Cash's small hand in hers and placed his index finger on the clock's smooth face. "When the big arrow's up here," she said, "that's twelve, see? Those two numbers at the top? Twelve. And here, this is nine—where the little arrow will be. Nine. Like this, see?" She held thumb and forefinger up at right angles: "That's nine o'clock." She tousled his hair. "Understand?"

Cash nodded solemnly. He was such a serious little boy. She traced the sweet curve of his lips with her fingertip. "Now you take this," she said, placing the clock in his small hands, "and off you go and play. And when it says nine o'clock, then you come back, okay? And wake me up if I'm asleep."

"And then pancakes?"

"Pancakes."

His smile was so joyous it hurt her to see. "Off you go."

And after all that, of course, she couldn't get to sleep again. There was no escaping; the day was here to stay and so was the feeling the day brought with it.

"Fan, you confound me," her old headmaster had once remarked, and that was the word for the feeling that took hold of her these days; that was it, exactly. She was confounded. Sometimes, when the endless hours of the mornings slipped into endless afternoons and then into evenings, which would bring night and then morning all over again, she couldn't stand to be in the house one moment longer. She'd bundle Cash into the stroller and go walking—up and down the streets of the town she went, or around the lake, or over the bumpy tracks that crossed the common. "I want to get out!" Cash would occasionally protest as the stroller rattled over ruts and stones, but Fan couldn't stop. She felt she didn't have the time, that she had to go faster and faster, though there was nowhere in particular to go. There was this feeling that she had to have something: she didn't know what that something was, only that if she walked fast enough she might find out. And if she didn't hurry, then it might disappear for good, dissolve into the endless paddocks and the wide empty sky.

Nothing was like you expected, was it? She'd always imagined she'd be a good mother—not like Mum, never like her—and when Cash was born and the nurse at the cottage hospital had placed him in her arms for the very first time, she'd vowed she would never do anything to harm him.

And yet here she was doing stuff no proper mum would do. Last Friday night when she couldn't get to sleep because the feeling of restlessness had been so strong it actually hurt her, like a rope pulled tight and chafing around her body, she'd gone out and left Cash alone in the house. Sure, she'd checked that he'd been sleeping soundly, and she'd only meant to be away a few minutes, and she wouldn't go out of sight of the house—except once she was through the gate and walking, she forgot all that.

She'd walked for miles that night; all the way out to the common and then down around the lake to the place where her old friend's camp had been. *Yirigaa*, he'd called her. Morning star. Some morning star she'd turned out to be! And where was he now, that old man who'd said he was her *miyan*? Was he still alive, wandering over the old countries in his stories, or was he dead long ago, gone back into the earth or climbed up into the stars? She'd sat there for a long time, her arms clasped around her knees, listening to the water lapping among the reeds, calling up the words he'd taught her as if they might somehow bring him back, or make her spirit strong again. *"Guriyan,"* she'd whispered. That was "lake," and *magadala* was the red earth, and *wir* was the sky, the air, where the winds of heaven blew.

Then a fox had barked out on the common, and she'd jumped to her feet and begun to run: along the shore, down the track toward Palm Street, panic swelling inside her, because how long had she been away from the house? How long had she left Cash by himself? What if he'd woken up and found her gone? She pictured him wandering through the house looking for her, peering into all the rooms, unable to find her, thinking she'd gone forever, tears on his cheeks, his little mouth square with grief.

She'd heard the sound of his crying when she was still only halfway down the track, long before she reached the house. And she'd run faster, the panicked breath crashing around her heart, afraid he might have hurt himself. When she'd turned into Palm Street she'd seen someone standing at the gate, an adult figure, a woman with a small child on her hip, so she knew Cash was all right, at least. Half blind in her panic, she'd thought the woman was Mrs. Darcy from next door, but as she came closer she'd seen it was her sister, Caro—an angry Caro clutching a bawling Cash, his eyes red slits from weeping, holding out his arms the very second he saw Fan. She'd grabbed him from her sister and held him close to her thumping heart. "Sorry, sorry, sorry," she'd whispered into his hair, which was warm and damp with sweat.

"Sorry?" Caro had hissed at her. "What do you think you're doing, Fan? How could you go out and leave him all alone in the house? Anything could have happened! Where have you been?"

"Nowhere," Fan had replied. "I just went for a walk."

"A walk! Do you know what time it is?"

It was one o'clock in the morning; she'd gone out at ten. And she'd totally forgotten how Caro had been coming on the late bus to spend the weekend with them. She forgot a lot of things these days.

In the room next door, Cash's cars still swooshed across the floor and pinged against the wall. "I'm only seventeen," Fan whispered into her pillow. She had to keep reminding herself, because all the forgetting was starting to make her feel old. Older than Mum even, because when Mum wrote a letter describing her latest ballroom dancing costume, she sounded like a kid of fifteen. The whole thing was crazy: it was like she and Mum had changed places, or Mum had gone backward in a time machine. There were girls of seventeen who were still at school—her cousin Clementine, for one. Though she'd never got around to writing that letter about the old shop she'd seen in the hills, with its tattered sign for Griffiths Tea up in the corner of the window, and though Clementine had long since given up on her, Fan often thought of her cousin. She daydreamed about visiting Clemmie in Sydney one day, and some nights when she couldn't get to sleep, she'd make up lists of clothes in her mind—clothes she would buy, and then pack in her suitcase, for visiting Clementine. One night she'd got up and gone out into the kitchen, taken the writing pad and a pencil from the sideboard, and written the list down.

One dark green skirt with patch pockets
Two pairs pedal pushers (one red, one pale blue)
One blue shirtwaist dress (circular skirt)
One white sleeveless blouse ...

She hadn't had clothes like that for a long time, not since she'd been working down in Mr. Chiltern's hardware store. There wasn't the money, for a start, but perhaps one day things might be different, they might. No one said they couldn't be, no one said that for ever and ever she would have to be like she was now.

"Nine o'clock!"

Cash was back beside the bed, the clock clutched tightly in his hand. He held it out to her. "Nine," he repeated, tracing the hands with a small finger. "See? The big arrow's on twelve."

"Hand." This time she corrected him, because she wanted him to get stuff right, even though he'd only just turned two.

Once you got to school, they thought you were dumb if you didn't use the right words for things, or if you didn't think in the same way as them. They'd thought she was dumb, except for Miss Langland in second year, who had wanted her to stay on at high school, at least until she'd done the Intermediate. Stay on! As if she would have! As if those other teachers wanted her! She was a loser, that's what they thought, a no-hoper from a no-hoper family. That sort of thing repeated itself, so that she knew Cash would cop it too, the minute he turned five and went through those bloody gates into the playground and the redbrick building with its smells of chalk and milk and squashed banana and something unnameable that made you feel you couldn't breathe.

No one was going to get a chance to call Cash a no-hoper, not if she had anything to do with it. No one was going to say that he was dumb. "They're called hands, not arrows," she told him gently. "The big hand's on twelve, and the little hand's on—nine."

"Hands," said Cash, and he smiled at her.

"You're my clever boy," she said.

"Up?"

"Yes, Mum's getting up now." She flung the sheet back and swung her legs onto the floor. "You've made your bed, now you lie in it," Mum said whenever Fan complained about anything, but enough was enough; you couldn't stay in bed forever, no matter how much you might want to do just that. Not when you had a little kid.

Fan stood up and entered the day. She wandered down the hall to the bathroom, where she washed her face and brushed her teeth and ran a ratty old comb through her sleep-tousled hair. Then she took yesterday's dress from the hook on the wall and slipped it over her head. Out in the kitchen she took eggs and milk and butter from the fridge and flour from the cupboard and mixed pancake batter in a big china jug. *"Oh my darling, oh my darling, oh my darling Clementine,"* she sang, ladling the batter into the frying pan.

"What's that?" asked Cash.

"It's a song your great-grandpa used to sing."

"What's a—"

"Great-grandpa? It's your nan's dad."

"Nan." He wrinkled his nose. "Where?"

"Down in Coota. You know that's where Nan lives. With Trev."

He waved his hands. "No, no. Where's great, great—"

"Great-grandpa? Gone to heaven," said Fan. "A long, long time ago. Before you were born. Before your mum was born."

"Long," said Cash.

"Long ago," echoed Fan, ladling golden syrup onto his pancake and thinking how Clementine used to say their house smelled special, of wild honey and kerosene.

Now she remembered that she'd dreamed of her cousin last night. It had been the oddest sort of dream. Nothing had happened in it; they were simply standing together, side by side, and yet though they were so close she could see nothing of her cousin, or herself, except their feet. Her own left foot, in one of the ratty old black sneakers she wore around the house, and Clementine's right foot, elegantly shod in the most beautiful shoe Fan had ever seen, more beautiful even than those red dancing shoes Fan had had when she worked down at Mr. Chiltern's. Clementine's shoe was made of soft green leather with a narrow strap across the instep and a small square heel. And though nothing had happened in the dream, there'd been this feeling of closeness and ease between them that was like a kind of special love. Like being sisters, thought Fan. *Gindaymaidhaany.*

She would never get to visit Clementine in Sydney, at least not for a long, long time; not until Cash was a big boy and even the baby that was coming had begun at school. Years, that would be, six or seven whole years, and only then if Caro could look after them down at Temora while Fan was away.

And where would Clementine be by then? She could be anywhere. She could have gone overseas, to England or America like lots of Sydney girls. She might even be married herself, with a husband who didn't care for visits from distant relatives. And Fan would be distant by then; she was distant now. Would Clementine even remember her after all that time? *"Thou art lost and gone forever, dreadful sorry, Clementine,"* sang Fan sadly as she flipped another pancake over in the pan.

But why should it have to be like that? Perhaps it needn't be. . . . Why shouldn't Clementine visit her? Why shouldn't she?

A surge of excitement rose in her. It was a long time since she'd been excited about anything, and the feeling was strange to her, like suddenly seeing a person coming toward you down the street whom you'd thought was dead and gone. She turned the gas off under the pan and hurried to the sideboard drawer. She took out the pad and pencil, cleared a space at the table, and began at once to write.

"What?" asked Cash, pointing. "What?"

"I'm writing a letter."

"To Aunty Caro?" He clasped his sticky hands together

like a little kid in an old-fashioned storybook—the kind they used to have at school—a kid from the poorhouse who'd seen someone else's Christmas dinner on the table. "Aunty Caro coming?" The joy in his voice made her shiver. "No," she said. "No, she's not."

She put down the pencil and smiled at him. The letter was finished, her pencil had flown; she'd drawn three kisses underneath her name.

"Aunty Caro isn't the only aunty in the world, you know."

"Yes she is!"

"No she isn't."

He scrambled down from his chair, ran around the table, and climbed up into her lap. "Is."

"Isn't." She put her arms around him and rested her cold forehead against his warm one. "You've got another aunty, Cash."

He looked up at her, astonished. "'Nother one?"

"Yes. Her name's Clementine. Aunty Clementine. She lives in Sydney. That's who I'm writing to, see?" She showed him the pad with the half page of writing on it, pointed to the neat little row of crosses on the bottom. "See these? They're kisses."

"Kisses?"

"Mmm. Like this." She kissed his cheek. "Mwaa. Only these are on paper, see? So we can send them to Aunty Clementine. Now you make one."

"Me?"

"Yes, you." She turned him around in her lap and placed the pencil between his fingers, closed her hand around his, guided it onto the page. "Like this, see? One line that way, one line this way. There!"

He stared at the kiss for a long moment, then turned to her, beaming. "Mine?"

"Yours."

They both thought it was the most beautiful kiss in the world.

CHAPTER

12

Clementine was walking home down Leary Street when she saw old Mrs. Sheedy leaning over her front gate, peering up and down the road. Old stickybeak! She could keep you hanging there for ages while she found out all your business and told you the business of everyone in the neighborhood. And Clementine, a crisp brown paper parcel tucked beneath her arm, which held the dark green linen she'd bought at Grace Bros. to make a summer skirt, was in a hurry to get home.

"Clementine! Clementine Southey!"

She'd been spotted; it was too late to cross the road and pretend she was going home by Newley Lane. Anyway, Mrs. Sheedy would know she never went by Newley Lane if she could help it—Raymond Fisk lived there. He was thirteen now, and the scourge of Lowlands Tech, which everyone said was the worst school in the whole of Sydney, possibly the worst in Australia. You never actually saw him when you passed his house, but things flew out at you: bricks and sharpened garden stakes, chunks of rusty scrap iron, wet parcels of tea leaves and ancient mutton fat.

Tom had been taken away. He'd gone to live with his proper parents. Clementine hoped they'd won the lottery and bought a mansion on the harbor; she hoped they'd taken him to Disneyland for his birthday. She hoped they loved him now.

"So you're off to uni, eh?" Mrs. Sheedy greeted her. "Off there in March?"

She even knew the month! Clementine would take a bet she knew the very date of Orientation Day as well. "Yes," she answered.

"Uni!" marveled Mrs. Sheedy. "Imagine that! I don't think there's ever been a girl from 'round here went to the uni." Her round blue eyes took on the distant scholarly expression that told you she was flicking through seventy years of oral research on the neighborhood. "No, wait, I tell a lie. There was a girl called Sally Lomas lived down the end of Irrawong Road—ever heard of her?"

"No."

"She was before your time, I expect; it was well before the war."

Before the war!

"But Sally Lomas, she was a Chisholm College girl all right, just like you."

What was that supposed to mean?

"And she got this idea into her head of going to the Teachers' Training College—"

"And did she go?"

"She went all right." Mrs. Sheedy sucked her teeth and then shook her head sadly as if to imply that no good had come from Sally Lomas's venture into higher education.

"What happened to her?"

"Well, no one knows, do they? And her mum and dad

weren't saying. Off she went to that dreadful teachers' hotel place in the city—"

"Hostel."

"What?"

"It's a hostel, where the teachers' college students live. Not a hotel, not a pub or anything."

Mrs. Sheedy's plump face mottled with outrage. "Well of course I didn't think it was a pub! Don't you give cheek to me, young lady!"

"I wasn't," protested Clementine.

Mrs. Sheedy looked her up and down. "Big ideas," she muttered.

Better than having none, thought Clementine, and began to move away.

"Hang on, where's your manners, miss? I haven't finished talking yet."

Clementine sighed and retraced her steps.

"Now where was I?"

"Sally Lomas."

"Ah, yes." Mrs. Sheedy settled her enormous bosom more comfortably on top of the gate and went on with her story. "Well, when that young lady took herself off to whatever that place was, that teachers' hotel, or hostel"—she glowered on the word—"that was the last we saw of Sally Lomas 'round here." She sniffed. "Home wasn't good enough, it seems. As for what happened to her, I suppose the little madam became a teacher somewhere. Then again she mightn't have; for all we know she could be at the bottom of the harbor."

"Oh."

Mrs. Sheedy looked suspiciously at Clementine, as if that one small syllable, like a primly dressed teachers' college student, concealed more than it showed. "I'll tell you one thing, Clementine," she said.

Only one?

"Teachers' Training College is one thing—and I won't deny the teachers do a good job, mostly—but the uni!" She narrowed her eyes and examined Clementine's face intently, as if searching for some sign of latent criminality, or rot. "There's never been a girl 'round here got up to that!"

"Well, I'll be off then, Mrs. Sheedy. Nice to have a chat with you."

"Wait on!"

Clementine kept on walking.

"Posh."

The single word stopped Clementine in her tracks. She turned around.

"What?"

"Posh. Going to the uni."

Clementine flushed. Lots of people said this. They'd said it five years ago when she'd been accepted for Chisholm College and her mum and dad had let her go. The snob school, they called it, and university was ten times worse.

"You won't want to know us," said Mrs. Sheedy, and the metal curlers beneath her hairnet seemed to gleam with malice.

"Yes I will," protested Clementine, though she would have given a great deal, at this particular moment, not to know Mrs. Sheedy. Did that mean she was a snob? Probably, but she didn't care. She didn't want to be like the other girls in the neighborhood: she didn't want to get a job at the bank until she got engaged, or go into nursing because then you might catch a doctor for a husband—or a rich patient who was too sick to say no. Jilly Norris had left school at the end of third year and was training to be a nurse at Parramatta Hospital. Imagine if you got run over and woke up on the operating table to find Jilly Norris leaning over you. . . . No, Clementine didn't want to be a bank teller or a nurse. She didn't even want to go to teachers' college: teachers' college was for old maids, and so was library school.

"Now, I know you young girls these days don't like us old chooks putting our oars in," said Mrs. Sheedy.

Don't, then, thought Clementine.

"What was that?"

"Nothing. I didn't say anything."

"I thought you did."

"I didn't."

"Well, I'll give you the benefit of the doubt, though there's hundreds wouldn't." Mrs. Sheedy stared hard into Clementine's eyes. "Now, as I was saying when I was so rudely interrupted—"

"But you weren't."

"Eh?"

"I didn't interrupt you—"

Mrs. Sheedy glared.

Clementine went silent.

"Now, as I was saying, the thing about us oldies you young ones don't seem to realize is that we've been around a long time and we've seen a thing or two. Come here."

"What?"

"Come up a bit closer and I'll give you some free advice."

"What advice?"

"Just come here and find out."

Clementine stayed where she was.

"What's the matter?" demanded Mrs. Sheedy.

Clementine blushed. "Nothing."

"I don't bite, you know. Least no one's complained to me yet."

Clementine took a tiny step nearer the gate. She didn't like being so close to that enormous wobbly bosom, which, beneath Mrs. Sheedy's green polka dot pinny, looked as if it might lead some secret, untrammeled existence of its own. Like Sally Lomas, she thought.

"What advice?" she asked again.

"I don't think too much education's good for a young girl."

"Why don't you?"

Mrs. Sheedy lowered her voice confidentially. "Well, the boys don't like it, do they?"

"Don't they?"

A faint expression of shock passed over Mrs. Sheedy's battered features; her small pug nose twitched as if she'd scented something—not bad exactly, but definitely on the turn. "Oh no," she said, and then paused for a moment, seeming to study the dust motes dancing gaily in the sunlight between them. "Boys like a girl to be—" She paused again, and Clementine waited, silently filling in the words she thought were coming: Prettier? More stupid? Handy with a duster? Unable to answer back because they didn't have the vocabulary?

"Unspoiled," said Mrs. Sheedy.

Unspoiled! A hot red rage surged through Clementine's spoiled veins. What did Mrs. Sheedy know? Stuck at her gate all day, hoping for something to happen: the thuds and curses of a good domestic, some careless kid skittled down the corner, some stuck-up little madam passing by, nose in the air, dreaming of going off to the uni. . . .

"No, you take my word for it, nice boys like girls who know—"

Their place, thought Clementine.

Mrs. Sheedy didn't finish her sentence, her attention suddenly diverted by the parcel under Clementine's arm. "What's that you've got there?"

"Just some material for a new skirt," answered Clementine. "For when I start at university."

"A new skirt? For when you go to the uni?" It was as if Mrs. Sheedy couldn't allow that skirts might be worn in such a place. What else then? wondered Clementine. Not jeans, Mrs. Sheedy might not have heard of jeans. Sackcloth and ashes, that was it. Penitential robes.

"Mum's helping me make it," she said. "And sorry, but I've got to rush, Mrs. Sheedy, Mum's expecting me."

"But—"

"Bye!" Clementine hurtled away down the street, and she was still hot and angry when she burst in through the kitchen door.

"What's the matter?" asked her mother.

"Mrs. Sheedy!"

Mrs. Southey laughed. "Caught you, did she? Hope you didn't give her any cheek; she's an old lady, after all."

"You can still be awful if you're old."

"Like me, I suppose."

"Not you." Clementine tossed her parcel onto the kitchen table and enveloped her mother in a hug.

"What's that for?"

"Oh, nothing."

Her mother smiled and picked up the parcel. "Is this the material for your skirt?"

"Yes."

Mrs. Southey took the kitchen shears from the drawer. Snipping the string, she folded back the crisp brown paper and the two of them looked down at the deep green cloth inside.

"Oh, Clementine, it's beautiful! How much is there?"

"Four and a half yards."

"A full skirt, then."

"With patch pockets."

"Oh, yes."

"And buttons down the front, don't you think? In the same color?"

"That might be a little difficult," said Mrs. Southey. "You hardly ever see that shade of green. Tell you what, though, I'll make you covered ones, in the same material."

"Oh, will you?"

"Of course. Didn't I just say I would?" Her mother lifted the fabric from its wrapping and held it up against the light. "Oh!"

"What is it?"

"I forgot, there's a letter for you over on the sideboard."

"A letter?" Clementine went to the sideboard. She picked up the single envelope lying there and looked at the post-mark. Even after all this time, those two words, *Lake Conapaira*, could make her heart move strangely beneath her ribs. It was a little like the feeling she'd had so long ago when she'd seen those signs for Griffiths Tea from the windows of the train. As if she expected something wonderful.

"From your cousin, that must be." Clementine's mother was looking over her daughter's shoulder at the envelope. "Since she's the only one left up there." She gave a little *tsk* of disapproval. Mrs. Southey hadn't been able to get over the fact that Aunty Rene had gone off to live with another bloke when she was still officially married to Uncle Len. "At her age!" And the photograph Aunty Rene had sent a year back, of herself in a slinky gold dancing dress, with a headdress of bright pink feathers on her electric curls, had been the very last straw. "Off to the Roxy again, it looks like," Mrs. Southey had commented, studying the picture hard. "Rene always was a fool."

"But why? Why can't I go?"

The three of them were sitting around the kitchen table discussing the letter from Lake Conapaira. Fan had asked Clementine to come and visit. "Only for a few days," she'd written. "I know you must be busy and have lots of other things to do. But it's so long since we've seen each other. . . ."

There were three kisses at the bottom, and a fourth one, big and wobbly, which had come from little Cash. And now Mum was saying she couldn't go.

"But I've got a whole week free when my summer job finishes!" protested Clementine. "Why can't I go then?"

"Clementine—"

"I've been up there on my own before, when I was only thirteen."

"That was different," said Mrs. Southey.

"How was it different?"

Mrs. Southey didn't reply.

"I'm nearly seventeen, Mum. I'm going to university in a few weeks' time."

"Don't count your chickens," said Mrs. Southey, who would occasionally sound as if she couldn't quite believe that Clementine's bright future was actually going to happen, and was every day expecting another letter to come: one that would inform them regretfully that Clementine's matriculation score, her scholarship, her place at the university had all been a mistake.

Clementine regarded her mother scornfully. "I don't know what you're worried about."

Her father cleared his throat. "Things are a bit unsettled up there now," he said. "That's what's bothering your mum."

"Unsettled?" But she knew what they meant, she'd known it all along, how Aunty Rene had taken off and how Fan was mostly on her own with the baby because her husband was away working more than he was home. They acted (or rather Mum acted—Dad wasn't quite so bad) as if Fan on her own wasn't a suitable person for their daughter to stay with, as if having to get married at fifteen because you were having a baby made you somehow unreliable, even dangerous.

When little Nerissa Parr at school had got pregnant at the end of third year and had to leave Chisholm College, Ba Purcell had remarked to Clementine, "It's always the good girls who get caught."

"Why?" Clementine had asked.

"Because they are kind, and nice," Daria, the Hungarian girl, had answered. "And because they don't know anything, of course. Which is good for the boys, I think."

"Fan's a good person," Clementine said to her mother now.

"I know, love, but—"

"She'd never hurt anyone, ever!"

Dad was reading through the letter again. "Poor lass sounds lonely. Must be rough on her, all by herself with the little fellow."

"Well, nobody asked her to go and get herself—" began Mrs. Southey, and then she fell uneasily silent, because both Clementine and her father were gazing at her sternly.

"No more than a kid herself," said Dad.

That night Clementine heard them talking in their bedroom when they thought she'd gone to sleep, Mum saying things like "Rene let her run wild!" and "No wonder she turned out like she has!" while Dad just kept on murmuring, "It's a shame, Cissie! A crying shame!"

It made her hate the pair of them. They didn't know Fan like she did. They didn't know how kind she was, how loving, how there wasn't a streak of meanness in her, and how she always understood. Or perhaps they thought kindness and love and understanding didn't matter, not if it went with stuff like failing in school and going all the way with boys and having to get married because you'd got a baby.

"No better than she should be," Mum was saying, and Clementine didn't know if she meant Fan or Aunty Rene but she jumped out of bed and ran down the hall and burst into their room, where, across a stretch of shadowy carpet and a dark wash of Onkaparinga double blanket, she could see the gleaming of their eyes.

"Fan's good," she said again. "You don't know. It's not her fault what happened. That—that she had a baby and everyone went away."

"Of course it isn't," said her dad, and her mum said, "Of course she's good, I didn't say she wasn't," which was a downright lie.

"There's no need to go getting all upset," her mum went on. "Go back to bed and get your sleep. We'll talk about it in the morning."

"I don't want to talk about it," bawled Clementine. She didn't, either—because what was the use? It was awful not being able to explain, having the words but not knowing how to arrange them so they'd understand. It made her hate them more.

"I don't want to talk about it," she said again. "I just want to go to Lake Conapaira and see Fan."

She ran back to her room but she didn't go to sleep. She knelt up on her bed like she used to do when she was little and gazed at the lights of the Brothers' house shining through the trees. "Fan's good," she whispered, and the lights shone back at her, calm and accepting, constant in the night.

In the morning at breakfast her parents said she could go to Lake Conapaira.

Clementine loved them again.

The mirror in the Cootamundra restroom was positioned in the strangest place, tucked right behind the door, so that going inside, Clementine hadn't noticed it was there. Leaving, she was suddenly confronted by a young woman walking toward her, a slender, brown-haired girl in a full green skirt and gingham blouse. And just as she'd done that time in the bathroom of the house in Palm Street, when she'd seen the skinny kid in Snugglepot and Cuddlepie pajamas, Clementine recognized the stranger by her clothes. That was her skirt, the green skirt with patch pockets that Mum had made for her from the green linen she'd bought at Grace Bros. That brown-haired girl was her. And though the girl wasn't beautiful, wasn't even really pretty—as Mum was always saying, "You'll do." She would do. She would always be small, of course, but she was no longer small as a child. She had breasts and hips and a firm, narrow waist; her freckles had faded, and her mousy hair had darkened to light brown.

She looked at least seventeen, and Clementine was glad of this unexpected revelation, because she'd begun to feel shy about meeting her cousin again. Fan had always been older, and beautiful, and more experienced, and so much had happened in her life since Clementine had last seen her. Fan had done real things; all Clementine had done was go to school.

She thought she might have grown up a little bit. She knew that if she ever met a boy she liked she'd never behave in the silly way she'd done with Simon Falls, daydreaming about him all the time and never doing anything, walking past the King's School for months after he'd gone away. And if David Lowell—well, not David Lowell, because he'd vanished as completely as Simon Falls had—but someone like him, ever asked her out she wouldn't get angry like she had with David. She wouldn't be mean to someone just because he was a Home Boy. Or because he'd liked her when she'd never wanted him to.

But these were small, trivial steps, she knew. Fan's growing up was big and serious. She was a married woman. She had a husband and a child, and this seemed amazing to Clementine: to be someone's wife, to be able to say "my husband" of another human being. Fan was an adult. When would she be one? When she started at university? When she left it with her degree? When she became a teacher or whatever else there was to be? When she was married, if she ever found someone, or when she was—and here Clementine stopped short in her reflections, because she had almost concluded them by saying to that girl in the mirror at the Cootamundra restroom, saying right out loud, "When I'm grown up, someday—"

CHAPTER

13

It was well into the morning: it was half past nine. Clementine wandered up the hall toward her cousin's bedroom and stood for a moment outside the door, yawning and rubbing at her heavy eyes. She couldn't understand why she felt so sleepy. It was three whole days since she'd got here, long enough for the tiredness of the journey to have ebbed away. Three days since Fan had met her at the station and Clementine had barely recognized her.

There'd been no one else waiting on the platform to meet the Sydney train, only this woman with the little boy in the stroller—a tall woman in a drab cotton dress with the hem coming down. Common sense should have told her that it was Fan, and yet even when the woman turned and Clementine had seen her face, thin and gaunt as Fan's had never been, she could still hardly believe it was her cousin. A thought had rushed into her mind before she could stop it: she looks like she's been left out in the rain.

She'd had to struggle to stop herself from crying out loud, "What's happened? What's wrong?"

"Clementine!" Fan's slow, sweet voice was just as it had

always been. "Oh, Clemmie!" And then the corners of her down-turned mouth had lifted and her great eyes shone, and she'd loosened her hold on Cash's stroller and held out her arms—and then Clementine had wondered how on earth she could ever have doubted that this was Fan.

Perhaps it was the hair. Fan's beautiful long hair had been cut, shorn off into a thick, ungainly bob that barely reached the tips of her ears. It had darkened, too, lost its treacle and wild-honey colors and become an ordinary brown that was almost the same shade as Clementine's.

Fan had caught her staring and put up a hand as if to cover it. "Oh, you're looking at my hair! I cut it off. It was too much trouble, seeing as—" Here she'd smothered a giggle. "Seeing as I didn't have good old Mum to help me keep it proper. Remember that? Remember how she used to drag the comb through, and I'd yell and she'd yell, and you'd put your hands over your ears. Oh—" She'd begun laughing then, that sound that made you think of bright water flung into the air. So it's all right, Clementine had thought as they'd walked down the lane toward Palm Street, the stroller rattling over ruts and stones and Cash leaning back in it, waving his small hands at the big bright stars. Fan looked different because she was tired, that was all. Hadn't Mum warned her that she might notice a change in Fan, because young mothers often got tired, especially when they had to manage on their own?

"Fan?" she whispered now. "Fan, are you awake?"

There was no answer. Softly she pushed the door open and glanced inside. Fan was still asleep, sunk deep into the hollow on one side of the huge double bed, one arm flung out across the pillow, her fingers curled like those of a child. She was smiling faintly, and asleep her face looked young and beautiful again; the lips softened, the frown lines eased away.

"Fan?" she whispered again. Fan slept on. But that was all right, thought Clementine, she'd have slept longer herself if a curious little noise hadn't woken her: a small rushing sound followed by a sharp metallic *ping*. She'd lain there for ages wondering what it could be before she'd realized the sound was made by Cash playing with his Matchbox cars: spinning them across the floor of his bedroom until they crashed against the skirting board. He'd been doing it last night while she and Fan sat talking in the lounge room. He was a funny, quiet little kid who seemed to be able to amuse himself for hours. Too quiet, she knew her mum would say.

She closed the door softly and walked down the hall to Cash's room.

"Cash?"

He was sitting on the floor in the middle of the room, his back to the door. "Cash?" she said again, and he turned toward her.

"You want some breakfast?"

He shook his head, one small finger spinning the wheels of the tiny red fire engine in his hand.

"You want to come out to the kitchen with me?"

He shook his head again and slid the fire engine across the floor. *Swiiish! Ping.* He was shy of her. She thought it possible he might be shy of anyone.

She looked around the room and with an odd little sense of shock saw something she hadn't noticed before: it was the same room she'd shared with Fan on those earlier visits to Lake Conapaira. She hadn't realized because the furniture was new—special children's furniture in pale gold varnished pine—a small bed, a chest of drawers, a little kinder desk and chair. The old linoleum with its pattern of urns and flowers had been replaced by plain green vinyl tiles; but the pale green curtains drawn back from the window showed the same view outside: the bare backyard, the woodpile in the corner where she'd hidden from Aunty Rene, the rickety paling fence, and beyond it the gray-gold paddocks stretching away to the hills.

It was all so achingly familiar that for a moment Clementine thought she'd slipped back in time. She floundered, disoriented—it might have been years ago, she could have been a child again, and Aunty Rene out there in the kitchen, slamming a pan down on the stove.

Her gaze dropped quickly to Cash's little desk and the color photograph that stood there proudly in its shiny wooden frame: two people, a man and a woman with their arms around each other's waist.

Cash saw her looking and jumped up from the floor. His face, which seemed too old for him with its high forehead, flat cheeks, and large square jaw, had lit up with a sudden eager joy. He ran to the desk, snatched up the photograph, and then, his eyes fixed steadily on her face, crossed the space between them and placed it in her hands. Clementine studied it: the man, sturdy and middle-aged, with a freckled face and kindly eyes, was unfamiliar, but she recognized the woman beside him as an older version of the girl with dark plaits whom she'd once imagined running away over the paddocks to Gunnesweare. It was Fan's sister, Caroline.

"Aunty Caro," breathed Cash. He was right beside her, she could feel the warmth of his skin; he'd never come so close before. "See—that's Aunty Caro. And Uncle Frank." He reached up a tiny hand and outlined his aunt's face with one finger, then looked up at Clementine.

"She's lovely," said Clementine. "And Uncle Frank looks nice too."

He nodded fiercely.

Clementine placed the photograph back in his hands, and he bent his head and kissed his Aunty Caro's face.

Clementine stood there. She didn't know what to do next. "You sure you don't want anything to eat?" she asked again.

"No."

He would wait until Fan woke up, as he'd done on the other mornings she'd been here. Fan never got up before eleven; it was like she was sick in some vague kind of way. "Just tired," Clementine told herself again, remembering her mother's words. But she knew it was more than that, and the thought of Fan and Cash's mornings going on and on like this after she'd gone back home made Clementine feel uneasy, even a little afraid. There was something wrong in the house and she couldn't work out what it was, though she felt it might be a wrongness made up of things that were missing rather than things that were there. She reached out a hand and touched Cash's soft, fine hair. "I'll be outside if you want me for anything," she told him. "I'll be in the laundry, okay?"

She roamed through the house gathering up towels and tea towels and abandoned clothes. "Give her all the help you can, love," Clementine's mother had said to her on the platform at Central. "It's hard work bringing up a little kiddie, when you're that young. And there's nothing like housework to get you down. Piling up on you . . ." Here Mrs. Southey had sighed and brushed a strand of hair from her damp forehead, for it had been hot, and Tuesday—ironing day—and when she got home from seeing her daughter off at Central it would be waiting for her, piled right up.

There was an old washing machine in the laundry of the Palm Street house now, squeezed in beside the copper and the tubs. The copper was huge, like Clementine imagined the witch's oven in "Hansel and Gretel" might have been. "I hid in there once," Fan had confided when they were little, "when Mum was chasin' me with the strap. I crawled in and I pulled the lid down on the top, and it was so-o dark, Clemmie, like you were right down buried in the ground. Mum didn't find me." She'd grinned at Clementine and then her face had darkened. "But she did the next time."

Clementine had gone cold all over when Fan had told her that, not for the darkness of the copper, or even Aunty Rene's gleaming strap, but for another picture that had flown unbidden into her head: Aunty Rene slipping through the laundry door without a sound, creeping over to the copper and holding the lid down firmly so Fan couldn't get out, feeding dry sticks through the little door at the bottom, lighting them, stooping to coax them up into a fine, fierce blaze.

The old machine rattled noisily through its single cycle. There was no spin like there was on Mum's machine at home, only a big wringer with a handle almost too stiff to turn. Clementine didn't bother with that; she piled the wet clothes into the basket and dragged them out to the line, which was empty except for a pair of old fawn-colored overalls—Gary's, she supposed. They were stiff and dusty, as if they'd been hanging out there through the storms and dust of summer and winter and summer come back again. Left out in the rain.

She'd almost emptied the basket when the back door

banged. Glancing over her shoulder, she saw Fan coming across the yard toward her. The way she walked was different, Clementine observed sadly: it was ordinary; her feet no longer skipped and danced and whirled. She was wearing the same faded dress she'd had on when she'd met Clementine at the station, and in the bright morning sunlight Clementine saw how its pattern of gray urns and branches of purple flowers was almost identical to the pattern of the worn linoleum that had once been in her cousin's old bedroom. That pattern had been visible only beneath Fan's bed, another place she'd tried to hide when Aunty Rene came seething with the strap. How many times? wondered Clementine. How many times had Fan had to run and hide? And did she know how the pattern on her dress resembled the floor of one of her old hiding places? Of course she didn't, Clementine told herself, and yet the idea of this strange coincidence, and Fan's innocence of it, set up a funny little tingling all along her spine.

The dress itself was the kind old ladies wore, a shapeless buttoned shift with no waist and short capped sleeves, light-years away from the beautiful tiered skirts and silky blouses her cousin had worn on Clementine's last visit. It was hard to imagine Fan choosing it, but then there wasn't much to choose from in Lake Conapaira. The cramped windows of Lindsay's in Main Street, the only store that sold women's clothing, displayed dresses of this style. If you wanted something different you had to travel hundreds of miles to a larger town, or choose from the mail-order catalogue like Fan used to do in the days when she worked in Mr. Chiltern's hardware store and had money of her own.

She wasn't working now. She was married with a little kid, and perhaps Gary "kept her short," a phrase Clementine's mother used for the kinds of husband who didn't give their wives much money; who spent their wages down the pub or betting on the horses out at Randwick or Rosehill. A wife could be poor, even if her husband wasn't, Clementine knew that. "People don't wear shabby clothes and live in slums because they choose to," she remembered Miss Travers telling them in a social studies class. "And it's not because they're slack. Don't any of you ever think that! They live this way because they're poor and they have no choice. Poverty restricts your choices. I want you all to remember that."

"Sorry," Fan was saying. "Sorry I went and slept in again. You must think I'm awful!"

"Course I don't!"

"Well, you should!" cried Fan with some of her old vigor. "I ask you to visit and you come all this way and you've only got a few days and then what do you find? Me snoring my head off half the time!"

"It's all right."

"Course it's not all right. You always were too soft, Clementine Southey!"

"Me too soft!"

"Doing all the washing! And it's not even Monday!" She grinned at Clementine.

"Monday washing day," chanted Clementine.

"Tuesday ironing day," Fan chanted back. "You know, I couldn't believe it when you told me how your mum used to do stuff like washing and ironing on certain days. Does she still do it?"

"Sure. That's why she got her job part-time, Wednesday to Friday."

"You're kidding me. Aren't you?"

"Yeah. But she still does it Monday and Tuesday. I think it must be carved in stone somewhere."

"Oh, well. She's nice, your mum. I used to wish she was mine." Fan went quiet for a moment, twisting a lock of her shorn-off hair. Then she said, "I don't know what's wrong with me. I think it's just—I get so tired." A kind of bafflement spread across her face. "And it's not as if I'm doing much, all day. Doing nothing, most of it. Nothing days."

A brisk breeze had sprung up and set the wet clothes flapping on the line and the clouds running fast across the sky: a cloud like a big lizard, another like a kitten with three legs, a long, skinny white arm. Fan looked up at them. "The winds of heaven," she said.

"Did your friend teach you that?" asked Clementine. It was something she'd always wondered. "The old black man?"

"Teach me what?"

"Those words—'the winds of heaven.'"

"I don't think so. I don't remember him ever saying them. They were just there, you know? Sort of in my head. Always."

"They sound like poetry," said Clementine, and she stooped and took the last clothes from the basket: the green skirt she'd worn on the train, a pair of blue child's shorts.

There was no more room on the line.

"Oh, we'll just chuck these," said Fan, and she reached up to the stiff, jigging overalls and ripped them from the wire. They fell in a heap at her feet. She kicked them. "Bloody Gary," she said.

"Where is he?" The minute the words were out she knew she shouldn't have spoken them. Fan's face went hard in a way Clementine could never have imagined, and her voice was cold and distant when she answered. "Out west some place, last time I heard. God knows where."

"Oh."

Fan laughed, a dry little laugh that didn't sound like hers. "Remember when Mum used to say that about Dad?"

"Say what?"

"'God knows where,' when anyone asked where he'd gone, and you used to think it was a country, a special far-away place called Gunnesweare."

Clementine scuffed at the red earth with the toe of her sandal. "Yeah." She didn't know if it would be all right to smile, even though her cousin was laughing now.

"You were a funny kid, all right," said Fan. Her face softened and she took Clementine's hands in hers and gazed at her intently. "But look at you now! You're lovely!"

Clementine pulled away in embarrassment. "No, I'm not."

"Oh, come off it, of course you are." Fan glanced down at her cousin's feet in their brown leather sandals. "Only I thought you'd be wearing green shoes."

"Green shoes? Why? To match the green skirt, you mean?"

"Didn't even know you had a green skirt, how could I? It was just—" Fan swiped at her windblown hair. "I had a dream about you a little while back."

"Honest? What was it about?"

"Nothing, I guess. Well, I don't know—we were just standing together, you know, side by side. Like this." She moved up close to Clementine, so close their hips touched, and their shoulders, too. Fan looked down at their feet. "And all I could see was one of your green shoes, right next to these old things of mine."

"Green shoes?"

"Only one," said Fan. "But it was beautiful, your shoe. It was made of leather and it had a thin little strap across the middle and a square heel. And there was this feeling in the dream, you know? Between us, like—remember when we were kids, and I said I'd be your sister? Your *gindaymaid-haany?*"

"Yes."

"Some sister I turned out to be! Anyway, in the dream it was sort of like that. Being close, in a special kind of way. Perhaps that's why I wrote and asked you up. At last."

"I'm glad."

The wind was playing a game with Gary's discarded overalls, twitching at the stiff brown cloth till it looked like a leg was kicking at the air. Fan nudged them with her foot, like you might nudge a lazy old dog to get him moving. Then she hooked them with the tip of her sneaker and kicked them right across the yard. "Ugh!" she exclaimed, scrubbing the shoe into the earth. "Filthy things!"

The wind was really roaring now, ripping and tearing at the washing on the line. Fan shook her head from side to side.

"You think it's them," she said in a dull voice.

Clementine was bewildered. "Who?"

"Them." Fan's voice rose. "Your mum and dad. You think it's all their fault. Making a mess of things, you know"—she waved a hand toward the house—"fighting and hating each other, like mine did. You think it's because they're stupid." Her face hardened again, and Clementine saw suddenly how it was becoming the face of a person who might do dangerous things.

"You think it won't happen to you," Fan went on. Her

voice was louder now. "You think, 'Oh no, you're not stupid like them, you'll know how to choose the right person, you'll know how to—love properly.' You think you'll be loved, and you won't make a mess." The bitter words spilled out of her like dirty water from a pail. Instinctively, Clementine stepped back. Fan didn't notice; she might have forgotten Clementine was standing there. Above their heads the clouds were changing shapes: the big lizard swallowed the three-legged kitten, the skinny white arm threw roses into the sky.

"But you're too young, see?" cried Fan. "You have to make these big decisions before you know anything—before you even know you're making big decisions. And—and then you find out it wasn't only your parents who got into a mess. It's you—it's everyone."

There was a silence, except for the wind. A tea towel flipped off the line and sailed away over the fence. Clementine moved to go after it but Fan grabbed at her arm. "Let it go," she said. "It doesn't want to live here." She caught sight of her cousin's stricken face. "Oh! Oh, Clemmie, you're crying!"

"No I'm not."

"Yes you are." Fan took a gray hanky from the pocket of her old lady's dress and dabbed at her cousin's eyes. "There you are. I'm sorry, Clemmie. I shouldn't have said all that stuff. I shouldn't have."

"It's all right."

"No, it's not. But I didn't mean you, you know. I didn't mean you'd get into that sort of mess. Because I know you won't. You'll choose properly, and someone will love you, someone lovely, I bet, and—"

She broke off. Beyond their clamor, the screen door had burst open; Cash came running toward them across the yard.

It was plain that while Clementine had been in the laundry, Fan had bathed and dressed her little son. The winds of heaven ruffled his clean hair into feathers, his face shone. He wore small blue jeans and a finely knitted sailor's jersey— beautiful clothes you could never come by in Lake Conapaira and which Clementine knew at once his Aunty Caro must have bought for him, just like she'd bought the new furniture for his room. In one hand he held a shape made from bright red Lego blocks, a shape that was recognizably a car. "Mum!" he shouted. "Mum! Look!"

Fan bent down to examine it. "It's wonderful," she said.

"It's for you!"

"Thank you," said Fan. "It's exactly the kind of car I've always wanted." She raised it to her lips and kissed it loudly. "Mm-mwaa! It's so good I want to eat it." She opened her mouth.

Cash squealed with delight. "No! No, Mum, don't!"

"Okay, I won't then. I'll put it in here, right?" She slipped the toy into the pocket of her ugly dress. "So then I can take it out and look at it when I want to—all day!" She rolled her eyes at Cash and he giggled joyously. Then she turned to Clementine and said, "Clemmie, I'm really, truly sorry for upsetting you."

"It's all right, honest."

"No. I don't know, something sort of comes over me sometimes." She smiled shakily. "Don't take any notice of me, okay? Because there are lots of good things, lots." She bent down and swooped Cash up into her arms, kissing his cheeks and the ends of his feathery hair. "And this is my best, special, great good thing!"

———

On Clementine's last evening Fan strapped Cash into his stroller and they set out for a walk around the lake. "For old times' sake, eh?" she said.

They went slowly along the track, where the tiny pieces of glass still glittered in the red earth, and the water made its familiar old-dog lapping sound among the reeds. "So you're going to university," said Fan, and Clementine noticed how she used the whole word, instead of saying "uni" like everybody else. "Soon?"

"Next week."

"Not long," said Fan, and after a few seconds' silence she added, "I saw it once."

"Saw what?"

"The university."

"You did?" Clementine heard the note of surprise in her voice and realized how snobby she must sound: as if she thought even a glimpse of such a place was impossible for a cousin in Lake Conapaira. She flushed. "You mean," she floundered, making things worse, "you saw it on a school trip or something?"

Fan laughed. It was a laugh without bitterness or offense in it and might even have held a kind of sympathy for Clementine's embarrassment. "They didn't have trips at our school, not back then, anyway—it's too far from anywhere. I didn't mean I actually went there; I saw it on the telly, at Mrs. Darcy's place. It looked really—"

Posh, they all said. Fan didn't.

"Beautiful," she said. "It was like one of those places I used to think might be in the blue hills." She snatched a quick sideways glance at Clementine. "You're lucky," she said, and there was no envy, she was simply stating a fact.

Clementine didn't know how to reply. The idea of her luck, of—of privilege made her want to sit down on the pebbly track and weep. It wasn't fair. Instead she looked out toward the horizon, where the color of the sky was fading and the hills showed darkly against it, their primitive humped shapes seeming to possess a strangely living quality. They might have been huge prehistoric creatures asleep on the edge of the plain.

Fan followed her cousin's gaze. "The blue hills," she said softly. "We went there once, me and Gary. Remember how I used to think anyplace you could dream of might be there?"

"Of course I do. What was it like?"

Fan shrugged. "Just a small town, a bit like this one. Mostly trees, and rocks, and then more rocks and trees."

"'Rolled 'round in earth's diurnal course,'" recited Clementine, "'with rocks, and stones, and trees.'"

"What's that?"

"Oh, nothing. Just a bit of this poem we had at school."

"Say it again."

"'Rolled 'round in earth's diurnal course, with rocks, and stones, and trees.'"

"What's *diurnal* mean?"

"Sort of 'on every day, for always.'"

Fan gazed thoughtfully across the darkening water of the lake. "It was a bit like that up there," she said. "So quiet you could feel the earth going 'round and 'round, forever." She paused and peered over the hood of the stroller to check on the sleeping Cash. "It snows up there sometimes, you know? And I thought how when the snow fell on those treetops it would be like a big fat white quilt you could jump into and pull right over your head and snuggle down to sleep."

"Cold."

"Soft," said Fan. She touched her cousin's hand. "And guess what? I saw a sign for your Griffiths Tea."

"On the way there, you mean? Along the road? They aren't by the railway line anymore. I looked coming up in the train, but they'd all gone."

"It was in the town. In a tea shop window—only it was closed, the tea shop, boarded up ages ago, by the look of it. Remember how you thought if you could find that tea it would taste like—what was it?"

"Ambrosia."

"That's right. The nectar of the gods."

"Metaphors," sighed Clementine. "That's what they were, the blue hills and Griffiths Tea. Our metaphors."

Metaphors. How bookish and prim the word sounded out here. Useless.

"Like in poetry, you mean? Oh, you needn't look so surprised; I did listen to some things at school. We had a good teacher in second year, Miss Langland. She found out I could read."

"What?"

"They thought I couldn't, all of them. Because when I had to read out loud in front of people, I couldn't do it—not with everybody waiting to see if I could. You remember—remember how Mum used to make me read those messages? And I couldn't?"

Clementine nodded.

"But I could read in my head all right, when no one was around. As good as anyone. Only after a while I didn't want them to know. Miss Langland was the only one who ever worked it out."

"Good," said Clementine. "I'm glad she did. I'm glad there was someone."

"She wanted me to stay on at school, Miss Langland did, but I couldn't stand the thought of it, not back then. Three more years of school! That place seemed like a prison to me. Only now I think—"

"What?"

"Oh, nothing." Fan peered over the stroller's hood again. "He's really sound asleep."

"Perhaps when he starts school you could—"

Fan cut her short. It was as if she didn't want to hear what Clementine thought she could do. "Funny, isn't it," she said, changing the subject quickly, "how your Griffiths Tea was in the blue hills? If we'd been born thirty years ago, when that shop was open and everything, we could have gone up there like we said we'd do, and drunk Griffiths Tea in the blue hills, and it wouldn't have been a metaphor then. It would have been real."

They came to the spot where the old man's camp had been. Even the blackened stones were gone now, but there was still something about the shape of the land that made you know it was his place.

"Remember when you took me to see him, that time? And he was asleep, and you said not to wake him up, because his spirit had gone walking?"

"Did I? He was a magic man—that's what he said, anyway. Reckon he put a spell on me, eh? It would have been a good spell, though, because he liked me, you know. He thought I was good." She smiled. "Bit of a laugh, that, eh?"

"No, it isn't. You are good."

"Come off it. Even good spells wouldn't work on me. You

know what? Sometimes I feel like I didn't get through into the world properly, like other people. That I left a bit behind, up there." She waved a hand at the dusky sky, where the stars were beginning to show, like pale faces looming behind a screen. "Some really important bit of me, and I'm no good without it." She nudged at Clementine's arm. "Reckon it might have been my brain, eh?"

"No it wasn't! Don't say that! There weren't any bits left behind! You're just as clever as me! Cleverer!"

"Hey, don't get all upset! I was only kidding." Fan kicked on the stroller's brake so she could put her arms around Clementine. "You're a great kid, Clemmie, and don't let anyone ever tell you different; don't let them put you down. Promise me?"

"Promise," whispered Clementine.

"'Specially not some bloke," added Fan, releasing her cousin and grasping the stroller again. "Don't let some thickie bloke put you down."

"Of course I won't."

"That's okay, then," said Fan, and they stood for a moment by the water, listening to the lapping of the little waves and the secret rustling of the nighttime reeds.

As the train pulled away from the station next morning, as it passed the wheat silo and the crossing gates, as Fan's tall figure with little Cash astride her hip dwindled and then disappeared, Clementine grasped what she'd failed to see while she was in the house at Palm Street with her cousin. She realized that Fan had asked her to come, not simply because she was lonely and longed for company, but because she'd wanted her to understand something. And Clementine hadn't been able to see what that something was. She still couldn't, not properly, though as the train rattled on through the plains, where the boxy trees stood in their little groups like people whispering, talking, waiting, she caught some faint, ghostly sense of it.

Last night she'd walked into the kitchen and found Fan with a book in her hand, one of Clementine's books that had spilled from the bag she'd tossed carelessly onto the table. Fan was riffling through the pages, pausing for a second and riffling on again, then stopping for a long moment, so absorbed in what she was reading that she didn't hear her cousin come into the room. She'd jumped when Clementine gently touched her shoulder.

"Oh!" Fan had snapped the book shut and dropped it back onto the table.

"Would you like to borrow it?" Clementine had asked. "Or you can keep it if you like."

"Oh no, no," Fan had protested, picking up the book again and bundling it hurriedly into Clementine's bag. "I was just looking, that's all." There'd been an expression on her face that Clementine hadn't been able to identify.

Now she realized what it had been: a hungry expression, the look of someone in a shop who wanted something badly and hadn't the money to buy. "I was just looking, that's all."

"Oh, Fan!" whispered Clementine. And pressing her face to the dusty window she peered back along the empty railway track. The boxy trees stood waiting, the gray-gold paddocks streamed away, but Lake Conapaira had vanished into the haze of heat and distance, had slipped from sight, was gone.

PART FOUR

1962

CHAPTER

14

Fan was out on the back veranda shelling peas. Her fingers worked deftly, mechanically, scooping out the small, fleshy green globes, tipping them into the white china bowl on her lap, discarding the pods on the sheet of old newspaper beside her. Her gaze wandered carelessly across the yard, over the bare red earth, the woodpile, the shed and the big gum tree by the gate—she was thinking, trying to remember something.

For three whole days and nights, ever since she'd woken from a dream whose tail had flicked from sight the minute her eyes sprang open, two lines of poetry had been swimming around inside her head:

> *If a star were confin'd into a Tomb*
> *Her captive flames must needs burn there;*
> *But when—*

But when what? She couldn't remember any more of it, though these two lines were fixed so solidly inside her head they seemed like a part of it. She wanted to know the rest, she wanted to know what had happened, what had become of the star. In some way she couldn't have explained to anyone or even get clear to herself, knowing the rest of that poem, which already she'd come to think of as "her poem," had become important to her.

Where had the lines come from? At first, because she hadn't read any poetry since she'd been at school, she thought they might have come from one of those poems Miss Langland used to read to them.

In those long double English periods on Wednesday afternoons, Fan had surprised herself by listening and occasionally remembering phrases and whole lines, lines that reminded her of the words the old black man had taught her, because they seemed to bring feelings and pictures to her mind in the same sort of way.

But though it sounded like a poem Miss Langland might have chosen, it also seemed closer than school. It was more like she'd read this poem herself, seen the words printed out on a page. There was even a memory of touch, as if her hands themselves remembered holding the book: a small book, she thought now, a small book with a green cover. But where could she have been, to have a book like that in her hands, if it hadn't been at school?

> *If a star were confin'd into a Tomb*
> *Her captive flames must needs burn there;*
> *But when . . .*

At the bottom of the veranda steps, the baby was sleeping peacefully in the big old-fashioned wicker pram that used to be hers and Caro's.

She had called her Madeleine, the name her cousin Clementine had loved so much when they were kids, and which Fan had promised she'd give to her first daughter. She'd wanted to write and tell Clemmie, and she'd begun the letter—only then she couldn't seem to get on with it. For weeks and weeks, half finished, the letter had hung about the house—on the kitchen table, on the arm of the sofa in the lounge room, even on the floor beside her bed—until eventually it had got lost before she'd found the right words to finish. When she discovered it was missing, she simply hadn't had the heart to start again, and anyway, Clementine had probably forgotten all about that promise. She might have forgotten the name itself, or wondered how she could ever have liked it. She might be embarrassed now to have a little kid given the name she'd liked when she was only thirteen. Fan herself liked it because it reminded her of Clementine.

Gary had laughed like a drain when she'd told him the name she'd chosen. "Jeez, why do you want to saddle the poor little bitch with a stupid name like that?"

"It's not stupid; it's beautiful," she'd said, and he'd gone on and laughed some more. But in spite of all the laughing, the big joke he made of it, Gary hadn't tried to stop her giving the name to Maddie. She knew now that had been because he was all ready to take off for good and he didn't give a shit what his little daughter was called.

Clementine would be nearly eighteen now. She'd be in her second year at university. Gary was at Gunnesweare.

Clementine! Fan's fingers stilled suddenly above the bowl of peas. Of course! That small green book of poems had belonged to Clementine. She'd brought it with her on her last visit. The night before she went back home again, she'd left her big cloth bag of books lying on the table in the kitchen and the small green book had spilled out, and Fan had picked it up and riffled idly through it, and her poem had been there, at a place where the page had fallen open easily. She'd begun to read it, first carelessly without even noticing what she was reading, and then eagerly, because there was something about this poem that was both mysterious and achingly familiar. She'd recognized it, like a long-abandoned child, grown up, might recognize his unknown mother walking toward him through a crowded room.

Then Clementine had come into the room and Fan had dropped the book back onto the table as if it had set her fingers alight and they burned.

It wasn't that Clementine had minded her messing about with it; in fact, she'd offered to lend the book to her, even give it to her for keeps. But somehow Fan hadn't wanted her cousin to see how much she'd longed for it. That longing had seemed a shameful thing to Fan, shameful because she'd had her chance, hadn't she? She'd had her chance and thrown it right away. Not that she'd ever put this feeling into words. It was more like a poison running through her blood, all mixed up with the teachers at school and then Mum saying over and over, "You've made your bed and now you have to lie in it."

So when Clementine had held the book out to her, Fan had shaken her head and refused. "I was just looking," she'd said.

If a star were confin'd into a Tomb
Her captive flames must needs burn there;
But when . . .

How could she find the rest of it?

She didn't know anyone who had proper books, especially books of poetry. And she wasn't going up to the school. How the teachers would look at one another, slyly, gloatingly, to see Fan Jameson, Fan Lancie that was, come up there begging for a book!

And there was no library in Lake Conapaira.

There was one in Lachlan. It was new, opened only last month. Caro had told her about it; she'd said it was a pity they'd built the new library in Lachlan instead of Lake Conapaira, because it had a children's section and Fan would have been able to get picture books for Cash. It had never for a second entered Caro's mind that her sister might want to get books out for herself.

"Mum?"

Behind her, Cash's bare feet padded across the veranda. "Mum, what are we having for lunch?"

"Just a minute," said Fan. "I'm thinking about something."

"You're always thinking about something." There was no accusation in the little boy's voice; he sat down beside Fan companionably, picked up a pea pod, and began to shell it into the bowl. "Go on," he said. "Go on thinking, Mum."

Lachlan was seventy miles down the highway. There was a bus, the bus her next-door neighbor traveled on when she went to visit her married daughter. Fan knew from Mrs. Darcy that it passed through Lake Conapaira at a quarter past twelve, and took one and a half hours to get to Lachlan. If they went today, if they caught that bus, they could get there, she and Cash and Maddie, just on two in the early afternoon. Fan glanced up at the sun, a pale winter globe high above the branches of the gum tree, which meant it would be around eleven now. She jumped up and the bowl fell from her lap, scattering the peas.

"Mum!" Cash began gathering them up.

"Not now, Cash," she said. "We're going somewhere."

"But—" he pointed to the scattered peas. He was such a tidy little boy, so orderly; she didn't know where he got it from. Not from her, certainly. Not from Gary.

"It doesn't matter, sweetie. We'll pick them up later. There isn't time now. We're going out."

"Out?"

Energy streamed through her like sudden sunlight. "No one can help you if you won't make an effort," Caro was always saying. Well, she was going to make an effort now. She ran down the steps and scooped Maddie from the pram. The baby woke without a sound, her limpid blue eyes opening widely, fixing upon her mother's face. She smiled. "Oh, little one," whispered Fan.

How come she had such lovely kids? How come they had her? "You'll be all right," she whispered into Maddie's tiny ear.

The baby needed changing for a start, before they could go anywhere—and clean clothes; her pink knitted dress with the rosebuds on the bodice that Caro had made for her, and her little parka, because it was cold—

Cash was tugging at her skirt. "We're going out? Down the shops?"

"No."

He stared at her. "Where?"

"We're going on the bus."

"On the bus? You mean we're going to Aunty Caro's place?" His voice trembled with joy. He loved Caro.

"No," she said, and tried not to see how his face fell with the disappointment of her reply. "We're going to Lachlan."

"Lachlan?"

"There's a library there, Cash."

"What's a library?"

"It's a place with lots of books."

She looked him over. His jeans were grubby, but they would have to do; his other pair was in the wash. His fluffy blue pullover was new, another present from Caro.

"Go and get your parka," she said. Catching sight of his small dusty feet she added, "And put on some shoes. Your good black ones. And socks."

"I hate those shoes. Can't I wear my sneakers?"

"No. Not when we're going to the library."

To the library. Even to speak that phrase aloud gave her a joyful feeling. It made her feel different; sort of hopeful and proud. It made her feel real.

Cash was staring at her as if he, too, had sensed the beginning of some happy change.

"Hurry now," she said.

"You mean we're really going? Now?"

"Of course. Didn't I just say?"

"Yes. But sometimes you say things and then you don't do them."

"Well, I'm doing something now. Go and get your shoes on, sweetie. We haven't got much time. The bus goes at a quarter past twelve."

She wouldn't take the pram, decided Fan. It was too big

and heavy to get on the bus. She'd take Cash's old stroller instead. Steadying Maddie against her shoulder, she hurried up the steps.

Inside the house she flew: it was later than she'd thought, almost twenty to twelve, and it would take them a good ten minutes to get down to the bus stop. She changed Maddie, dressed her, bundled clean nappies and a bib into a bag, made up the feeding bottle, and then an extra, just in case. But when she began to strap the baby into the stroller, Maddie started to howl.

Cash came running. "She hates the stroller," he said.

"I know. C'mon, Maddie," she begged, wrestling with the straps.

"Here y'are." Cash put the dummy into his sister's mouth. She spat it out and went on bawling, flinging herself from side to side, her tiny hands clenched into fists.

Fan's own hands were shaking; she couldn't get the buckle fastened around Maddie's struggling little body.

"Mum, it's five to twelve!"

Fan tossed the straps aside and grabbed the squirming baby up into her arms. She'd have to carry her. Maddie wasn't heavy and it wasn't far to the bus stop. It was outside the baker's shop, where the end of Palm Street met Main Street. She snatched her purse from the table and Cash grabbed the nappy bag, and they ran out of the house and down the path and through the gate into the wide red road.

And then, after all that, the bus was late.

"I'm hungry." Cash stared into the window of the baker's shop. "Mum, can I get something to eat in there?"

Fan looked down the road; there was no sign of the bus.

"All right," she said, reaching into her purse. "But be quick. And if I call you, come straight away, okay?"

"All right." He took the coins she gave him and ran into the shop; in less than two minutes he was out again, a bag of jam doughnuts clutched in his hand. "Want one?" He held the bag out to her.

She shook her head. "Don't get jam all over your clothes."

"Hello, Fan."

She turned round.

Evie Castairs and Maggie Carmody had paused on their way into the baker's shop to buy their lunch. They were girls she'd known at school, though they hadn't really been friends. Now they worked in the council offices across the road, and she knew they were both engaged; she'd seen the notices in the local paper. In Lake Conapaira, at eighteen, any decent girl would be engaged—any later and it began to look like you never would be. Engaged at eighteen, working in a shop or with the bank or at the council offices, saving for your home, married at twenty-one, first child at twenty-two—that was how things should be. That was the proper way.

"Waiting for the bus?" enquired Evie.

"Yes."

"Off to see your sister, eh?"

That was the thing about Lake Conapaira: everyone thought they knew all about you, even if you hardly ever spoke to anyone.

"No. Just going into Lachlan."

"Oh?" They waited, bright eyes fixed upon her face.

If she told them she was going all the way into Lachlan, dragging two little kids with her, simply to look for a book in the library, to try and find a poem she liked, they'd think she was crazy. And selfish. *Selfish.* Once you were a mother, people got busy with that word. They'd spread it all around. None of that mattered. What mattered was that she possessed only this one secret, this half-remembered poem that made her feel a kind of hopefulness, and she wanted it for herself. It was hers. She didn't care if wanting it was selfish.

"Lovely baby," said Evie, and she reached out her pretty hand, the nails varnished a soft pearly pink, and stroked Maddie's cheek. "What's her name?"

"Madeleine."

"Madeleine. Ooh, posh!" She winked broadly at the baby. "Whose little girl are you?"

The question drifted painfully along the winter street. Fan knew there were rumors around the town that Madeleine wasn't Gary's child.

Let them say anything they liked.

"She's ours," said Cash, laying a small protective hand on Maddie's little arm. "She's Mum's and mine." He didn't mention Gary.

The two girls looked at each other. Madeleine turned her face into her mother's shoulder.

Now Maggie Carmody was gazing avidly at Fan, like a sharp-eyed bird sizing up a worm. Despite herself Fan felt angry tears welling in her eyes. She hated being stared at. If only the bus would come! "Had your one and sixpence worth?" her mum would have said to them, but Fan wasn't like that; she wasn't good at fights like Mum. Mostly she didn't let people get close enough to really look at her; she kept herself and the kids well out of their way. Only now she was trapped here, waiting for the bus. And she wasn't going to walk off and miss it—she needed to find the book. She wanted to know the rest of her poem. She had to have something.

"Do you know you've got your cardie on inside out?" asked Maggie.

"What?"

"Your cardie." Maggie leaned forward and pointed to Fan's arm, where the seam showed plainly, wrong way around.

"Oh!"

"Here, I'll give you a hand," said Evie, and she lifted the surprised Madeleine from her mother's arms so Fan could take off her cardigan and put it back on right side around. "Whose little girl, whose little girl, whose little girl are you?" she sang to Maddie, and Fan realized, from the tenderness in Evie's voice and the gentle way she was jogging the baby in her arms, that there was no malice in the girl's words; it was, quite simply, a question you sang to little babies, anyone's little baby. And she saw that these two girls might be well-meaning after all.

"You never give people a chance," Caro was always saying. Caro wanted Fan to get out more; she'd offered to pay Mrs. Darcy to look after Cash and Maddie while Fan joined the Young Country Wives Association, or helped out at the school canteen.

Only Fan had become scared of things like that. She imagined walking into a room where a group of proper Young Country Wives sat round a table, imagined how they'd all stop talking and stare at her. . . .

"People are kind," Caro said. "If you meet them halfway. If you're kind to them. If you'd stop thinking about yourself for a change, Fan."

"They're kind to *you*," Fan had retorted.

But perhaps Caro was right, she thought, as Evie gently placed the baby back into her arms. Fan gave the girl a smile of such extraordinary sweetness that Evie would remember it later and say to herself, "Oh, I wish, I wish—"

"Thank you," said Fan.

"That's okay." Evie smiled. "Anytime. It was lovely having a little hold of her; she's gorgeous."

Gorgeous.

"Oooh! Aren't your feet cold?" Maggie was pointing.

"What?" Fan looked down. She saw it wasn't her feet Maggie was exclaiming over: it was Cash's. They were grimy and bare. "Where are your shoes?" she demanded.

He blinked at her.

"I thought I told you to put them on, your good black shoes, and a pair of socks!"

"Yeah, but—"

"But what?"

"I told you, I hate those shoes."

"Why didn't you put your sneakers on, then?"

"You said not when we're going to the library."

"But I didn't mean for you to—"

"Here's your bus!" cried Evie.

It was crawling slowly up the hill that was Main Street, and you could see the lake shining behind it, so that the battered old bus with its thick skirt of red dust resembled some tired old monster rising from the deep.

Fan was still staring at Cash's bare feet as if she couldn't believe her eyes. Would they let him into the library with no shoes? No, they wouldn't. She'd have to buy him something for his feet in Lachlan.

"It'll be okay," said Evie, following her anxious gaze. "Joe'll let him on the bus."

"Plenty of kids with no shoes 'round here," said Maggie stoutly.

"It's not the bus I'm worried about, it's—" She was almost going to tell them about the library, but the squeal of brakes and a churning of the ancient engine drowned out her words. Evie took a hanky from her pocket and caught hold of Cash's hand. She pulled him to her. "Here, love, let me give you a bit of a wipe; your mummy's got her hands full."

He had jam all around his mouth as well. And a sticky, screwed-up paper bag in his hand, which Evie took from him and lobbed at the waste bin up the road. It missed and fluttered farther up the street.

"Don't forget this," said Maggie, picking up the nappy bag.

Fan took it wordlessly in her free hand.

"You comin' or not?" called the bus driver. "I haven't got all day."

"Haven't you, Joe?" cried Evie.

"You could've fooled me," said Maggie.

The small family climbed on board. The bus drew away. Cash pressed his face close to the window and smiled against the glass. His hand sketched a small, uncertain gesture. "Those ladies are waving to us," he said shyly.

CHAPTER

15

The library was almost empty at this time of day, the drowsy hour after lunch when people had gone back to work and Lachlan's children were still in school. An old man sat reading the newspaper in a chair by one of the big windows that faced onto the street; two ladies stood chatting quietly to the librarian behind her desk. All four of them looked up as the doors opened and Fan walked in with Cash and Madeleine. The ladies at the counter stared, and one of them leaned across and murmured something to the librarian. Fan was glad she'd stopped off at the store and bought a pair of rubber flip-flops for Cash's bare feet.

"Flip-flops?" the storekeeper had marveled. "You want a pair of flip-flops in the middle of winter?" He'd winked at Cash. "Mum takin' you to the beach, eh?"

Cash had looked down at the floor. "No," he whispered.

"It's only for today," Fan had explained. "Just till we get home. He forgot his shoes when we were coming out."

"Forgot his shoes, eh?" The storekeeper's disapproving eyes had flicked from Cash to Fan; they'd traveled all along her body and fixed midway down her legs. When she'd followed his gaze she'd seen that the hem of her skirt was coming down again; she must have caught it with the edge of her heel as she came up the steps of the bus. She could see he was the type who thought forgotten shoes and broken stitches made her a bad mum.

"Born lucky, you are," he'd observed.

"What?" She'd looked at him blankly, and he'd sighed, and when he answered it was very slowly and carefully, as if she wasn't quite right in the head and might have difficulty understanding.

"You're lucky we have flip-flops in stock this time of year. They're normally a summer item."

"Oh."

As they left, he'd shivered and rubbed his hands together in a parody of chill. "Bit nippy outside, eh?" He'd rolled his eyes at Cash. "Better watch out Jack Frost doesn't get those toes."

"Oh!" Cash spotted the children's section the moment they came through the door. You couldn't really miss it: a wide bright space to the side of the main room, the shelves at child height, fat with books in all shapes and sizes, small chairs and tables painted in vivid primary colors, posters of fairy-tale scenes all along the wall.

"Mum?" Longing made his voice go loud. He tugged at Fan's skirt. "Mum—can we—can we go there?"

"Shh." She put a finger to her lips. There hadn't been a real library at her old primary school; only a shelf of books at the back of the senior classroom. You were allowed to read them only in the last slow hour of Friday afternoon, and total silence was demanded. "No talking in library!" the sixth-class teacher, Mr. Pell, would roar, puffing his cheeks out like the big frill-necked lizard Fan had once disturbed at the bottom of their backyard. If you talked you had to go and stand outside in the corridor. Fan had often been sent outside; something about school made her feel so jumpy and nervous that even when she wanted to be quiet, talk and giggling simply burst right out of her. She understood now that she'd been trying to shut things out. She was still shutting them out. You had to live.

Now she took one of Cash's small hands in hers. "You have to speak softly in libraries, Cash. People are reading. They're reading all kinds of lovely things and they don't want to be disturbed, okay?"

"But can we, can I, go there?" He pointed across the room. "Am I allowed?"

"Of course you're allowed. But quietly."

He ran. His flip-flops made only the faintest mutter on the carpeted floor; the three ladies at the desk turned their heads and watched him narrowly. Fan followed, Maddie slung across her hip, ducking her head as she went by the desk, sensing the gazes of all three watchers upon her, expecting any second to hear a stern voice demanding, "And just where do you think you're going?"

No one said anything, no one stopped her; she heard their whispered conversation begin again the moment she'd passed by.

When she entered the children's section, Cash had found himself a place on the floor beside the shelves of picture books. He sat cross-legged, a book already open on his lap.

"Why don't you sit at the table?"

"I like it here. It's soft." He stroked the carpet. "And then when I've finished this book, I can just reach out and get another one. See?" He beamed up at her, his face flushed with delight.

It was warm in the library; she took off Maddie's parka, revealing the beautiful rose pink dress with the scalloped hemline that Caro had knitted, and which made Maddie, with her silky curls and soft flushed cheeks, look like a little flower. Fan laid her lips against her daughter's tiny, perfect ear. "My little rose," she whispered.

"I'm going now, Cash," she told him. "Keep an eye on our things for me, eh?" She nodded toward the nappy bag.

Cash looked up, alarmed. "Going? Where?" He dropped the book from his lap and began to get to his feet. "I want to come with you."

"No, no, it's all right, sweetie, I'm only going to the desk to ask the library lady something, and then I'll just be over there. See those shelves?" She waved a hand toward the adult section of the library. "You'll be able to see me from here. Don't worry, I'm not going outside or anything, I'm looking for a book, that's all." She kissed the top of his head, and he sat down again and returned to the pages of his picture book.

He was afraid of being left, she knew that, though she didn't quite know why. Was it because his father had left? But Gary had gone before Cash had turned two. And he hadn't been around much anyway; it had seemed to Fan that Caro was right and Cash hardly knew that Gary was his father. He never asked her questions about his dad, like you'd think he would. Never.

She knew Cash loved her. She thought he loved her more than she deserved, but despite the love, she could sense he didn't feel quite safe with her. Perhaps it was because there were only the three of them—Cash and Maddie and her—and he was scared she might vanish and there'd only be Maddie and him and he wouldn't know what to do. It was only when Caro came that he relaxed and felt safe. You could tell: the minute Caro came in the door, alone or with her husband, Frank, you could almost see Cash grow solid, as if some hollow place inside him had suddenly been filled and he wasn't worried anymore.

Fan walked toward the desk, the flowery Maddie in her arms. The two women who'd been talking to the librarian had gone now, and in the corner by the window the old man had fallen asleep over his newspaper.

The librarian was sorting cards into a box, and she didn't look up as they approached, though she must have heard Fan coming. She didn't even look up when Madeleine stretched her hand out toward the vase of flowers on the desk, making a little sound of joy.

"Excuse me," said Fan.

The librarian flipped the lid shut on her box. "Yes?"

"I'm looking for a poem."

"A poem?"

There was something about the woman behind the desk that seemed familiar to Fan. Or was it simply that these ladies—ladies who had the kinds of job where they could tell people what to do, or refuse to tell them something they needed to know—all seemed to have the same sort of face? The teachers at school, the nurse at the Cottage Hospital, the Welfare lady, and now this librarian, all had the same alert, reproving eyes, the long, floppy cheeks, the tight lips that reminded Fan of the steel clasp on an old leather purse her mother had once owned. And they were all so much older than her.

"Um, y-yes," she answered, stumbling even on that simple, single word.

"Just the one poem, is it?"

The librarian made it sound as if there were something not quite right with wanting only one. The color rose in Fan's cheeks; she said bravely, "Yes. I saw it in a book that belonged to my cousin. A long while ago."

The librarian was silent.

"It had a line which went—" Standing tall and straight before the desk, Fan recited, "'If a star were confin'd into a Tomb, her captive flames must needs burn there; But when—'"

The old man over by the window jerked awake in his chair and clapped his hands. "Bravo! Clear as a bell!" he said, smiling.

The librarian took no notice of him.

"Name?" she asked Fan.

"Name? You mean my name? It's Fan—"

"Not yours. I meant the name of the author. Or of the poem."

"I don't know."

"Do you know the title of the book it was in?"

"No. I told you—it was a long time ago and I only saw it for a few seconds."

"Was that the first line of it? The line you recited?"

"No." Fan was quite sure of this. The lines she had remembered had been near the end of her poem; she could picture them quite clearly in her mind. And she had the astonishing feeling that this poem, her poem, might save her if she could only see it once again. She felt it might somehow tell her what to do.

"That's a pity," said the librarian. "Because poems are indexed by their first lines, as well as by authors and titles, and if it had been a first line it might have been easier for you to locate it." She paused, and her eyes fixed on Fan's hand, the right one, where she'd torn her thumbnail last night, trying to open a tin of condensed milk. "If you remembered it correctly, that is."

"I remembered it correctly."

"Well, you're going to have your work cut out, if that's the only information you have. Are you sure you don't remember anything else?"

"It had a green cover. The book it was in."

The librarian smiled at that, and when she smiled Fan remembered her. She knew now who she was: Mrs. Stuckey, who'd lived down the bottom of Palm Street years back, and who'd taught religious instruction at their school when Fan had been in first class. In those days Mrs. Stuckey had owned a wonderful brown polished box in which she kept her felt board to tell Bible stories, with lots of tiny little figures, hundreds and hundreds, it had seemed to Fan: people and animals and birds and even angels. She wouldn't let you touch them, she wouldn't let you stroke the little lamb's fleece or the zebra's stripes or touch the tiny golden beads that made the knowing eyes of Elijah's ravens.

Fan had stolen one of the little zebras. She had never stolen anything before, and she'd never stolen anything since. It hadn't felt like stealing because Fan had loved the little zebra so much that it seemed almost as if it belonged to her. Mrs. Stuckey had never noticed its absence; she had so many little figures, and there was another zebra, though he wasn't so special or lovely as the one Fan had taken. She'd called her zebra Clementine, and for a long time she'd kept it under her pillow to show when the real Clementine came on her next visit, but eventually it got lost, as tiny beloved objects often do. *Thou art lost and gone forever, dreadful sorry, Clementine.*

"A green cover," repeated Mrs. Stuckey. "That's not going to help you very much, I'm afraid." She raised a hand and pointed. "The poetry section's over there, 821. We haven't got all that much, but there's enough for you to be getting on with."

Fan found the section marked 821. The poetry books took up two small shelves near the floor. She knelt down and placed Maddie gently on the carpet, and the baby put a finger in her mouth and gazed up at the ceiling, where small round lights were set at regular intervals, like orderly stars. Fan began to go through the books, volume after volume, poem after poem after poem. Words jumped out at her, lines and whole stanzas, names and titles, but never the line she was searching for, never the same brave sound of it. Never her poem.

"Mum?"

She looked up. Cash was standing there, a picture book open in his hands.

"What is it?"

He knelt down beside her and pointed to the page. "Look, Mum, it's the magic kingdom! Exactly! Exactly like you told! Isn't it?"

At bedtime she sometimes told him stories about a place she called the magic kingdom. The magic kingdom was a little like the countries she'd once imagined might be in the blue hills, though she never suggested to Cash such a place could be real or in the world. It was a fairy place, she told him, a place in your imagination, to think about before you went to sleep at night. To make you happy and give you good dreams. That was all.

"Look! It's even got snow!" His voice trembled with the wonder of it. "I could look at this for ever and ever!" He clasped the book to his chest.

"You can borrow it if you like," she told him. "You can take it home for a few weeks."

"Can I? Can I really?" His whole face blazed. "To our house? You mean I can have it in our house?"

"Of course," she said. "That's what libraries are for. You can take out five books and keep them for three weeks." She'd seen the notice on the librarian's desk. "So you go and choose some more you like, while Mummy finishes looking here."

He raced back to the children's section. His feet, in their blue flip-flops, seemed barely to touch the floor.

They didn't have much longer now. The bus back to Lake Conapaira came through at half past four. They had spent too much time on other things before the library—buying Cash's flip-flops, feeding and changing Maddie in the council restrooms, getting fish and chips and eating them at the windswept picnic table in the Memorial Gardens.

"Maddie, no!"

Maddie had crawled to the bottom shelves and dragged out a book with her small fat hands. Now, before Fan could stop her, she raised a corner to her mouth and began to chew.

"No." Fan took the small volume from her, wiped the damp corner, and replaced it on the shelf.

Maddie began to cry.

"Oh no, sweetheart, no," pleaded Fan. "Please, not now."

She took the dummy from her pocket and held it out. Maddie made a grab and then sat examining it carefully, as if she'd never seen such a thing in her life. She thrust it in her mouth, and, books forgotten, fell once more to gazing at the little lights on the ceiling. The windows of the library were darkening now; Mrs. Stuckey flicked a switch and the lights shone out and Maddie murmured, "Ah!"

Fan had found a fat book, 657 pages long: an anthology of English poetry; she wasn't quite sure her poem was English, but she had a sense that it might be. There was no time to go through the anthology now, but, like Cash's book of magic kingdoms, she could borrow it and take it home. She gathered up Maddie, found Cash, and together they took their books to Mrs. Stuckey's desk. Too late, she saw that one of Cash's books had a large greasy thumbprint on its cover, like the signature of a poor person from the olden days who couldn't read or write. The cover was plastic. Hastily, she took a tissue from her pocket and wiped the thumbprint off. When she placed the book back on the librarian's desk she knew that Mrs. Stuckey had been watching the whole operation, though her tight purse face gave nothing away. "Now, you're not a member, are you?" she said. "Mrs.—?"

"Jameson," said Fan, though she sensed that Mrs. Stuckey already knew her name. "No, I'm not a member, but my sister told me anyone could join if they lived in Lachlan shire."

"That's correct," said Mrs. Stuckey. She opened a drawer beneath the desk and took out a clean white card. "Now," she said. "Proof of residency?"

"What?"

"Written proof that you reside in Lachlan shire."

"But—but I do."

"Yes, I know that, but for the purposes of our records, and as a safeguard against loss—"

"Loss?"

"You'd be surprised how many of our books go missing, Mrs. Jameson."

Fan flushed, remembering the little stolen zebra. "What kind of proof?"

"A driver's license would do."

"I don't have a license. I haven't got a car."

"Ah," said Mrs. Stuckey, as if she had expected that. But why did she make you feel not having a car was wrong, as well?

"Any kind of identity card?"

Fan shook her head. "I've got a bankbook," she said, reaching into her bag.

"A bankbook won't be any use, I'm afraid," said Mrs. Stuckey. "It doesn't have your address on it. How do I know it's yours?"

"But—"

"We need something that has your name on it, together with your address. An electricity bill would do, or a rates notice?"

"No," said Fan. She was almost crying now. "I didn't bring anything like that with me. I didn't know you had to."

"Well, you understand, Mrs. Jameson, that we do need to have documentary proof of identity—we can't go lending our books to every Tom, Dick, or Harry now, can we? To anyone who walks in off the street?"

"But, Mrs. Stuckey, you know me. You used to live in the same street as me, when I was little. In Palm Street, at Lake Conapaira, remember? I was Fan Lancie—we lived up the top of the street, and you lived down the bottom. We were the

Lancies, remember? Mum and Dad and my sister, Caroline, and me. And you used to teach RI up at the school, remember? When I was in first class?"

Mrs. Stuckey sucked in her lips and frowned. "That was a long time ago, Fan. You can't expect me to remember that far back!"

Fan didn't believe her. She could tell from the way Mrs. Stuckey said her name that she remembered, though it was so long ago. She'd known who Fan was the minute she'd walked through the door.

"And even if I did remember," said the librarian, as if she could see the thoughts swirling around inside Fan's head, "even if I lived right next door to you now, Fan, I still couldn't issue you with a card without documentary proof of residence. Do you understand?" She reached across and slid the fat anthology and the picture books onto her side of the desk.

Standing quietly beside his mother, Cash gave a small shocked gasp.

Mrs. Stuckey pretended not to hear.

"Now what I'll do for you, Fan, is I'll put these books down here, under the desk, so no one else can take them out, see? And when you come back with your documentation, they'll be right here, waiting for you." The librarian's eyes slid uneasily toward the stricken Cash. "Right here, see?"

Cash said nothing. He didn't protest or cry. He stood silent, as if all along he'd expected just this, as if it was an experience he knew all about and expected to have again.

Fan was silent too. What was the use of speaking? There was a deep, unbridgeable chasm between the pettiness of Mrs. Stuckey's demands and the intensity of their longing that no words of hers could ever get across.

She tried all the same. "If I promise to bring the proof first thing tomorrow, could we just take one book out today? That book?" She pointed to Cash's book of magical kingdoms.

Mrs. Stuckey shook her head. "Rules are rules, I'm afraid, Fan."

They always said "I'm afraid" when they were taking stuff away from you.

What was the use?

Fan took Cash's hand and they walked out through the door.

They struggled up Palm Street toward home.

It was a bad, wild night; a night filled with noise, for the winds of heaven had broken loose and were raging in the sky. Doors banged and windows rattled, somewhere a sheet of iron clattered to the ground. Dust and grit flew through the air and an old chaff bag capered along in front of them like the ghost of a small white dog.

People of Mrs. Stuckey's kind made you feel like a beggar, thought Fan, anger boiling up inside her. They made you hold your hand out for what should by rights be yours—and then they teased you, like they'd tease a pup with a bone. And they enjoyed it; they loved what they could do.

"Mum! Mum!"

She swung around. Cash was trailing along behind her, dragging the bag along the road.

"Mum! Wait! Don't go so fast!"

Fan slowed. Cash was such a serious, responsible little boy that she kept forgetting he was hardly four. She waited until he caught up with her, then she bent down to him. "Here, let me take the bag."

"No, let me! I can carry it. Just walk slower."

She did. Only then she saw something she wouldn't have noticed if she'd been walking fast. It was nothing, really, an everyday sight around Lake Conapaira, especially in the evenings; a girl and boy in the shadows of a sheltered laneway, their arms locked fast around each other. Only tonight, because of what had happened at the library and the feeling of shame that had taken hold of her, this ordinary little scene reminded Fan of something she kept shut out, tamped down fast inside her. Deep, deep down, concealed yet always present, like a spirit hiding in a haunted house, waiting for exactly the right moment to leap out and take you for its own.

Now it sprang.

It was how Gary had left.

Oh, she hadn't minded him leaving; she'd been glad. He was a useless bastard, they were better off without him. It was the way he'd left that had been unbearable: how, at the door, he'd suddenly put down his bags and moved toward her. She'd thought he was going to kiss her and she'd backed away. But kisses hadn't been what he was after. Instead he'd taken her hand in his, and with his other hand he'd reached into his pocket and taken out a wad of notes. He'd put them into her hand and closed her fingers on them. They'd had a dead, greasy feel and a smell had come from them, of beer and the old fat chips had been fried in, over and over again. The smell that came off Gary's skin.

"There," he'd said. "That's two hundred pounds." And then, picking his bags up, he'd paused in the doorway and smiled at her. And he'd said, "I bet you've never had so much money in your hand in your whole tiny little life."

Struggling up Palm Street, Fan gave a low, choked sob. How could anyone do that to you? Say that? How could they make you into a beggar? Make her into a beggar? Cast a bad spell on her, take away her real true self, like a stolen baby in a bag?

Because all along, no matter what Mum had said, or the teachers at school, or any of them, she was *Yirigaa*. She was the person her *miyan* had once called her: *Yirigaa*, the morning star.

"I was *Yirigaa*!" Fan cried out loud in the windstruck street. "I was!" Tears poured down her face and were whipped away by the wind. "I was!"

"Mum?"

She looked down and saw Cash. He was staring up at her with big frightened eyes. "Mu-um?"

"Yes?"

"Mum, when is Aunty Caro coming? Is she coming to-night?"

"Don't say that!" she screamed at him suddenly. "Don't say that! You're always saying it. Don't ever—"

"Mum! Stop! You're hurting!"

She hadn't realized she'd grabbed his arm. That she was shaking him, and shaking Maddie, too, who rocked on her hip, wakened and screaming.

She didn't know which one to comfort first. "Oh, Cash, I'm sorry, so sorry. Oh, Maddie, sweetheart, it's all right—"

Cash pulled away from her and ran.

She stood there, pressing Maddie's head into her shoulder.

Distantly, she heard the bang of their back door.

What frightened her most was the way there'd been the echo of another voice inside her own.

A familiar voice.

Mum's voice in the old days. Mum when she'd lost it. And gone for the strap.

Mum's.

CHAPTER

16

As Clementine rushed out through her front gate, late for her train and her early morning lecture, the postman handed her a letter. "One for you," he said cheerfully, and Clementine shoved it into the pocket of her jacket without even looking and raced off down the road toward the station. Then she forgot all about it until her train was passing through Strathfield, when she reached for her handkerchief and found the letter there.

It was a plain white envelope, postmarked Temora. Temora? The name had a familiar ring; it was one of the stations you passed on the way to Lake Conapaira, wasn't it? Who could be writing to her from Temora? Clementine turned the letter over. The name and address of the sender was written on the back: Mrs. Caroline Waters, 15 Meridian Street, Temora, NSW.

Caroline. The image came back to her, as it had ten whole years ago on the train to Lake Conapaira, of a long-legged girl with dark plaits, running over the rough straw-colored paddocks of the central western plains. Running away from Aunty

Rene and the house in Palm Street, leaving her little sister behind. Mrs. Caroline Waters was Fan's big sister, Caro.

Why would Caro write to her? Foreboding gathered like cold in Clementine's heart. Her hands trembled as she snatched the two folded sheets from the envelope. Another image rose before her: Fan in her faded dress, standing on the platform of Lake Conapaira station with little Cash, both of them waving; waving and waving until the train was out of sight. That was over a year ago now; she hadn't heard from Fan since, and she hadn't written either. And when Clementine thought about that last visit it seemed to her as if a much longer time had passed: those fifteen months might have been years. Lake Conapaira had become as dreamlike as the jeweled palaces where she'd once imagined princesses and fine ladies sipping the ambrosia of Griffiths Tea. It was hard to believe it was a real place, that she could actually get out at Central in ten minutes' time, walk across to the booking office, and buy a real ticket that would take her there.

What had happened to Fan? The letter had to be about Fan; there was no other reason Caroline would write to her. Was Fan ill? Or was it something worse than that? With a little stir of fright, she remembered how Fan couldn't get up in the mornings; she saw her standing outside by the clothesline, shouting, and how her beautiful face had taken on the look of a person who might do dangerous things.

Clementine unfolded the sheets and began to read. As her eyes sped swiftly over Caro's neat blue sentences, the sense of dread lifted a little. Nothing bad had happened to Fan. Nothing really bad, anyway. Fan would be all right. Clementine folded the letter quickly and pushed it back into her pocket;

but when the train passed Newtown she took it out and read it again, and walking up Broadway toward the university, even though she knew she was late and would miss her lecture, Clementine sat down on the low stone wall of St. Barnabas's church and read Caro's news once more.

Dear Clementine,
You may think it strange that I am writing to you, when we have never met (I am Fan's sister, your cousin Caroline) but I am doing it because I am worried about my sister. Fan has not been herself for a long time, and especially since the new baby was born.

New baby? Clementine hadn't known Fan had had another baby. Yet how could she know, when Fan never wrote, and even Aunty Rene had stopped writing to Mum?

As you know [though Clementine didn't] she and Gary separated for good last year, and though he was never around much I think Fan gets lonely in that old house with only the children for company and nothing much to do. I'm afraid she has rather let things get on top of her. I try to get her to go out more and I visit as often as I can, but it is sometimes difficult for me, what with running a house and having a job as well. Fan often talks about you, and I was wondering if you could write to her—a letter from you might cheer her up a little, only don't expect an answer in a hurry! I know it's a lot to ask, with all *the studying you must have to do—Fan told me last year that you were at the uni—but perhaps when you have holidays you might be able to visit her for a few days. I have tried to get her to write to you herself, and she always says she will, but then she never seems to get round to it.*

With best wishes,
Your cousin Caroline (Waters)

PS Please don't mention to Fan that I wrote to you. She wouldn't like me interfering. Only I felt I had to do something.

Clementine stared blankly at the sheets of paper in her hand. She couldn't go up to Lake Conapaira! Not just now, anyway. The midyear exams were only a few weeks away, and then in the holidays her boyfriend, Phillip, wanted them to go camping with his law school friends, and then the last half year was always a big rush. Perhaps in summer, thought Clementine; in summer she might go up there. She would write to Fan, though, she would write to her this evening, as soon as she got home.

As Clementine began to fold the letter she noticed two grains of bright red dust stuck to the center crease, and they tugged at her heart, they stirred her memory, they brought back the narrow red road that led to the lake, and the tiny pieces of glass that glittered in the earth like diamonds. Red ocher. There was no other substance in the world that held so true a color. It was like an ache in the soul, thought Clementine, and then she wondered where that thought had come from.

She sat there for a long time, staring at nothing, while the traffic roared by along Broadway and passersby glanced at her curiously, then she got up from the low brick wall and hurried up the road toward the university.

She meant to write, of course she did, only she kept putting it off. And when she did try, sitting at the small desk in her room, pen poised over a blank sheet of paper, she couldn't think of anything to say. She would begin awkwardly, write one or two rubbishy sentences, crumple the page and toss it into the wastepaper basket. Then she would sit there, chin on hand, and puzzle over why her last visit to Lake Conapaira seemed so very long ago.

It was because so much had changed for her, she decided. Yes, that was the reason, surely. In these last fifteen months she'd moved beyond the small world of Chisholm College and her parents' house in Willow Street. She was a second-year arts student now and her world had become that of the university, of lectures and tutorials, of student parties and long, earnest discussions in the little cafés of Glebe and Camperdown and Chippendale. She even had a boyfriend—Phillip Massinger—a third-year law student who took her to cricket matches and dinner at the Malaya, to law school parties, and once, last month, to afternoon tea with his widowed mother in her big white house on the north shore.

And all of this was a long, long way from Lake Conapaira. Beautiful though it was, and however painfully its images— the grand sky and the endless paddocks, the red grains of its soil—might stir her heart, it had now become part of the landscape of her childhood; it was left behind. And Fan? She hardly ever thought of her cousin these days, and she never dreamed of her. The closeness, the feeling of being like a sister, had melted away. This was the reason she couldn't think what to write in her letter.

I suppose Cash is quite big, she began, and then crumpled the page again, because she thought it sounded patronizing, and anyway, she couldn't remember how old Cash would be now. And she couldn't write anything about the new baby, because Caro had asked her not to mention that she'd written—and how else could Clementine have known there was a baby, now Mum and Aunty Rene weren't writing to each other anymore?

But though she couldn't write the letter to her cousin, Fan lingered now in Clementine's mind. Once she even thought she saw her. It was a rainy Monday afternoon and Clementine was hurrying down a long, dark corridor in the Old Arts Building, on her way to a philosophy tutorial in room 34, and there, at the shadowy end of the passage, she had a sudden glimpse of a tall girl with dark blond chopped-off hair. A girl in a faded blue-gray dress with the hem half coming down, who vanished around the corner the moment Clementine caught sight of her.

"Fan?" whispered Clementine. "Fan, is that you?" And then more loudly, almost shouting, running to the end of the hallway, peering down the narrow passage where the girl had disappeared, "Fan! Fan! Fan!"

The passage was empty. Even if there had been a girl there, Clementine told herself, surely it could never have been Fan. If her cousin had come to the city looking for her, she'd have gone to the house in Willow Street first, and waited for Clementine to come home. She'd never have come to the university, a place she didn't know, which she'd seen only on her neighbor's television. She wouldn't have known how to get there; Fan had never been to Sydney, and Clementine guessed that she might be shy of asking city strangers, and shy of the city itself. And if she had somehow managed to find the way, why had she run off the moment Clementine had appeared?

It had been some other girl, it must have been. It was only because she was tired that she'd thought it was Fan, because she'd stayed up so late the night before, trying to write the letter and finding nothing she could say.

Only she'd thought the hem of that girl's dress was coming down. Fan's hems were always coming down; she wore her skirts too long, her heel kept catching at the cloth. . . .

Simply to walk through the quadrangles now, or along the shady cloisters, past ivy-covered buildings and tall spires, brought Fan to Clementine's mind: Fan saying shyly, "I saw it once," and then confiding how her glimpse of the university had reminded her of those magical places she'd imagined waiting for her up there in the blue hills. It's not fair! thought Clementine childishly. It wasn't fair that a beautiful person like Fan should be stuck in that old house in Palm Street, while she, who'd never once longed to be in a different world, had entered one so easily.

This sense of luck and privilege made the letter even more difficult to write. "It's not my fault," she said one day, walking across the quad, speaking her confusion out loud. Phillip, who was walking next to her, leaned closer. "You're talking to yourself, do you know?" he whispered. "First sign of madness, that." He tweaked at a strand of her hair. "What's not your fault?"

So she told him about Fan and Lake Conapaira.

He waited until she'd finished and then he said briskly, "Of course it's not your fault. Don't be silly, Clementine."

She hated it when he said stuff like that. He was handsome as Prince Charming and her mum thought he was wonderful, but she hated it all the same.

"Why is it silly?"

"You worked hard to get here, didn't you?"

"I suppose so."

"You suppose so?" Phillip's reedy voice was incredulous. "Of course you bloody did. While that little cousin of yours—" He paused, his elegant nostrils flaring with distaste.

"My little cousin what?"

"Oh, nothing. But Lake Conapaira sounds a good place to keep away from."

"It's beautiful," said Clementine. "The lake, the red earth—you should see it, Phil! And at night, the stars! They're so big, they look like faces shining through the windows."

He smiled faintly. "The situation, Clementine," he said. "That's what I was referring to: teenage mum with two kids, all on her ownio—it sounds a good situation to stay away from."

"But—"

"Write her a letter by all means, but I don't think it would be wise to go up there and get involved. You can't go now, anyway; it's only a week till the midyear exams and then there's the camping trip straight after." He frowned. "I hope you're not thinking of reneging on that?"

"I—"

"Bob's girlfriend won't go if you don't come along too."

Clementine hadn't really been planning to go up to Lake Conapaira, not right away. But when Phillip spoke in this manner she felt mutinous, almost tearful. He always sounded so cool and sensible, yet with him she sometimes got the feeling that being sensible could be an excuse for not doing the more difficult thing.

"She was my *gindaymaidhaany*," she said in a low trembling voice.

"What? What's that when it's at home?"

"It means, like a sister. It's an Aboriginal word. When Fan was little she had this friend who was Aboriginal—"

"Figures," he said.

"What do you mean?"

"Well." He cleared his throat. "Those kind of girls, they always get mixed up with blacks."

She didn't ask what kind of girls. "He was an old, old man," she said coldly. "He told her stories, that was all. He was kind to her; her dad and sister had gone away, and her mum—" Clementine faltered. "She didn't get on with her mum. There wasn't really anyone to care."

Phillip didn't reply. They walked on in silence, down a shadowy cloister, over lawns and through gardens, and out by a small gate into the busy road. It had been a heavy gray winter's day in the city, but now, in these dying minutes of the afternoon, the sun pierced through the clouds at last.

Clementine turned, straining against Phillip's hand, and gazed back at the university, which had caught this extraordinary light and become a golden city, the kind of place where she and Fan had imagined the pair of them might sit and drink Griffiths Tea. "It just doesn't seem right," she said.

"Right." Phillip grinned. "Who are you to judge what's right or wrong, little Clementine?"

"Fair, then," she said. "It doesn't seem fair."

"Life isn't fair," he replied smugly. "However . . ." He leaned closer and kissed her on the corner of her mouth.

"However?"

"Write your little cheer-up letter by all means. Can't do any harm."

Clementine didn't write. She still couldn't think of anything to say.

At one of the parties given by Phillip's friends, Clementine saw Daria, the Hungarian girl from Chisholm College, who was now doing second-year law. There was another person from Chisholm Clementine occasionally glimpsed around the university—the Home Boy, David Lowell. He was in med school, a scholarship student like Daria and Clementine, and when she saw him it was always at a distance, across a street, in a crowd at the station, going up the steps of the library. He never came and spoke to her. Catching her glance, and one uncertain smile, David Lowell looked away. He was taller than he'd been at Chisholm, and thinner too. She wondered where he lived now. She never saw him at parties or other student gatherings.

Daria was sitting on a sofa, a glass of white wine in her hand, and when she saw Clementine with Phillip, she smiled a narrow, catlike smile. Later in the evening, as Clementine was searching for her coat in the jumble of clothes left on someone's bed, Daria came up to her. "I see you have found someone," she observed.

Clementine flushed, and Daria stood silently, watching the color mount and then fade in the other girl's cheeks. "You will get married, I think," she said, and Clementine knew from her cool, dispassionate tone that what Daria really meant was

"You'll *only* get married." Get married to Phillip and live in a big house on the north shore or in the eastern suburbs, the kind of houses she and her parents had passed by on those long-ago bus trips through the city. They would have two children, who would attend private schools, and Clementine would go to coffee mornings and play tennis in the afternoons.

"No, I won't," she said.

"Oh?" Daria glanced down the hall to where Phillip stood talking with a friend. She gave her catlike smile and waited.

"I don't really like him," said Clementine unexpectedly. The words had rushed from her lips before she'd thought them out; she hardly knew where they'd come from. And yet now that they were there, spoken aloud to someone else, she saw that she meant them. Oh, she might like having Phillip for a boyfriend, she might like going out with him, even like him making love to her in his cautious, prudent way. But she didn't like him. She didn't like the way he'd criticize her clothes: "That dress doesn't really suit you." She didn't like the way he bossed her around: "Time to go, I think," he'd say at parties, without asking her if she wanted to leave. Most of all, she didn't like how he never seemed to understand anything she really cared about. He hadn't understood about Fan and the place where she lived; she could see he thought her feeling for them was childish and ridiculous. It was the same when she tried to share some discovery she'd made in her reading, or in a friendship; he'd brush it aside, like he'd done with Fan. "Nothing to get excited over," he'd say. "Nothing to get all worked up about, little Clementine." And he would put his arm around her and murmur softly, smiling into her hair, "You're a little bit crazy, do you know that? My crazy little Clementine."

She didn't want to be his crazy little Clementine.

"Don't let some thickie bloke put you down," Fan had said on their last walk around the lake. "Promise me."

She had promised.

"You will have to do something, then, I think," murmured Daria now. She brushed a light, cool kiss on Clementine's hot cheek and said, "Good luck to you, my darling."

She would have to tell him. She would have to break it off. He would be angry—of course he would be. He'd accuse her of leading him on. There wouldn't be an engagement after all. Mum would be disappointed, but Clementine knew she could count on Dad. "Ah, there's plenty of time yet," he'd say, and she knew he'd say the same thing if she were pushing seventy.

She would wait until after the exams, Clementine decided. And she wasn't going on that camping trip with his mates and their snobby girlfriends. She hated them. She hated him. And when it was all over she'd write to Fan. Fan was better than him—better in a way Clementine couldn't put into words. How could you? It would be like comparing one of Shakespeare's sonnets to an article in Phillip's *Financial Times*.

And straight after the exams, in the midyear holidays, she would pack away her books and go up to Lake Conapaira.

CHAPTER

17

Fan's leaving. She's leaving the old house at the end of Palm Street, where—except for that brief spell with Gary in the rented house out near the common—she's lived since she was born.

For nineteen years, eight months, and fifteen days.

"I'm not even twenty," she says to herself again. She's been saying it for the whole of the past week, ever since that windy night when she and Cash and Maddie struggled back from the Lachlan library, without Cash's picture book and without her poem.

She doesn't care about the poem anymore. She's forgotten it. Even the two lines she could remember have vanished from her head. She made them go. It was stupid to think a poem might help you find out what to do. Stupid.

She's leaving, yet she doesn't need to pack. She doesn't need to sit up at the kitchen table and write out a list of shoes and clothes and little bits and pieces, like she used to do in the days when she daydreamed about visiting Clementine down in Sydney.

All she really had to do was to decide.

And she's decided.

She doesn't feel at home anymore. Perhaps she never has felt at home, ever, except for those long-ago afternoons when she used to sit with the old man who called her *Yirigaa* and he'd tell her stories that made her feel she belonged in the world.

If a star were confin'd—

Her poem's coming back; Fan pushes it away.

She's not a star. A star would shine gloriously. It would blaze. Her light, if she has one, is very small. It's flickering and uncertain; people like her mum and Gary and even Mrs. Stuckey can almost blow it out. They can make her feel like she hasn't a right to be.

But it isn't how she feels or what happens to her that really matters.

It's them. It's her children, little Cash and Madeleine.

Because what use is she to them?

What kind of mum is she?

That man in the shoe shop at Lachlan thought she was no good, and he was right.

Look at those times she left Cash alone in the house when he was hardly more than a baby, for no better reason than to walk by herself, around and around the town. Look how late she gets up in the mornings, later and later every day. And how Cash has learned to look after little Maddie, all by himself while his mother lies in bed: to change his baby sister's nappy, to take the cold off the bottle Fan leaves ready in the fridge by holding it between his small warm hands. Look how he knows how to make cornflakes and Weet-Bix and even spread jam on the sliced bread. And he's only just turned four.

Look how she shook him last week, on the way back from the library, right in the middle of the street, and how she didn't know she was doing it until she heard her voice sounding exactly like her mum's used to. And look how she hasn't taken him back to the library yet to get the book of magical kingdoms, even though he asks her every day.

Just because she can't bear the thought of Mrs. Stuckey's disapproving face, and being made to feel like a beggar again. She's told Cash that Caro will take him there next time she comes to visit; Caro will get the book for him.

She will, too. Caro will walk through the door of the library in her good clothes and high-heeled shoes and with her hair done properly at a hairdresser's. She'll walk with a sure and certain step, she won't sneak in expecting that at any moment someone's going to call out, "And just where do you think you're going?"

Mrs. Stuckey will be nice to her. Mrs. Stuckey will call her Mrs. Waters and ask how Mr. Waters is and what the weather's like down in Temora. There won't be any bother about taking books out even if Caro has forgotten to bring her proof of residency. But Caro won't have forgotten; Caro always remembers things like that.

And if Cash is with Caro, Mrs. Stuckey will be nice to him as well.

There are marks on the top of Cash's little arm where she shook him, faint blue shadows of her fingers. He doesn't hate her for it; he follows her around the house, he's got sort of clingy since that night. And Fan can remember this from when she herself was very little: how she'd follow Mum around, trying to please her, trying to get Mum to like her, because she was afraid.

Cash is frightened of her. Look how he keeps asking for Caro. Look how he always runs to Caro when she visits, how he's in her arms the minute she comes in the door. Even little Maddie smiles when she sees her aunty—when Caro leans over the cot, Maddie crows and holds up her chubby arms. They know Caro is good, that's what it is. It's almost as if they can scent the air of a calm, solid world which she carries about with her: the good job she has, and the education (for Caro has done her Leaving Certificate at night school), her lovely husband, Frank, the beautiful house in the best street in Temora. When Fan takes them to visit, the children cry when it's time to go home; they know that beautiful house is where they really belong, that's why.

How strange the world is! How strange it is that two lovely people like Caro and Frank can't have children. They've done all the tests and the answer has come back, quite plain: they never can.

When Fan caught hold of Cash and shook him on the night they came back from the library, it was the first time she'd ever done anything like that. But she knows it mightn't be the last.

Things go around and around. She feels scared all the time now, and the thing she's most scared of is that she'll turn into a mother like her own mum was: a mum who said every morning as Fan went off to school, "One of these days when you get home you'll find me with my head in the gas oven." So that for years and years when she was little, after Dad had gone and Caro moved away, Fan had run up Palm Street from school, her heart bumping like a ball inside her chest, bouncing high up into her throat so that she could hardly breathe, and at the front gate she'd stop dead and whisper the first two lines of a prayer she'd learned in Infants with old Miss Greely: "Gentle Jesus, meek and mild, look upon this little child—"

She didn't know the rest of it. She'd never been good at memorizing stuff, because how could you keep your mind on schoolwork when all the time you were worrying and worrying about what you might find on the kitchen floor when you got home?

"Gentle Jesus, meek and mild," she'd whisper, and then she'd push the gate open and tiptoe up the path (as if a dead mother might hear) and up the steps to the veranda. There she would stop again, take a deep breath if she could, and push the screen door open, gently, slowly, with one fingertip, little bit by little bit (as if a dead mother might jump out at you), and then she'd creep on down the hall and edge into the kitchen with her eyes screwed up tight. "Gentle Jesus, meek and mild, look upon this little child—" And she'd open her eyes and there Mum would be, sitting at the kitchen table, reading the paper or calmly slicing vegetables for tea.

Fit as a fiddle. Right as rain. As if she'd never said that stuff to you in the morning before you left for school, as if that had been another person altogether. And Fan knew that if she'd asked Mum about that other person, Mum would have shrieked at her, "What? Who? What are you talking about?"

For a little while you might feel safe.

Only you could never feel properly safe, could you? Because then there was the next day, and the next. "One day when you come home from school," Mum would say, and one day, well, that could be any day, couldn't it?

That's why she'd stolen Mrs. Stuckey's little zebra, Fan realizes suddenly. The soft little felt zebra she'd called

Clementine and hidden beneath her pillow. It was because she had to have something.

Oh, imagine saying that sort of thing to Cash! Imagine, in a year's time, saying to him as he went out the door in the morning, his little schoolcase in his hand, "One day when you come home from school—" Imagine if it was poor little Cash running up Palm Street, heart clenched in his chest like a panicked fist, terrified of what he might find in the house.

She'd never say stuff like that to him—she wouldn't; never, never, never.

Only you can't ever really know what misery might make of you, over years and years. Even Mum had been nice once. Caro had told her this. She'd said, "Mum was nice once, when I was little and Dad was here."

No, Fan doesn't want to get like Mum. She doesn't want to pass her sorrows on to Cash and little Madeleine, like Mum had passed hers on to Fan. And she doesn't want to pass on her beggary. She doesn't want her lovely children turned into beggars like her. And it will happen, she knows. Because it wasn't only her that Mrs. Stuckey had treated like a beggar in the library, she'd done it to Cash as well. She wouldn't have treated him that way if he'd gone in there with Caro. Caro would have seen that his hands were clean before he touched a book. Back at the house, before they left, she'd have noticed he wasn't wearing shoes.

It's time for Fan to leave. Cash will be starting school next year. She doesn't want the teachers picking on him because he's hers, because he's that awful Fan Lancie's child. "Another no-hoper from that lot in Palm Street," that's what they'll say. And the things that had happened to her would start happening to him, and then to Maddie, and later on to their kids, on and on and on. It's like a wheel, she thinks, going around and around, spinning senselessly because no one knows how to stop it. No one's game.

She has a sudden flash of that rainy morning years ago when Mum had given her a belting and she'd tried to ride away to the blue hills on Dad's old bike. Only she couldn't get there, and when she came back Clemmie was waiting for her in the middle of the paddocks, bawling her eyes out in the rain. She'd been bawling too, and she'd chucked the bike down on the track to run to Clemmie, and its wheel had gone on spinning, hissing in the rain. And she'd put out her hand and stopped it with a finger. She'd been strong in those days. . . .

If Cash and Madeleine belong to Caro, no one will put them down. They won't even be going to Fan's old school, they'll be going to some school in Temora that Fan has never seen. She may not have seen it, but Fan can imagine Cash quite plainly, going through the school gate on his first day, in his new clothes and with his little kinder case, clutching tight to Caro's hand.

A terrible anguish rolls over her. She gets up from her chair. It's time to go.

"It's only for tonight, Mrs. Darcy," she begs, standing on her neighbor's doorstep with the two children, a small cold wind from heaven tugging at their hair and clothes. "My sister will be here on the morning train."

It had been difficult with Caro.

"But what's the matter, Fan? Why do you need me there at such short notice? Is Maddie sick? Cash?"

Caro's voice goes tender on their names.

"No, they're fine. It's—"

"It's what?"

"It's me. I've—I've caught some kind of bug, Caro. It's just come on, and I can tell it's going to get worse by tomorrow. That's why I came out now to ring you, while I could still get down to the phone box."

"You're down at the telephone box? Where are the kids? You haven't left them in the house alone, have you?"

The telephone box is down in Main Street, outside the bank, a good ten minutes' walk from home.

"No, no, of course not. They're here, with me. Cash is outside on the bench, minding Maddie in the stroller. I can see them from here. Caro, look, I know the bus has gone, but can you come tomorrow, on the morning train?"

Caro grumbles a bit, and ums and ahs about how the train comes through Temora at three o'clock in the morning and she'll be up all night, but the thought of Cash and little Maddie with only a sick Fan to care for them wins her around, as her sister knew it would. "I'll be there in the morning," says Caro. "I'll be on the train. Look, go home and feed the kids and take some aspirin and all of you go to bed, okay?"

"Okay," says Fan.

"I can't leave them alone," Fan pleads with Mrs. Darcy.

"Alone?" Her neighbor stares at her, shocked. "Of course you can't. But what on earth's the matter? Where are you going? What—"

Fan interrupts. "They won't be any trouble, Mrs. Darcy, I promise." She turns to Cash. "You'll be good for Mrs. Darcy, won't you, Cash? And keep an eye on Maddie?"

Cash nods, his fist stuck in his mouth. He's always liked Mrs. Darcy. Fan often sees him down at the bottom of the yard, chatting to her through the gap in the fence while she pegs out her washing on the line. Except that this evening he seems wary of their neighbor; he won't look at her face. He keeps his head down, and his fingers bunch tightly on the hem of his mum's dress.

"And they've had their tea," adds Fan.

"As if that mattered," cries Mrs. Darcy indignantly. "As if I'd grudge a pair of little kids their tea."

"Sorry," whispers Fan. "I know you wouldn't, Mrs. Darcy."

"Fan," says Mrs. Darcy, softer now. "Fan, love, what's the matter?"

"I don't want to go and leave them, but I have to," Fan says. "It's an emergency, Mrs. Darcy."

"What emergency?"

"Someone—someone's sick."

"Your mum? Your mum's took sick?"

"No, no," says Fan. "Not Mum. She's away in America, with Trevor."

Mrs. Darcy is knocked all of a heap for a moment. Rene? Rene Lancie is in America? She wouldn't credit it except that Fan isn't the kind of person who tells that kind of lie, and anyway, Mrs. Darcy is old enough to know that wonders never cease.

"At a dancing competition."

"A dancing competition!" marvels Mrs. Darcy. So pigs do fly. "Who'd have thought it, a few years back, eh?" she says to Fan. "Talk about leopards changing their stripes! Or is that tigers?" She shakes her head wonderingly and then gets back to the problem at hand, which is Fan and the kiddies standing here on her front step. "So who is it, then, love, this emergency?"

"A friend," says Fan.

"A friend?" Mrs. Darcy sounds doubtful.

"Yes. Someone I knew at school."

"From 'round here, then?"

Fan doesn't answer. Mrs. Darcy knows everyone in town. Instead she says, "She's down at Stockinbingal and she needs me right away. She—she hasn't got anyone. There's no one."

"Ah," says Mrs. Darcy, and Fan can see she doesn't believe her. She probably thinks Fan's going off to meet some man.

"But, Fan, can't you—"

"I have to get the Coota bus tonight!" Fan cries out, and Cash's fingers tighten on her skirt.

"Tonight? The six o'clock, you mean? But, Fan, it's quarter past five now."

"I can still make it."

"You're not thinking straight, love. What if I'd said no? What if I'd been out, over at my daughter's place? What would you have done?"

Fan says nothing.

There's something funny about all this, thinks Mrs. Darcy. She can't put her finger on it, but definitely something's not quite right. "That's theirs, is it?" Her gaze fixes on the bag in the girl's hand. "Got their things in there, have you, love? Their little nightclothes, nappies for the baby, her bottle?"

"Yes. Everything's in there."

But where's her bag? wonders Mrs. Darcy. Where's her bag, if she's going down to Stockinbingal on the Coota bus? Ah well, perhaps it's still in the house. She thinks it's pitiful the way this girl's been left all on her own. And with two little kiddies now. "Sleep through, does she?" Mrs. Darcy asks, nodding at Madeleine. "After the ten o'clock feed?"

"Yes." Fan's voice is almost a whisper. "She sleeps right through."

"Well, come on then, lovies." Mrs. Darcy swoops Maddie into her arms. "Say bye-bye to Mummy," she tells her, waving the baby's tiny hand.

"Bye," whispers Fan, leaning forward to kiss the top of Maddie's head. "Good-bye, little Madeleine."

Thou art lost and gone forever,
Dreadful sorry, Clementine.

She won't remember me, thinks Fan. She's too little.

"C'mon, Cash, love." Mrs. Darcy reaches for Cash with her free hand. "Let go of Mummy's skirt and pick up your bag, there's a good boy."

Cash picks up the bag but the fingers of his other hand are still clenched tightly in the fabric of his mother's skirt. Fan loosens them gently and kisses each cold finger one by one. "There," she says. "There."

Cash's eyes turn up toward his mother's face. There's a terrible darkness rising in them, as if he actually knows.

She kisses his forehead. "Cash," she whispers. "My little Cash. Be good, little Cash."

Abruptly he draws back from her with a terrible, anguished howl.

Mrs. Darcy grabs his arm. "Come on, lovie, no waterworks," she tells him. "Be a big boy, now. Mummy's only going for a little while, and in the morning, when you wake up, your Aunty Caroline will be here."

For once Cash's face doesn't light up at the promise of Aunty Caro. Instead he goes all quiet. Pulling away from Mrs.

Darcy's grasp, he turns from his mother and slips around the neighbour's ample body into the lighted passage, and then through another door into Mrs. Darcy's kitchen. There. He's gone. Fan stands, staring down the empty hall.

"And you'd better get your skates on, love, if you're going to make that bus."

Fan sucks in her breath; she wants to howl like Cash did. She feels like an animal caught in a trap, a vixen who has to gnaw and tear her limb off to get free and give her cubs a life. She turns and runs toward her house, and behind her, back at Mrs. Darcy's place, she hears the front door slam.

Inside, she drags on her parka and zips it up against the coming night. Checking her purse is there in her pocket, she runs out again. Palm Street is unlit but all the same she keeps to the shadowy places and averts her eyes from Mrs. Darcy's house in case a small face is watching for her at a window. Halfway down the road she slips into a narrow lane behind the houses, a lane that turns away from the direction of Main Street and the bus stop and leads her eventually to the track beside the lake.

She walks on, slowly now, the small winds of heaven ruffling her hair and rustling the reeds beside the track, the lake lapping at the stones, the cold of the earth striking through the thin soles of her shoes. When she reaches the place where the old man's camp used to be, she lies down in the soft winter grass, her hands behind her head, and gazes up at the stars in the sky. Has her *miyan* climbed up there? Can he see her? What would he say if he knew where she was going? What would he say to her?

She doesn't know. "Come back," she whispers. "Just for a moment, please. Come back and tell me things." And she screws up her eyes and clenches her fists and curls her toes and wishes and wills him, but her *miyan* doesn't come.

She turns her face into the grass as if it was a pillow and whispers into it. *"Yirigaa,"* she says. And *"gadhaang,"* and Birrima. Morning star and happiness and a place far away. . . . All the words come back to her; she hasn't forgotten one, and it seems to her they are more beautiful than any poetry and carry the very sound of the earth. She closes her eyes and for a little while she sleeps, quite dreamlessly, and then wakes up again.

Long before dawn she's on her feet again, hands thrust deep into her pockets, eyes set straight ahead, striding on toward the road that leads to the blue hills.

CHAPTER

18

Fan reaches the mountain highway a little before dawn. It's wider than the narrow dirt road from Lake Conapaira and its surface is newly sealed; cars and trucks pass along it, speeding over the ranges to towns and properties on the other side. It's very early, still dark, but already there are people traveling: road and railway workers, tourists and salesmen, a farmer setting out to distant sale yards, or coming home again after a rough night in a Main Street country hotel.

Fan stands and waits by the side of the road, patiently. There's a gleam of light at the edge of the sky now, and paddocks and trees are separating, like pale blobs of cheese in turning milk. From here the blue hills look very close, rising steeply from the edge of the plain, but Fan knows there's still a long, long way to go. Headlights show far away down the road, and as they come closer she steps out from the shadowy verge, waving.

The town has grown a little since that time a few years back when Gary brought her here, but it's still small, the kind of place people pass through rather than linger or stay. There was talk of building a tourist park last year but nothing ever came of it. The views from the lookout have a rare splendor but there's not much else to see. Only trees, as Fan once told her cousin—trees and more trees, rocks and stones and trees.

"Sure this is where you want to go?" the old farmer asks as he slows his truck at the side of the deserted main street. Place looks dead as a doornail, he thinks, but then it always does. He'd been over to Condo to visit his married daughter; her eldest isn't much younger than this girl sitting beside him. He turns his head to look at her again—yeah, she'd be around Luce's age. Fan, her name is, a name you hardly ever hear these days.

"Yes," says Fan. "Yes. Just here will do." She points vaguely in the direction of the tea shop that had once sold Griffiths Tea.

"You'll need to dry off those clothes of yours properly," he says. The back of her parka and skirt were soaking wet when he picked her up, and though he turned the heater on full blast she still looks damp and cold. Shivering.

"Doesn't matter," she mumbles at him.

"You won't think that when you come down with bloody pneumonia," he says, but all she does is laugh. Kids!

"You got someone you know lives here?" he asks as she jumps out from the cabin. Luce would tell him he's an old stickybeak but he's concerned about this kid. What was she doing out there by the crossroads so early in the morning? She doesn't look like a hitchhiker; she's got no bag for a start. She's got nothing and she looks like she slept rough out there in the bush last night. When he left Condo at four this morning it was only 31 degrees Fahrenheit, cold enough to ice the windscreen over and freeze the puddles on the road.

"Thank you," she says softly. "Thank you for the lift."

She's not a city girl. He'd take a guess she's a local lass, it's there in her voice and the way she moves, a thing you can't explain, but it's there.

"Got someone you know 'round here?" he asks again, because she seems to be in a bit of a daze, standing out there on the footpath, like she doesn't know where to go.

"My cousin," she says quickly. "My cousin lives here."

"Want me to drop you off at her place?" He'd like to see this cousin.

"No, no!" she stares around the deserted street. "I've got to do something here, first."

"She know you're comin'?"

"Who?"

"This cousin of yours."

"Yes," she says angrily, flushing. "She does."

Now he's done it; he'll get no more out of her. He shakes his head and takes the brake off. What can you do? "That's all right then," he says, giving her a long, long look before he drives away.

It's only a little after eight o'clock. The post office isn't open yet. Fan wanders up the hill to the small memorial park and sits on the steps of the bandstand. There are bandstands just like this in little towns all over the Central West: there's one in Lake Conapaira, and one in Lachlan, and Temora, and Coota, and in other towns she distantly remembers driving through in Dad's truck when she was very little and he was still at home. She's seen a lot of bandstands but never once has she seen a band. The idea strikes her as funny and her lips curve in a smile.

At nine o'clock the slow main street begins to stir. A car noses out of the driveway of the service station, a man hurries from the newsagent with the morning's paper tucked beneath his arm, a woman sweeps the pavement outside the tea shop. As Fan walks down the hill toward the post office she notices that the shop is no longer boarded up; it's freshly painted, the windows shine. The old sign for Griffiths Tea has gone.

The woman is inside now; Fan can see her through the window setting out plates of cakes on the shelves: apple tarts and lamingtons, butterfly cakes and pink and white meringues. Fan walks in through the door and sits down at a small wobbly table near the counter.

"Do you sell Griffiths Tea?" she asks when the woman comes over to her.

"Griffiths Tea?" The woman laughs, a warm, lovely sound that challenges the cold of the day. "Gee, you're goin' back a bit, aren't you, love? Haven't heard that name for donkey's years."

"There used to be a sign on your window," explains Fan. "A few years back, when the shop was boarded up. Right up in the corner there." She points to the top of the window.

"Don't know about that," says the woman. "We bought it like it is, after old Fred Thoms done the place up and then sold." She pauses to wave through the window at an old woman pushing a shopping trolley up the road. "Old Mrs. Rellick," she explains to Fan. "Off to get her milk and bread. You can set your watch by her, most days."

Fan orders a pot of ordinary tea. When the woman comes back with it, she says, "Not Griffiths, I'm afraid, but you've jogged my memory—my gran used to drink Griffiths Tea, but that was way back before the war. Haven't heard of it since then."

"Did you ever drink it? Did she give you a little sip?" Because suddenly Fan has remembered how when she was very, very little she used to beg Mum for a taste of her tea and Mum would put the cup to her lips, very gently, and say, "Just one little sip; tea isn't meant for little girls."

"Now you mention it, she did. She did use to give me little sips!" The woman shakes her head, delighted at the memory, and Fan notices how she's got a little dimple in her cheek, like Clementine's mother, and tiny freckles across the bridge of her nose, like Clemmie when she was a kid.

"And what did it taste like?" asks Fan eagerly. "Was it different from other teas?"

"Well, you know, it's funny you should say that, because it was. Of course it might just have been because I was a kid, and they didn't let kids drink tea back then, so it was sort of special, you know? But I thought it tasted wonderful—heavenly."

"Heavenly?" smiles Fan. "Really?" She's smiling because it's so unexpected, this, it's like the gift in the very bottom of the Christmas stocking, the one you've been hoping for for so long that in some strange way you've forgotten all about it. "My cousin used to think it would taste like ambrosia," she confides.

"Ambrosia? What's that, love?"

"The nectar of the gods," says Fan.

"The nectar of the gods!" The woman holds out her hand. "By the way, my name's Jenny," she says.

———

When she's finished her ordinary, earthly tea, Fan walks down to the post office. She buys a stamp and a postcard of the town and writes inside it:

Dear Clementine,

There's a lady up here in the blue hills whose grandma used to drink Griffiths Tea. And the lady taisted it when she was little, and she says it taisted hevenly, just like you imajined, like ambrosea, the necter of the gods.

Love from Fan xxx

She fixes the stamp on slowly, carefully, like a fourth, last kiss. She wouldn't ever see Clementine again.

> *Thou art lost and gone forever,*
> *Dreadful sorry, Clementine.*

She addresses the postcard and hands it to the man behind the counter. "When will she get it?" she asks him.

He glances at the address. "Day or two," he grins at her. "Or three." And then, noticing the anxious expression on her face, he adds kindly, "Don't worry, love, it'll be there sooner than soon. Soonest. Promise."

Everyone is being kind—Jenny in the tea shop, the old man who gave her the lift to the town, this man behind the counter of the post office—and somehow their kindness reminds her of Evie Castairs and Maggie Carmody at the bus stop that day she'd gone to Lachlan with Cash and Madeleine: how Evie had taken Madeleine so Fan could put her cardigan on right side around, and how Maggie had said, "Plenty of kids with no shoes 'round here!" As if they were on her side. As if they really liked her. And how Cash said they'd waved as the bus pulled away. . . .

For a moment, a crack of light shines on a different world, or is it simply the same world, with a different light upon it? The world you hadn't believed was there but might have been, even though you hadn't noticed it. The thought makes Fan deeply uneasy, and she walks quickly from the post office and out to the telephone box in the street. She looks up a number in the book and dials. "Is that Lake Conapaira railway station?"

"Sure is!"

"Is that Fred Niland?"

"Yep."

"It's Mrs. Jameson here, Mrs. Fan Jameson. You know, I live up the end of Palm Street. I used to be Fan Lancie." The line crackles and she adds suddenly, "Francesca."

"Francesca?"

"That's my real name."

"Oh. Well, sure I know you, Fan. I mean, Francesca. Showed you how to tie your shoelaces, didn't I?"

He did, too. She remembers now. When she started school Fred was one of the big boys in sixth class who helped the little ones. Tying her shoelaces was the one thing Caro had never been able to teach her, but Fred had known this special, easy way, with two loops instead of one.

"And what can I do for you this cold, cold morning?" A small raspy sound comes over the wire, and she pictures Fred in his cluttered little stationmaster's office, rubbing his big red hands to get them warm, like he used to do on winter mornings at school. "Said on the wireless they might get snow up in the hills today," he tells her, "and if they do, it'll be only the second time this century!"

"Will it?"

"Yep. So what can I do for you?"

"Um, did you see my sister get off the train this morning? You know, Caroline? She's Mrs. Waters now. Mrs. Caroline Waters."

Fan thinks how when you say "Mrs. Waters" it sounds solid; when you say "Mrs. Jameson," it sounds like a girl with her hem coming down. "She was coming from Temora."

"Sure did," answers Fred. "Only passenger we had. How come you want—"

"Thank you," she says quickly. "Thank you, Fred," cutting him off before he can say anything else because the kindness in his voice is like the man in the post office and Jenny in the tea shop and the old farmer in the truck and Evie Castairs and Maggie Carmody, and she doesn't want to think how people might be kind. Not now. Not when she's made up her mind. She replaces the receiver and walks out into the street, past the tea shop and the little park with the empty bandstand, on up the road to the lookout on the top of the ridge.

It's a cold day in the very heart of winter. The thick gray clouds are so low that little misty wisps of them drift in front of her, dabbing at her face like small cold fingertips—like Cash's fingers last night when she'd plucked them from her dress.

"You'll be okay," she whispers to Cash and Madeleine, who would be safe with Caro now. "In a little while, you'll be all right."

Below her are the soft billowy crowns of the trees, like

pillows, like a big fat quilt you could jump into and pull up over your face.

"I grew up so fast I didn't have time to look," she says to no one in particular, and not at all complainingly. Though it was true.

Then she says the first lines of old Miss Greely's kindergarten prayer. They're still the only lines she remembers, but as she stands there a strange thing happens: into the stillness she hears her old teacher's voice speaking the last two lines: "But in the kingdom of Thy grace, Give this little child a place."

Fan stepped out into the air.

There was a majestic silence.

It began to snow.

2009

On the bench beside the flat suburban lake, Clementine's friend Sarah says sadly, "Ah, the poor little love."

It's good to hear the dead called "love," thinks Clementine. You feel the word might reach them and lay a calm, gentle touch on their souls. She remembers Fan's small hand lying light as a moth on the hand of the old black man, and she looks away to the horizon, almost expecting to see the blue hills there instead of the rooftops and smudged greenery of city trees.

"Are you all right?" asks Sarah.

"Yes." Even after all this time loss can still sweep over her. "You know, I dreamed of her that morning, the morning after she—left home," she confides to Sarah. "Of Fan. Before they found her."

Found tangled in the treetops, Caro had told her after the funeral. Her neck was broken. "They said it was instantaneous," said Caro. "They said she wouldn't have felt a thing, but they always say that, don't they?" Caro's eyes had been red with angry tears; she'd added in a whisper, "She was all covered with snow."

Snow. "Like a fat white quilt," Fan had said that last time they'd walked beside the lake, imagining how the treetops of the blue hills would look when it snowed. "A fat white quilt you could jump into and pull right over your head and snuggle down to sleep."

"What did you dream?" asks Sarah, and Clementine tells her friend how she'd dreamed her cousin was climbing up into the black night sky of Lake Conapaira. She'd been a child again, fat wild-honey-colored braids tumbling down her back, small, slender feet freckled with red dust, gamely scaling the rungs of an invisible ladder set down among the cold-faced stars. "She's looking for her friend," Clementine had murmured in her dream. "She's looking for the old black man."

And then she'd woken with a start because her mother had come into the room and was tugging at the blankets. "Oh darling," she'd whispered when her daughter opened her eyes. "Oh darling, there's such bad news."

"What?" Clementine had jerked upright in her bed. There'd been dark at the window of her bedroom; it wasn't even morning yet. "What?" But she'd known it was Fan, even before her mother started telling.

"That was Caroline on the phone. Fan's sister."

"I know. I know." Clementine had wrenched at her mother's arm. "What is it? Tell me! What's happened to Fan?"

"No one knows yet. She's gone and disappeared. . . ."

Clementine and Sarah get up from the wooden bench beside the lake and take the path toward the car park. "Do you need a lift?" asks Sarah. "Only I noticed you got dropped off this morning; you haven't got your car."

"Thank you," says Clementine. "But someone's coming to pick me up at twelve."

It's almost noon now, and the sky has turned hazy; frail white streamers of cloud float there, like prayer flags or bridal veils or the gauziest of shawls.

On Fan's funeral day the clouds were small and white and fluffy, children's clouds: kittens and ducklings and little lambs on a bright blue kindergarten frieze. The townspeople stood in small clusters, whispering to one another: neighbors and shopkeepers, younger people who might once have been at school with Fan; Fred Niland from the station, a teacher called Miss Langland who'd come all the way from Parkes. Old Mr. Chiltern from the hardware store was crying into a big checked hanky; beside him Evie Castairs and Maggie Carmody were crying too.

"And she a mother!" a woman's voice exclaimed harshly, suddenly, and then another, softer voice said, "Hush!"

There wasn't a sign of the young man who might have been Gary, no sign of the vanished Uncle Len. Even Aunty Rene had been absent, far away with Trevor in Tucson, Arizona, dancing on a competition stage. "'Too far to come,' that's what she said," an angry Caroline told Clementine. "Couldn't be bothered, more like!" She'd stamped her foot, but gently, so as not to alarm the small fair-haired baby she was holding in her arms, and a puff of bright red dust rose up around her shoe. "Oh, I hate her! Mum! Bloody old dancing fool!"

"Ah, come on, love." Her husband put an arm around her shoulders.

Caro's anger was the kind Clementine had instantly recognized, an anger with oneself. "I'd give anything . . . ," Caro had begun, and then fallen silent, her unfinished sentence drifting away on the air of the bright winter day.

The baby she was holding was Fan's daughter. "We left Cash with the neighbors," Frank explained. "We reckoned this might be too much for him, seeing he's old enough to understand what's going on—" He gestured around the little cemetery, the scrubby grass, the dry, lopsided stones, the small heaps of deep red earth beside the hole where Fan's casket had been lowered into the ground.

"And it was so-o dark, Clemmie, like you were right down buried in the ground. . . ."

Frank chucked a big finger under the baby's chin and she grinned up at him. "But we thought we'd bring the little one along for her mum." He took her small hand and held it out to Clementine. "This is Madeleine," he said.

Madeleine.

Clementine felt the ground falling away beneath her feet. She could hear Fan's voice, her actual laughing fourteen-year-old voice: "Okay, tell you what. When I have my first little girl, I'll call her Madeleine for you."

Clementine looked up at the small frisking clouds, the kittens and ducklings and baby lambs, and fought back angry tears. "Why didn't you tell me?" she cried out silently. "Why didn't you write and say, 'I've had a little girl and I've given her your favorite name like I promised. Madeleine!'"

Why hadn't she? If Fan had done that, then Clementine would have written back because she'd have known what to write about, and she'd have come up to see Fan and the baby in the holidays, and—

And then perhaps none of this would have happened. There'd have been no vanishing, no death, and she and Fan might this very morning be walking around the lake with Madeleine and little Cash, the fluffy clouds frolicking above them, the small winds of heaven riffling through their hair. Distantly, she heard Caroline saying, "It was good of you to come."

She spun around in anguish. "But I didn't!"

"What?"

"I didn't come! Not when I should have, anyway! I didn't even write to her when you sent me that letter. I didn't—" Clementine burst into noisy tears, and Frank took the baby so that Caro could put her arms around her cousin. "Shhh," Caro whispered. "Shhh."

"It's not your fault, love," said Frank. "Even if you'd written a letter she mightn't have got 'round to opening it. Fan sort of—left things lying."

"She would have opened it," said Clementine. She was sure of it. And she couldn't help remembering the girl she thought she'd seen on that rainy afternoon a few weeks ago, the girl at the end of the corridor in the Old Arts Building, in the faded blue-gray dress with the hem coming down. Fan had still been alive then, so it couldn't have been her ghost. But what if she'd learned to send her spirit wandering when she was asleep, like she'd told Clementine the old black man used to do—sent it roaming down the red land to Sydney, searching for her *gindaymaidhaany*?

"Was that you?" Clementine whispered, gazing up at the great blue arch of sky. "Was that you, Fan? Francesca?" The beautiful name, suddenly remembered, so long forgotten, settled in Clementine's heart like a sweet white dove. Francesca.

"Grief is the worst thing, I think." Sarah might have been tracing the silent passage of her companion's thoughts as she and Clementine made their way slowly along the path toward the car park.

"Yes," agrees Clementine. "Oh, yes."

In a fourth-year English exam, a whole two years after her cousin's death, Clementine had opened the poetry paper and unexpectedly begun to cry. It had been the question on Henry Vaughan that had undone her, the poem for analysis printed out on the page. It was the eighth stanza:

> *If a star were confin'd into a Tomb*
> *Her captive flames must needs burn there;*
> *But when the hand that lockt her up, gives room,*
> *She'll shine through all the sphere.*

She had read those lines many times, but never before had the connection to her cousin revealed itself, as it did that December afternoon in the middle of the English honors exam. Oh, that was like Fan! It was! Perhaps it was the heat of the summer day pouring through the high windows of the exam room, or the sound of the wind roaring outside, or the smell of red inland dust in the air, but Clementine couldn't stop crying; she'd had to be helped from the examination room to sit outside in a chair in the corridor, an invigilator beside her, until she'd got herself together and could go inside again.

"Fan would have shone, she would have, if only," she'd sobbed out in the corridor, "if only she'd stayed!"

"Do you want to go to the sick room?" the invigilator had asked.

"No, no, I'm all right." Clementine had rubbed at her eyes. "I'm better now." And she'd marched back into the exam room, sat down at her desk, and answered the question on

Henry Vaughan. She was living life for both of them now, and it had to be good, it had to be "brushed with light," as old Henry Vaughan would have said.

Then there was the time, at a party in a terrace house on Glebe Road, where she'd gone with David Lowell, when Clementine had turned pale and quiet as Johnny Cash's rich deep voice flooded out into the room—"Oh!" she'd gasped, because he was singing about a girl from a far country, a girl with long hair that curled and fell all down her dress. Like Fan's hair used to do, once upon a time.

How Fan would have loved that song, and how bitter it had seemed to Clementine that Fan had never got to hear it.

Never, never, ever.

David Lowell had taken her to that party. It was the first time they'd gone out together. He'd seen the shock bloom on her face when she'd heard that song.

"What's the matter?" he'd asked her. And she'd told him about Fan, and he'd put his arms around her and whispered, "Your poor cousin."

"And you keep on thinking," Sarah goes on, "you keep thinking, if only one little thing had been different."

Oh, yes! Clementine has puzzled over this so many times: if she'd written that letter to Fan, would it have made a difference? Or had it been too late, even then? Would Fan have left it lying unopened on the kitchen table, or never even taken it from the postbox, already too far along on her last mistaken journey to the blue hills?

Would it have been different if Fan had grown up in the city, instead of far away at Lake Conapaira?

Or if she'd had a different family?

If she'd married someone else instead of Gary?

If things had gone better at school?

If the old black man hadn't gone away?

There were so many "ifs"—"ifs" beyond number, countless as the stars that peered in through the window of Fan's old bedroom, or the grains of red earth that made up the land. The closest Clementine can come to any reason is something Fan said herself, on that last evening by the lake: "Sometimes I feel like I didn't get through into the world properly, like other people, that I left a little bit behind—"

Clementine had protested, thinking Fan was putting herself down, but perhaps she'd been right after all. Perhaps there was a little piece missing, something hard and thoughtless and self-serving, which most people needed to survive and which Fan didn't possess, or bother to call out and use. The only thing that would have saved Fan for sure was this: quite simply, if she'd been a different kind of person.

If she'd been a different kind of person, then Fan would have lived. If she'd been more cautious, less defiant, less sure that happiness would come to her, less eager for life, then she'd probably still be here.

But then she wouldn't have been Fan. There'd have been no Fan ever on this earth, no sweet Fan, Francesca, *Yirigaa*, the morning star.

"Ah, it can be a difficult old place, this life," grumbles Sarah, and as she says this Clementine has a sudden unaccountable image of the Brothers' house across the road from her childhood home, and remembers how she used to sit up on her bed and lean her elbows on the sill and gaze across at the lighted windows, long into the night. She remembers how she dreamed that the Brothers were seated around a table busily sewing their big net and how Fan was dancing in the center of it, close to the weak place they hadn't finished yet.

"You missed her," Clementine silently accuses the industrious Brothers. "You let her fall through."

It's strange how some dreams stay with you all your life, so that when you're old they seem as real as the actual people and places that you've known. Clementine can still see, quite plainly, the soft red dancing shoes Fan had been wearing as she danced up and down, happiness shining out of every little bit of her.

"What beautiful shoes!" Caro had exclaimed on the day after the funeral, as Clementine was packing to catch the train back home.

They were green shoes, like the ones in the dream Fan had told her about that morning when they'd hung the clothes out together: green leather shoes with a slim strap across the instep and a small square heel. A few months after she'd come back from that last visit to Lake Conapaira Clementine had seen them in the window of a shoe shop on Broadway. "I should have written and told her," she thinks now, almost fifty years later, as she and Sarah make their way through the last stand of dusty eucalyptus. And then, suddenly: "That's what I could have said in that letter I didn't know how to write. I could have told her about the shoes!"

They turn into the car park. Only two cars remain there now: Sarah's blue Datsun and a battered green Toyota with a thick band of red dust along its sides. As they approach, the Toyota's driver's door swings open and a young girl leaps out, a tall girl, with hair in two thick braids the color of wild honey. She rushes forward and stops abruptly just in front of them, lifting the braids in both hands, twisting them into a crown on top of her head. Then she lets them fall, tossing them back over her shoulders. "You're late, Aunty Clementine!" she cries. "You're late, but I forgive you. Seeing as it's so hot, and you're so ancient!"

"This is Fan," says Clementine to Sarah.

"Fan?"

"My cousin's granddaughter. Cash's child." Clementine laughs at the amazed delight on Sarah's face. "She's staying with us for the holidays. Before she goes back to university."

"Ah," breathes Sarah, and she stands quite still, gazing steadily at Fan, like someone gone quiet before a painting where it seems some rare and lovely truth of life is unexpectedly revealed. "So," she says, clasping her hands together. "So." She smiles at Clementine. "There are good things after all, eh?"

Clementine takes Fan's thin brown hand in hers and holds it fast. "There are great good things," she says.

Acknowledgments

My thanks to friends and helpers:
Erica Wagner and Sue Flockhart
Margaret Connolly and Jamie Grant
Frances Floyd and Frances Sutherland
Laurie Mooney and Marnie Kennedy
Cathy Jinks and Kathleen Stewart
Robyn Barlow and Roswitha Dabke
Tracey and Tyrone Johnstone
Reis and Nima Flora
Allan Baillie and Graham King
Wendy Dickstein and Bryan Gray
And to the librarians of Lithgow, Blackheath,
   Katoomba, and the Lachlan shire.
And to Dr. Jo Tibbetts of Active Computer Support
   (for many rescues).

Fan's poem in Part Four and the Epilogue is the eighth stanza
of Henry Vaughan's poem "They Are All Gone into the World
of Light!"

The lines Clementine recites to Fan in chapter thirteen are from William Wordsworth's "A Slumber Did My Spirit Seal."

The custom described by Daria in chapter six is related in Henri Troyat's biography *Gorky*.

The poem Clementine reads in the school library in chapter five is A. E. Housman's "Into My Heart an Air That Kills."

The song "Oh My Darling, Clementine" is a folk song about the American gold rush.

The story Fan tells Clementine in chapter two is "Revenge of the Magic Child (Bidjandjara)," collected in *The World of the First Australians*, by Ronald M. and Catherine H. Berndt.

Words of the Wiradjuri language are from *A First Wiradjuri Dictionary*, compiled by Stan Grant, Sr., and Dr. John Rudder (language copyright Wiradjuri Council of Elders).

The National Suicide Prevention Lifeline at 1-800-273-TALK (8255) is a free, 24-hour hotline available to anyone in suicidal crisis or emotional distress.